CLEAR and a MILLION

A SIERRA HOTEL NOVEL

PRAISE FOR KENT MCINNIS & *SIERRA HOTEL*

"Balancing pathos and comedy is a challenging task for a writer, and McInnis does this beautifully. Lead protagonist Rob Amity's internal conflict is carried throughout the book in both tragedy and hilarity."

—Alan B. Hollingsworth
Author of *Flatbellies*

"An exciting story of American history and patriotism, a gifted author and historian, and a former USAF pilot. What better formula for your next page-turning thriller than Sierra Hotel?"

—John J. Dwyer
Will Rogers Medallion-winning
Author of *Shortgrass* and *Mustang*

"Kent McInnis is a man who has served his country. We are fortunate that God made men like Kent who was willing to do the tough job, and still continues to have a smile on his face."

—Harvey Pratt
Designer, National Native American Veterans Memorial, Washington, D.C.
Cheyenne Peace Chief, U. S. Marine

"Kent McInnis is the consummate storyteller. His vivid description of life as a T-37 IP brought back a flood of memories for me...."

—Lt. Col. Glenn R. Schaumberg, USAF (RET.)
B-52 Pilot during Operation Linebacker II

"Author Kent McInnis's depiction of young Air Force airmen in wartime is raw and honest—a man's book that will also appeal to women."

—Major General Donald F. Ferrell, USAFR (Retired)
Former Oklahoma Adjutant General

"The genius in Kent McInnis's writing is his ability to submerge you into the good, the bad, and the ugly of military life."

—Bob Giel
U.S. Army Veteran and Author of *A Crow to Pluck* and *Shawnee*

also by

Kent McInnis

Sierra Hotel

CLEAR and a MILLION

A NOVEL OF LIFE AFTER WAR

Kent McInnis

HAT CREEK

HAT CREEK

An Imprint of Roan & Weatherford Publishing Associates, LLC
Bentonville, Arkansas
www.roanweatherford.com

Library of Congress Cataloging-in-Publication Data
Names: McInnis, Kent, author
Title: Clear and a Million/Kent McInnis | Sierra Hotel #2
Description: First Edition. | Bentonville: Hat Creek, 2023.
Identifiers: LCCN: 2023930752 | ISBN: 978-1-63373-813-3 (hardcover)
ISBN: 978-1-63373-814-0 (trade paperback) | ISBN: 978-1-63373-815-7 (eBook)
Subjects: | BISAC: FICTION/War & Military | FICTION/Historical |
FICTION/General
LC record available at: https://lccn.loc.gov/2023930752

Hat Creek hardcover edition May, 2023

Jacket & Interior Design by Casey W. Cowan
Editing by Amy Cowan & Anthony Wood

For Cheryl...
wife, lover, best friend

PREFACE

BY THE AGE OF THIRTY, I learned the heartache of losing my best friend to combat in Vietnam. I also learned the value and virtue of a good woman. I don't believe men fully mature before they are forty. The Vietnam War turned boys into men well before they should have. It also turned men into angry cynics—often with opposing opinions of a war no one seemed to want and only some tried to win. To my surprise, the ambitions I had entering college but saw dashed by my country's call in the war were blessings in the end. Plan B was a path to a happy life with a good woman at my side. I am proud to say I served my country, although it was difficult in retrospect knowing so many friends saw combat, but I never did. To hear someone call non-Vietnam combat veterans draft dodgers still offends me. We all sacrificed something. Some their lives. Many their dreams. Often their marriages. Perhaps their sanity. Time, tough love, and perhaps a few self-inflicted wounds are how we men mature. We learn by our mistakes. This is that story.

ACKNOWLEDGEMENTS

AMONG THE TEN COMMANDMENTS THERE is *"honor thy father and thy mother...."* I
strive to remember that every day as I practice the grammar they command-
ed me to speak and write to their strict standards. They also taught me the
joys of laughing and entertaining.

Before I began this work, I inspired my mother to write her own novel
at the age of 89. I was her editor for over two years. That is why I appreciate the work and meticulous detail my own editors at Hat Creek—Dennis
Doty, Anthony Wood, Amy Cowan, Casey Cowan, and countless others of
whom I am unaware. Editing is a labor of great value to me and is always
a learning experience.

Many former and retired airmen shared stories, both true and legend. As
the Laredo AFB Undergraduate Pilot Training Class 71-06, the Rio River
Rats, we worked together to either sink or swim. The bond among these
men has held for 50 years. All but a handful spent some time in Vietnam. I
write to honor them, my friends and fellow veterans.

Dr. Hugh Strickland, who achieved my dream to became a veterinarian
after leaving active duty, was my closest friend in the Air Force when I was
an instructor pilot. We shared many stories and some experiences which
inspired my imagination in writing fiction.

Retired Air Force pilots Lt. Col. Glenn Schaumburg, Col. Larry Hoppe,
Col. Chuck DeBellevue, and many other former pilot members of Order of

Daedalians shared their unique experiences spanning over six years of air combat in Vietnam.

I will always be grateful for nationally known author and surgeon, Alan B. Hollingsworth, MD, for giving me the sound advice of how to land a publishing contract. Also, I thank another successful author, John J. Dwyer, who introduced me to my publisher. Between the two men's help, it only took 15 years to work.

Finally, my wife Cheryl has let me write without complaint for all 40 plus years of our happy life together, although she occasionally insists that I come out to play. If my work effectively reveals my love for the fairer sex, it is because of her.

1

THE BARE, COLORLESS WALLS OF my apartment were dreary reminders that the choices we make are often turned to regret. With no furniture in view and no decoration to add cheer, a wave of fear filled my aching heart. As happy as I was at first to leave the Air Force in late 1973, I soon found, to my shock, that I missed it. I had departed from the only friends I had left, and there was no one worthy to hear my tale. The blandness of an uncertain future replaced my high intensity life in the cockpit of a jet airplane. I already had lived the greatest moment of my life at the age of only twenty-seven.

I was a returning veteran from an unpopular war in Vietnam, having no allies on either side. To some I was a draft dodger because I did not go to Vietnam. Others called me a war monger, simply because I put on the uniform to support the cause. I caught disdain from both ends of the political spectrum. I longed to be worthy of any respect from anyone. My only solution? Run away.

I cancelled the lease on my apartment. With months of uncut hair and a heavy beard to match, I went to see my parents to explain that I was leaving my hometown behind to find the excitement that I craved.

Only God knew where I was going, and He wasn't talking. Like an Okie from forty years before, I headed out west early in the morning on Route 66 for parts unknown. The road had changed like everything else in my time away. At first, I was disappointed because I didn't get the feeling of excitement that I experienced as a child when my own parents took the same journey to the Southwest United States. For the first hundred miles the road was uninspiring, until an idea came to my head. I pulled my car to the side of the road and rolled down the windows of my Datsun 240-Z to take in the fresh morning air. It all came back to me. With the scent of morning air and the faint odor of hay bales, my long-lost childhood memories came rushing back to me. I continued back on the road west. The smells and the sounds of buffeting winds in ways were different now. It was a chilly winter day, not summer, but there were no parents to guide me. I could go as far as I wanted, be as cold as I chose, and stop on a whim. For now, I simply soaked up the taste of my childhood like a cake with adulthood as icing.

Being a bachelor, who spent little money in the service to my country, my portfolio was quite flush for a man my age. Being grounded from flying after several medical episodes in the air gave me hope of some compensation from the Veteran's Administration. I was well positioned to throw away a bit of money to help me find myself.

I grew up watching Martin Milner and George Maharis on the CBS television show, Route 66. The series ended just before the Corvette Stingray changed the styling of Corvettes. I still love seeing those Vettes with their four headlights. How cool was that? Like me, Tod must have been flush with cash because he had a brand-new Corvette every season. Lucky guy. When the season ended in 1964, there must have been thousands of high school graduates who dreamed of recreating the television's Route 66 experience. Most would not have the wheels that Tod and Buz enjoyed but still ventured as a pair of young men looking for action and likely trouble. My problem was that my car, a Datsun 240-Z, was long in the tooth after years of abuse in the hot sun of Laredo, Texas. So, like a crazed teenager without a lick of sense, I headed west to Albuquerque, New Mexico, to buy a new car more fitting to my current mood.

The Chevrolet dealership was obviously my first stop, but still being in love with the old style four-eyed headlights of the 1962 Corvette, I chose to rule out Corvettes from my list. I was too much of a nonconformist to go with the conventional formula Route 66 adventure. I next stopped by one of those dealers who sold cars from companies less mainstream. It was a large conglomeration of Volvo, BMW, American Motors, and Porsche. To add to the allure of this place, the first salesman to come out to me asked a surprising question.

"I hope you want to trade in that 240-Z, son, because I have a ready buyer who is looking for one."

It sounded like an old sales trick. The man looked to be in his early fifties, clean shaven with salt and pepper hair cut short with fashionably long sideburns. He carried himself erect and looked physically fit. Unlike the stereotypical used car salesman, he wore a conservative pair of black Sansabelt slacks with a long sleeve white shirt and paisley necktie.

"What branch of service were you in?" he asked. The question surprised me since I sported a heavy beard and long hair.

"Air Force," I said, worried that I could be so easily singled out. "How could you tell?"

"I have a knack," he replied. "We see a lot of veterans through here. I can spot them as soon as they get out of their cars. They just have a look about them."

"Then you must have served also," I said. His face was expressionless at my comment.

"Oh, yes," he said. "Different time but the same war. Retired Marine. I'm Mike Randall."

"Rob Amity," I said, shaking his hand. "Well, I'm sure you paid your dues, being a Marine."

"Can I sell you a car, son?" Mike asked, avoiding the topic of his service.

"So, who want's my car?"

"My son. I think he might like it. I'm fascinated with the new breed of sports cars out of Japan. It's sort of a poor man's Jaguar XKE."

"Without its hood up for repairs," I said with a laugh.

"That, too, but these Datsuns catch a lot of attention from my customers."

I looked him in the eye, knowing that by now I, too, could size up a man. Mike Randall obviously was not ashamed to keep his hair a conservative short length, in the face of a nation that seemed hell bent on being as anti-clean cut as possible. He took pride in his appearance, which could translate into taking care of his used cars. And I couldn't afford a new one. I decided to try the next level.

"Mike, what sports car could a retired Marine offer to a young washed-up jet jockey?"

"You been to the Corvette dealer already?"

"Yeah, and I don't like 'em. The old style is more to my taste."

"You'd probably like a Porsche, then," he replied. "I've got several choices of new 911s and S models."

"I'm sure they are out of my price range."

"I might have an answer to that if you are interested in a unique used Porsche." My car-dealer-red-alert warning horn started to kick in. "Come this way and let me show you this. With your Z in trade, we may have a match made in heaven."

I suspected he may have retired from the top enlisted ranks of Marines. At a rapid pace, Mike practically force-marched me over to the used car lot. As expected, the lot was filled with every American-made car of the past 20 years. Among sports cars were Mustangs, Camaros, one Dodge Charger Daytona with its ridiculously tall rear spoiler, and a couple of Volvo 1800s. There was a canopied area near the highway protecting a brand-new Porsche 911 in a rich racing yellow with a tasteful rear spoiler. My salesman lured me ever closer to the magnificent piece of German engineering to get a better look. The track of the rear wheels and tires seemed wider than other Porsches. The brakes were larger. The front end sported the new federally mandated bumpers in the same yellow. Compared to American cars, the interior was spartan.

"There's no radio," I said, after taking my first look inside the cockpit.

Mike laughed. "Son, once you turn over the engine on this baby, you will find that the sound of its power is all the music you need to hear."

Good point.

"What model Porsche is this?" I asked. I was now salivating.

"That is a 1973 Porsche Carrera RSR 3.0. They didn't make many, so I heard. I read up on it. It has a bigger 2.8-liter, 296 horsepower air-cooled engine," he described, then gave me its history. "It's a monster that got dumped on me one day by an oilman who bought it for his wife. She hated it, so he tried driving it for business. He brought it to me while on a road trip from Texas. Rich people are crazy. He said he didn't really like to drive a stick shift and needed a car he could operate comfortably to get back home."

"Are there many miles on it?"

"That's the even crazier part," Mike said. "It only has about 500 miles. The guy told me that he was in a hurry to get somewhere and needed a different car immediately and offered to swap cars with me for an even trade to save him time. I took him up on the offer, and by golly, when he left, we were both happy. A Rambler American for this beauty. The truth is, I've felt guilty ever since."

I looked at him again pensively, remembering all the times in my youth that I was afraid to ask for things because I was terrified that people would find me funny or naïve. After five years in the Air Force, I observed how pilots and NCOs got things done. The common thread in all of them was a lack of fear and an expectation of being taken seriously. With a jet jockey swagger of confidence, I charged forward with a ridiculous offer.

"Well, if it will soothe your guilty feelings, why don't we make the same deal? My car for yours. You will break even from the last deal and be rid of all that guilt."

He looked at me as if I were some wise guy who talks before he thinks. He began a chuckle that turned into shouting laughter that carried inside to the used car office. He again faced me and shook his head at me.

"You're a piece of work," he said. "You know, I own this dealership, but I have never had anyone make an offer that outrageous. You might want to come to work for me, of course, after you come back from your adventure."

I stood there in silence. I had faced down superior officers hellbent on ruining my life. Staring down a retired NCO Marine was easy. I remained silent and waited. From experience, I knew that the first one to talk loses. He began a deliberate shaking of his head then started a nervous chuckle.

"You really an Air Force pilot?" he asked.

"Yes," I replied. "Five years, mostly under Nixon at Laredo Air Force Base."

"You ever work with any Marines?"

"I had three in my pilot training class, all from the Naval Academy. I wrestled one of them in the gym on occasion."

"Did he whip your ass on the mat?"

"Well, how would a smart pilot answer that question?" I retorted.

"Honestly," he said.

"I mopped up the floor with him."

The Marine looked at me in silence for a prolonged time, then looked down at the ground and sighed.

"Son, you've got a deal."

There are times in life when a *you're-kidding-me* expression will ruin things. I struggled to stay calm and to breathe normally. These were obviously crazy times. I did not hesitate to finalize the deal. We exchanged signatures. There were a few fees I had to pay to the State of New Mexico, but I was glad to pay cash to expedite the process. He handed me my proper papers to secure a title in Oklahoma. I didn't know for sure when I would be back, but I figured I could pay for any fine beyond the state's 60-day grace period. I stepped into the beast, buckled the lap belt, and pulled out my new car keys. It took me a couple of minutes before I realized the key goes in from the left side of the steering wheel.

"It's the Germans again," I mumbled.

I turned the key to start the Porsche, and the roar of startup was instant, exhilarating, and sensual. How can a car make you horny? I don't know, but it did.

I pulled out of the parking lot, testing the clutch pedal and getting used to its feel. The departure was tempered, until I drove the Porsche to the entrance ramp to what once was Route 66 going west, but since 1970 called Interstate 40. Deciding the Porsche's engine was warm enough, I trounced on the accelerator and left a brief trail of black rubber on the road before the tires gripped the surface and second gear pushed me back in my seat. I was living the dream.

I now had my dream car purchased on a whim, but my Route 66 experience was still incomplete. I needed a sidekick. Who would be Buz? I now owned one of the fastest cars in the world with thousands of miles of American roads on which to test it out. There was only one man I knew who was a logical choice to ask. I exited I-40 on the west end of Albuquerque to stop at a pay phone. I called one of the few friends I had left who might be crazier than I was. I let it ring over five times before someone picked up.

"Bueno," said a male voice.

"Hal Freed? You still answering the telephone like you're in Laredo?"

"Rob Amity? Is that you?"

"You doing anything at the moment?"

"Just sitting here weighing my options while they shut down good old Laredo Air Force Base."

"You have any leave saved up?"

"About sixty days, I suppose."

"Then let's take a trip together on Route 66 and go kick some ass!"

2

I RE-ENTERED I-40 BUT THIS time going east. Entering Texas, the road name reverted to Route 66. I drove until I stopped for dinner. The following morning, at the cheap motel on the west edge of Amarillo where I had spent the night, Hal and I agreed by telephone to meet in Big Spring, Texas, near Webb Air Force Base, another Air Force pilot training base like the one where we served in Laredo.

I took the Porsche on Route 87 toward Big Spring. First, I made a stop at Palo Duro Canyon to drive through the second largest canyon in the United States. It was a spectacular drive in a sports car, with many climbing and descending turns in a canyon 800 feet deep, six to twenty miles wide and over a hundred miles long. I longed to compare it to the Grand Canyon in Arizona and committed myself to selling Hal on setting our sights to hike the big one in one of our first adventures.

I put the Porsche into high gear and raced south through the Texas high plains, down through the windy dust of Lubbock, and finally into the heat and land of giant Western Diamondback Rattlesnakes of West Texas at Big Spring. I found the agreed upon meeting place at Hotel Settles downtown. Fifteen stories high, the place was showing its age. Once housing the men of an expanding oil operation in the West Texas oil fields, the 1973 oil crisis had crushed the industry—and the hotel. As I gazed up at the only skyscraper in town, I was heartened to look overhead and see and hear the whine and the roar of T-37 and T-38 jets traversing the clear skies overhead.

Stepping inside, I found the hotel's Pharmacy Bar and settled down with a Cuba Libra cocktail to wait for Hal's arrival. Reflecting on the life I had left, what an incongruous relationship my friend and I had. He was older, a combat pilot, and a loner, whose tendency was to not take crap off anyone. By contrast, I was still in college when he was getting shot at. I was not in combat. I had many friends from my Air Force days, unlike Hal the loner. Something about his nonconformity appealed to me. After my close friend, John Alexander, died in a T-37 plane crash, Hal, a fellow instructor pilot, became my major sidekick. He became a good friend and mentored me by example in the ways of being cool. Having flown the F-105 in over a hundred combat missions over North Vietnam, Captain Hal Freed carried himself and comported himself like the real thing—a fighter pilot's fighter pilot. Because of his personality, his career was on a pathway to seeing him either court-martialed or promoted to general. He was still hanging on to make the Air Force a career.

The town of Big Spring was in a malaise, because of the depressed drilling activity in West Texas. Webb Air Force Base may have been the only saving grace for Big Spring. Unlike Laredo, this base was still open, and jets were flying everywhere. There was still no slump in making plans for war.

Having finished my Cuba Libre, I stepped outside once more to enjoy the warm dry air and to watch the aircraft taking off and landing southwest of the hotel. A wave of nostalgia hit me hard as the first T-37 jet climbed out on the distant horizon. The aircraft had been so easy to fly and so easy to take for granted. The smallest jet in the large Air Force inventory, it was easy to make light of. Nicknamed Tweet, because if its high-pitched whistle from the twin jet engines, it was the brunt of many jokes. It was a workhorse, not a T-38 supersonic sex object. It was easy to fly, but it could still kill you, as I all too well knew.

By contrast, my buddy Hal had flown an F-105 Thunderchief, the fastest airplane on the deck yet made. It was known for its ability to take a hit and keep flying. In a bit of gallows humor, the pilots renamed the Thunderchief the Thunderthud, adopted from the character many of its pilots grew up with while watching Howdy Doody on television. Military personnel tend to shorten any name, and in no time the F-105 was simply called Thud for short. Every pilot joked that thud was the sound it made when hitting the ground. Hal's Thud had never hit the ground, but both he and his F-105 faced lots of combat over North Vietnam, and Hal lived to tell about it. In truth, he did not talk about it willingly, and he did not take affronts from peaceniks without consequences. If you were looking to kick some ass, as I imagined myself doing, Hal was the one person I would invite to come along.

Because Hal was hitching a ride with a friend of ours who was reassigned from Laredo to Webb, his arrival was uncertain. I amused myself by standing on the corner and watching the girls go by, infrequent as they were. I struck up a conversation or two when people stopped near me. They were worried about their base closing in the future since the Vietnam War seemed over. I knew that not to be true, as we still flew a close air support role to aide South Vietnamese ground troops. North Vietnamese communists and the South's Viet Cong were cheating their way to victory—Paris Peace Accord be damned.

Pulling up to a parking space on the opposite corner of Runnels Street, I spied a familiar Ford Mustang with a not-too-pleasant green paintjob. Out of the driver's seat came red-headed, hyperactive, and skinny Johnny Wise, former F-4 Phantom driver and twice lucky enough to survive an ejection from a crashed fighter. A fellow T-37 instructor pilot with Hal and me, we had shared many days together at the flightline in Ragtop Flight. In the living room of his rented house, Johnny's easy chair was his Phantom ejection seat from his first bailout and parachute landing. His wife was a tolerant woman.

Hal emerged from the confines of the Mustang's passenger side door. Stepping to the corner together, Hal's half-a-head height advantage over Johnny was apparent. They strode across the street with smiles that only come from being with good friends. It had been nine months since my departure, but they already looked like different people to me. I realized at the same moment that I was more changed than they. I hadn't had a haircut or a shave in months.

"Hey, Amity!" Wise said as he crossed the street on a red light to my corner. "You look like a damn hippie now."

The shock of that comment caused me a moment of embarrassment.

"Too bad for you, Wise, but you haven't changed a bit," I replied as we grabbed a quick handshake and half a hug.

Turning to Hal, I laughed as I spoke. "Hal, you don't look much better yourself."

Hal grabbed my hand and almost pulled me over with an enthusiastic greeting.

"You wasted no time turning to crap," he said. "Goodness! You look awful. It's good to see you again, old friend."

I led them into the Hotel Settles Pharmacy Bar where we could cool down from the ample warm West Texas sunlight. The lighting was dim in the bar and furnished with elegant, overly worn, plush seating and leather sofas. It looked more like a smoking room than a classical hotel bar. It had been a pharmacy for years before its upgrade to a dual purpose. At first, my two friends enjoyed standing, after an over 400-mile drive from Laredo. After ordering a round of drinks, we settled down to share what meager news we had.

"Wise, I thought they were sending you Tweet drivers to Moody. How are you ending up at Webb?"

"The brass at Moody believes I am too hard on airplanes." It was a joke only Wise could tell. "It'll be okay. Half of the squadron is going back to assignments in FACs. Probably back to SEA shortly. I'm glad not to go back there and be a target again."

"Most got O-2s, but a few will be flying OV-10s, which would be fun," Hal said.

The FACs, or forward air controllers, mostly flew the slow and lightly armed O-2s from bases in Southeast Asia, or SEA. The larger and more heavily armed OV-10 was more rugged and flew like a fighter. Both were propeller driven and would be used to support the South Vietnamese ground troops that still expected trouble from both inside and north of their endangered nation.

"Wise, are you going back to Laredo, or is this it?" I asked.

"No, this is it," he said with a smile. "Sherry's already here and settled into our quarters. I have the rest of our stuff in the trunk. I'll check in at ops, and then I'm done for the day."

Hal looked over at Wise and smiled. "Well, go say hi to your wife and have a good time while we bachelors decide what to do for a month."

"Will do," Wise said with eagerness. "I've been TDY much too long to suit me."

The three of us stood up. Hal and I each shook hands with Wise before he turned to head home in his Mustang to be with his devoted wife. From past conversations, we knew the value of a loyal, devoted, and supportive wife. If we were forced to admit it, Hal and I envied Johnny Wise.

3

"WHY DON'T WE STAY IN this dump tonight?" I said. "That way we can file a flight plan for where we want to go tomorrow morning."

"I'm glad to get away to anywhere. Laredo is in sad shape. They're trashing everything on base."

"I knew that would happen."

"Remember all the airplane models we had in A Flight hanging from the ceiling? They trashed them. There were some valuable pieces." Hal spread his arms wide. "Remember that big, oversized B-52 up there? It must have cost a fortune to buy it and build it. It's trashed."

"What about the plaques on the wall?"

"All trashed."

"Was there anything saved?"

"I was talking to one of the flight surgeons that we used to make puke in the cockpit. Remember Doc Terra? He told me that the Pentagon ordered them to destroy all the medical equipment. X-ray machines. Exam tables. Drugs supplies. Scopes. Doppler ultrasound equipment. Everything."

"What a waste."

"Instead, Doc removed several loads of equipment from the base hospital into the trunk of his car and snuck it all off base. He brought it to Laredo's Mercy Hospital and donated it anonymously. His wife was a nurse there and made sure it got to the right place."

"What is the government thinking?"

"Terra asked the same thing. Their answer was that donations would compete with established medical supply companies who would object and raise hell."

"At least that's good news," I said. "Someone used common sense. That's a refreshing change. Doc Terra was always good to me. I'm proud of him."

Freed looked down at his empty glass, then up to me. "Are we going anywhere else tonight? Should we find a place to eat? We can figure out where to head tomorrow morning."

The bar tender, overhearing us in the empty lounge, came over to our easy chairs. He was a slender man with greying hair and a far along receding hairline. He looked close to retirement age, which in a farm community or an oil patch could be deceiving.

"You guys here for jobs in the oil patch?" he asked.

I looked up at the man and smiled, not sure what to tell him. Hal and I had no idea what we were here for.

"We just chose here to meet up before we head out tomorrow," I said.

"Road trip," Hal said. "Gonna find ourselves."

"Or what?" the man said with a laugh.

"Keep looking, I guess," Hal replied.

"Is there a good place to eat nearby?" I asked.

"I'd try right here," he replied. "Have you eaten here before?"

"We just got here," I said. "It's our first time in Big Spring."

"You knew about Hotel Settles, I see," he said. "It's THE historic hotel in town. A must to see and the best place to eat if you like a good Texas meal."

"I think you need to bring us a refill," Hal said. He held up his empty glass. "I have a question about the oil patch out here in West Texas."

"Comin' up," he said. "Things are starting to happen, since that blasted oil embargo started. You boys driving fifty-five like you're supposed to?"

"Hell no!" I said.

"Good for you," our bartender replied. "Texas has plenty of oil in the ground, so speed away. Prices are high, but this place may start humming again. You'll see."

While we waited for our man to come back, I reflected on the whole mess with oil in the world. The Yom Kippur War in Israel almost spelled the end of the nation, except for the military resupply efforts of America, Canada, Japan, England, the Netherlands, and other minor contributors. The Arab nations with most of the oil in the world cut off the oil spigot of every nation that supported their enemy, Israel.

I concluded that the dumbest thing President Nixon could have done was interfere with supply and demand for gasoline. Stations restricted how much gas you could buy. Thus, the lines were twice as long. By Congress mandating a fifty-five mile an hour speed limit, it clogged the highways with cars driving unpredictable speeds. Super compliant drivers were still driving the 50 mph speed first suggested by Nixon. Trucks in the expanding oil industry tied their speed on the highway to the growing price of a barrel of oil. The average speed on Interstate 40 was currently close to 85 mph. That meant that you were safer going 85 mph than going 50 mph. At least you got to see what you hit if you were speeding. Otherwise, the risk for slow drivers was getting rear-ended.

Citizen Band radios gained popularity. Soon anyone who frequently used the highways had adorned their cars with a whip antenna. Convoys of cars and big rigs, trying to outsmart state troopers, used their CB radios to avoid radar traps for those exceeding 55 mph. I had already learned that I didn't need a CB radio. Convoys of up to a dozen CB radio-monitoring big rigs, followed by several interspersed automobiles, routinely raced by at 85 mph or more. All you had to do was match their speed and slip in with them. Rumor had it that the cops would more likely pull over a vehicle if it had one of the CB whip antennas. So far, my system worked one hundred percent.

Our personal bartender brought over our fresh drinks, and we asked him again what the story was with oil in West Texas.

"Oil is coming up in price, which is fantastic," he told us. "If it gets to twelve dollars a barrel, we'll all be driving new Cadillacs by this time next year. That's good, because the air base we figure will close soon. The war is winding down. The military doesn't need pilots so much anymore. So, it's going to be goodbye flyboys."

"Do they drink a lot here in Big Spring?" Hal asked.

"No, siree! Not here they don't. Webb has their own bar at the officers' club," he replied, then with a smile, "but when the oilies start showing up again, watch out. It'll be like Dodge City. If I can hold down the fights and maybe dodge a few bullets, it'll be that Cadillac I'm talking about... maybe two of 'em."

We took a sip or two of our drinks as he stepped back behind the bar.

"You want to meet a bunch of oil field workers, Hal?" I asked.

"I'd rather not," he said. His more characteristic reticence was back.

"Then we better get to dinner so we can plan how to get the hell outta Dodge, while there's still time."

"I have no desire to drive around town, for sure."

"Same here. We've already been in cars all day, but before we go eat, you have to come outside and see the car I stole yesterday."

We left our drinks on the table by our plush oversized easy chairs. Stepping out into the February afternoon setting sunlight, Hal stopped for a minute to shade his eyes and wait for the effect of a darkened bar to go away. Looking east, his eye caught sight of a bright reflection from the racing yellow paint of a car parked nearby.

"You've got to be kidding. Is that what you bought? A Porsche?"

"No, Hal. That's the car I stole."

"I'm sure you did." He wouldn't for a second believe my fib. He headed over to the curb for a closer look. "What in hell have you done?"

"I swung the deal of the century, and I'll share my secret as soon as we get another sit down at dinner. I should name it, The Beast."

"How fast can this Beast thing go?" Hal asked.

"I don't know, Hal, but this is West Texas, and I'm sure that tomorrow we can find out."

4

MORNING WAS STILL WAITING FOR sunrise when we crawled out of bed and stumbled into the bathroom to make our presence at breakfast appear civilized.

"Do I *have* to share this bathroom every day with you," Hal asked with a ton of sarcasm.

"No. You're free to go outside and do whatever business you need."

"Why in heck are you up so early?"

"Because we're pilots, and we know the best sunrise occurs at ten thousand feet."

"Okay, sounds right. You go first. I'm older. I'll take longer."

"Three years make that much difference?"

"You'll see."

We came down to breakfast in tandem. I was already having a second cup of coffee before Hal came in the hotel café. He was already more animated, as was I. As pilots, we learned to enjoy early morning sorties. The air was cooler. The sky was cleaner. Sunrise was of a color that uplifted spirits, while sunsets were calming. For both of us this morning, we were looking for a sunrise high.

"We need a map," Hal said.

"Well, good morning to you, too." It was already clear that I would be the relative morning person in the road trip. "I want a haircut."

"You want a *what?*"

"I want a haircut. I want to be clean cut, so no one is confused about my credentials. I'm not going to be one of those Fonda loving peacenik hippy types on this trip. How are they going to know where I stand with a mop like this?"

"Great way to start the trip, eh?"

"I thought so."

Hal waved over our waitress and ordered his breakfast and coffee. We both ordered the standard fare of two eggs, sausage patties, hash browns, and toast with coffee and orange juice—my eggs scrambled, his over easy.

"Ma'am," he asked before she delivered our order, "is there a barber shop nearby, so this poor planner can get his mop cut short?"

She laughed at Hal after looking at me. "I think he's kinda cute," she said to Hal, then turned to me. "I think you look great right now."

I blushed. Hal laughed. Our waitress looked straight at me for an extra uncomfortable second. "We have a barber shop right here in the hotel. It opens at eight. Jake may come in early."

I looked at the young lady again. Long light red hair, petite, and full-figured, she was obviously enjoying flirting with us both. Attractive, personable, and comfortable in her own shoes, I couldn't help admiring the fine specimen of womanhood she was. That alone deserved a generous tip.

At 7:45 I found the barber shop with Hal in trail behind me. The man indeed was already there and ready to take my money. I sat down in his chair, and as he draped me with his barber cloth, I gave this morning's orders.

"See that Roger Ramjet character over there?" I said, pointing to my sidekick. "Cut my hair and shave my face like his, except I don't want his mustache—clean shaven. I want to look like a steely-eyed killer again."

I got my wish, leaving the hotel clean cut and deadly. Hal and I loaded the Porsche with our minimal luggage. We had the same mindset. Minimal personal gear. Nothing that would encumber the travel experience. Anything we needed we could buy along the way. It was the usual way we had flown together on cross country flights with students. The T-37 was a small jet. Any items we carried, we loaded into a hanging bag and hung it on our ejection seat. Too much baggage and the seat would be a drag on any ejection we hoped we never had to do again. As for the Porsche, it was no Bond car with an ejection seat. We crammed all our stuff in the front boot.

Hal climbed into the passenger seat for the first time to encounter the joys of the Porsche experience. I was only 400 miles of familiarity ahead of him.

"Now pay attention," I said. "You're going to have to learn to drive this beast, so watch and learn."

With that lecture I started the car's engine with a roar, put its gear in first, lifted the clutch, and killed the engine. Hal said nothing, only shook his head. I restarted the engine, listened to the notes of the exhaust momentarily, then carefully applied the correct proportion of power and clutch to get the Porsche moving. We were off.

"So, it's off to Route 66, eh, Hal? Only miles of miles to go."

"Let's put pedal to the metal,"

"Balls to the wall."

The music of the six cylinder horizontally opposed engine in town was like listening to a symphony of low drum rolls. We soon were at the edge of town where we could open up our powerful instrument, turning this percussion symphony into a mid-range snare drumroll. We remained good law-abiding boys until we passed Lamesa on Texas Highway 137. With 37 miles to go before getting to Brownfield, this was the time for a test track speed run.

"Are we ready to blow the cobs out of this motor?" I asked.

"Your ticket."

The truth of that statement was that, since Hal was still active duty, getting certain citations could become a career killer.

"The book says it has a top speed of 178. Are you up for that?"

"Hell, Rob. I've landed faster than that in a Thud."

The road ahead was straight enough and without other cars. Our eyes could see far ahead. There appeared to be no intersections. Without a word I shifted from fifth gear to third, put the accelerator to the floor, and waited for the 6300 rpm redline. Soon we were in fourth gear. The speed buildup slowed a bit. I checked ahead to estimate our distance to any obstacle, such as a turn or a hill. It still was clear when I reached 150 mph and shifted to fifth gear. I waited uncomfortably as the speed slowly increased from there. When we reached 165 mph, Hal and I turned to look at each other.

"Are we done?" I said over the roar of wind and engine that now screamed like six high-pitched trombones.

"We're done," Hal replied in agreement.

I lifted my foot from the accelerator and let it coast until I could downshift in succession to fourth gear, third gear, then second. When we were back to the legal speed limit, I heaved a sigh of satisfaction and put the Porsche back into fourth as we dragged along at the legal speed of 55 mph.

We hummed into Brownfield and past the town's police station with a smug satisfaction, knowing we were rebels who got away with it.

5

THE NORTH RIM OF THE Grand Canyon was at an elevation of around 8,000 feet. Neither Hal nor I had ever been on that side because it was difficult to get to. It was on the Utah side where the roads were tortuous and narrow. It was more prudent to visit the more popular South Rim. It still left a lot of time for talk as we passed through the Texas high plains on our way to New Mexico.

"What do you hear from Suzy Alexander?" It was the elephant in the Porsche that Hal hesitated to bring up and that I dreaded resurrecting.

"Suzy? I've talked to her several times. She's doing fine."

Hal was not satisfied with my answer. I knew he wouldn't be. Suzy was my best friend's wife and my former college girlfriend before I dumped her for all the wrong reasons. I was a fool, but my best friend was no fool at all. Suzy and John Alexander had a happy marriage. They had a son, Sean. Then John and I flew a T-37 into the ground. The resulting fire killed John. I failed to save him. His wife Suzy was left alone to take care of Sean, now one year old.

Hal was never one to be fooled easily. He knew exactly why I was on this road trip with no plan at all. I also knew why I was. I was in love with Suzy. I carried shame that I let her husband die. Their toddler, Sean, didn't deserve a drifter like me for a father. If I expressed love to Suzy, she was bound to see right through me as an opportunist taking advantage of a widow. In my heart I was convinced that she would always hold a grudge because I could not save her husband.

The irony was that she couldn't have been more supportive of me. And I to her during that time after that fatal accident, but it could never be anything but love like a brother to a sister. Otherwise, what would the world think of me and of her? In the meantime, I knew that in a perfect world, I would take her back in an instant. Unlike in college, this time I would never let her go. What would people think then?

"Does she have family nearby?"

"She does. Her parents live close. They help out and keep her spirits up."

"Is that what they say?" Hal persisted, "or is that what you suppose?"

I pondered long and hard before answering. "I suppose."

We fell silent for a while, driving into New Mexico. I could tell Hal was calculating how to say something. After covering another two miles at 60 mph, he responded to my answer.

"We should add a visit to Suzy on this trip. I think it would do you two some good."

"No, Hal. That would not be good. The nerves are still too raw."

"What nerves, Rob? Over John dying or Suzy living alone?"

"Hal, not now, damn it! It's too early. I'm not ready for that."

Hal knew to shut up. We drove on US Highway 380 toward Roswell, New Mexico, across the southwest segment of the Llano Estacado, the flattest place on earth. There was true beauty in the sheer starkness of such an experience.

"I'm pulling over," I suddenly said. "I want to try something."

The road was only slightly elevated. I invited Hal to step out with me and try an experiment. We hiked a quarter mile to the north from the highway, to take advantage of the Earth's curvature. The walk gave me a chance to explain to Hal why this exercise was necessary. He said little except for an occasional sound of acknowledgement. I stopped in a patch of arid-adapted shortgrass, checked for any critters that might object to my lying down on them, then placed myself face up on the Llano Estacado. Hal, now intrigued by the idea, joined me supine.

Shading our eyes with our hands, there it was. The giant bowl of blue, laced with a few brush strokes of cirrus clouds, just like I hoped it would be.

"Good idea," Hal said. "Quite a pleasant experience."

We lay there for a few minutes in silence. Then the first contrails of an airplane entered our view at high altitude.

We silently watched the jet streak by to ruin what our ancestors would have seen—nothing but sky.

"You know, Hal," I found myself confessing, "I think this sky is the perfect way to explain why I called you. I need to blot everything out for a few weeks. I need to see blue sky and no obstacles. Until we get back home, I'm going to kick the ass of every obstacle I find until my life is only blue sky."

We said nothing for another minute. The jet overhead was long gone, only leaving the elongated contrail in its wake. I said one last word on the subject.

"When I get those blue skies back, Hal, only then will I go find Suzy and pay her a visit."

6

WE PASSED THROUGH THE LLANO Estacado and hit the Caprock Escarpment, before rolling into Roswell for lunch. After flirting with a couple of waitresses, we paid our bills with generous tips and headed north to Interstate 40 and Flagstaff, Arizona. Having gained an hour by changing to Mountain Standard Time, Hal and I hoped to make Flagstaff by 8:00 p.m. Then it was just a challenge to avoid the winter weather and find a motel or hotel that would take us. We decided that we could divert around Albuquerque. If we did that, I specified that we would go nowhere near Mike Randall's Porsche dealership.

"You're going to have to explain this car," Hal said for the umpteenth time. I calmly showed him my name on the title and left him hanging for further explanations.

"Why do you not have a radio?" Hal asked in irritation.

"The Porsche engine is music enough," I replied deadpan.

It was an uneventful daytime drive of two hours to Clines Corners, with only a few slow-moving Winnebago campers and other ponderous vehicles to impede our progress. The Porsche turned out to be a dream at passing. Proceeding west on I-40/Route 66, we had an even more boring drive through Albuquerque, where we waited only ten minutes in line to get premium gas.

Hal and I successfully bypassed Mike Randall's generous car dealership.

I continued to worry that if he saw me, he would demand his Porsche back. The sun was lower on the horizon now, its glare making our westward direction harder to see the world as we intended. Passing through the lava flows of El Malpais, we made it to Gallup, New Mexico, and the El Rancho Hotel, perhaps the most iconic Route 66 establishment in the state. Because we were hungry and curious to stay at this historic rest stop, we delayed the last two and a half hours of driving to Flagstaff for the comfort of some overnight history. Some of the rooms bore the name of a celebrity who had stayed there—some famous, others infamous. We went first to the 49er Lounge, where Errol Flynn once took his horse along to the bar, according to Stan, our bartender. We bellied up to the bar and listened for a time, which beat sitting in what we now knew was a cramped cockpit of the Porsche. Customers were scarce. With all the spare time in the world, Stan fixed a fine and ice-cold shaken gin martini for both of us, then continued to tell us tales of life in Gallup. He had worked at the El Rancho for 20 years. He loved his job and was not shy in telling us about the great celebrities and the total jerks. John Wayne received an excess of glowing terms.

"He's a real gentleman," Stan said, "and the man is bigger than he looks on the picture screen."

"And the other side of good?" I asked.

"Errol Flynn was trouble. When he came to Gallup, it was best to hide the women, children, and all your small animals."

We finished our martinis, paid Stan with a large tip, and headed to the hotel restaurant for our evening meal. A menu posted at the hostess entrance gave me a chance to preview the food offered before I committed to a table. Hal was in an animated discussion with two attractive and unaccompanied women, as I reviewed the menu in more detail. He pointed in my direction, after ending his conversation. The ladies parted company, and Hal joined me.

"Now, what have you done?" I asked.

"Not much. Just meeting new friends."

"Is this going to cost us?"

"Oh, no. They aren't those kinds of girls. They're just two single girls who found us interesting. They're on a road trip, just like us."

"I guess there's no harm in asking them to join us for dinner."

"I already did." Hal turned back to the bar, giving a wave to the two. "They'll join us after they finish their wine and pay their tabs."

"This is like old times."

"Am I just getting better looking, or is the female population getting more aggressive?"

"I'm guessing more aggressive, which is not a bad deal. These are exciting times for dating."

We asked for a four-top table with facing chairs and gave Hal's name to our hostess. We waited to order drinks until they arrived. Within five minutes they approached our table with pleasant smiles and a touch of class in their introduction to me. We stood up to offer chairs to them, so that we each sat on either side of the two ladies. A waiter came up before we could do more than introduce ourselves. We ordered four different wines and talked while we waited.

Elizabeth on my right, with shoulder length light brown hair, wore white cotton pants, nicely fitted at her hips with an ornamental chain belt. Her pink linen blouse cut at the waist and opened at a most tasteful degree. She looked expensive with her gold chain and pendant slightly teasing the V in her cleavage. On top of that she wore a leather vest adorned with silver medallions arrayed in swirling patterns. She had a swarthy complexion and the most engaging beautiful eyes. I found this Mexican influence a most appealing trait in the native women of Texas and New Mexico.

On my left sat Catalina with a smile that men would die for—overly eager and happy. With an unconventional raven-haired pixie cut, it gave full view to her full red lips and her cute pixie nose. Like Elizabeth, her face and her brown eyes spoke of a Mexican heritage that was so appealing. She dressed in the Santa Fe style with silver-studded black slacks, an ornately embroidered denim blouse buttoned high, with a scarf tied at her neck. It was quite stylish but too harsh for my tastes befitting a girl with a pixie cut. I never got down far enough to see the shoes they wore.

When the waiter set the glasses of wine down at our table, we began a pleasant conversation. If Hal and I had to choose up sides with these ladies, it would be difficult. Elizabeth and Catalina were cousins from Southern California who were traveling together for the first time. They joked about how they learned what the other was really like the week before, when they began their trip. They had grown up in families that traced their roots to the early Spanish settlers of California. They both were out of college, had good jobs, didn't like hippies, and knew California was paradise. When Hal and I told them that we were friends from flying in the Air Force, they found it intriguing, positive, and honorable. That opinion of us was worthy of buying their dinner, but when we suggested it, they refused, saying it would be strictly Dutch treat. That was okay by me.

With dinner ordered, we learned about each other while sipping wine and finding what we all had in common, which was not much. The wines of four distinct varieties were perfect metaphors for our common interests. I found soon that Hal was turning into the Clint Eastwood "Man with No Name" of the group with few words. Catalina, the Pixie, seemed to find that appealing. Elizabeth did not. The choice was easy. They did the pairing for us.

What I found appealing about these two women was their ease with us as well as comfort in their own skin. They were physically attractive, but so are nearly all women. The difference was their smile, their comfortable conversation, and their interest in listening as well as talking. I was once again seeing the merits of brains as the sexiest part of a woman.

Our meals came soon enough. We ate with impeccable manners, had our plates cleared, and turned down dessert, coffee, and after dinner drinks. After paying our four separate tabs, we sat and talked for a while, but soon the two ladies suggested they needed to get back to their room. Hal and I, being officers and gentlemen, offered to escort them to their room. They accepted graciously.

Passing through the lobby, we agreed that the hotel was a spectacular find. That it was on Route 66 made it even more special. We soon got to their room and waited while Catalina found her key in her purse and unlocked the door. As the two stepped inside, Elizabeth looked at Catalina, then turned to us and asked.

"Would you boys like to come in for a while?"

To my surprise, Hal said the unexpected.

"Thank you, ladies, but I'm done for the night...." He looked at me. "...but Rob here, I'm sure, would take you up on your kind invitation."

The two women then turned to me. I had had a chance to assess their physical attributes as we had walked to their room. They were both magnificent physical specimens, but to men, every woman is a magnificent physical specimen. I was imagining what could possibly transpire if I joined them. Would it be a threesome? I had no experience with that. It would be exciting to have that notch on my belt. Would they roll me and take all my money? I had read about that. It took only a split second to decide that I wanted this experience and the fantasy of this one-night stand. I was already extremely turned on at the prospect. So, I replied.

"Well, thank you, ladies. I think I will..." and there I hesitated, "...go back to my room."

As surprised as they looked, Catalina looked at us with a hint of relief on her face. We bade our goodnights and suggested we would enjoy seeing them at breakfast. As their door closed, we turned toward the lobby for a sit.

"What were you thinking?" I asked Hal. "You... totally missed the chance of a lifetime."

"So, I should ask the same of you. I set you up with the opportunity of a lifetime, too."

"I have my reasons, but you? That isn't like you. What the hell?"

He looked down to hide his face. "I have my reasons, too."

As we walked in the splendid hotel lobby, I pondered what just happened. I found one of the heavy upholstered chairs and plopped myself down. Then a lightbulb of an idea came on.

"You have a girlfriend, don't you?"

Hal lowered his head and sheepishly responded.

"Yep."

"Good Lord!" I was laughing. "What has happened to my friend, Hal?"

"Her name is Lisa Anders." He sat down in the chair beside me. "She lives in Austin. She has a PhD from Texas University, and she's smarter than I am. That's what I need, and I'm not about to blow it."

"Thanks for telling me." I was sarcastic.

"I didn't want it to ruin your image of me."

"It has done that."

"So, tell me, truthfully. Would you have gone in their room with me if I had said yes?"

"No." I said, without hesitation.

"Then, what's wrong with you?" His voice showed his exasperation.

Could the truth hurt me to share? I only learned the truth five minutes before. An epiphany hit me with the clarity of the Golden Rule. With a modification to the actual Rule, I made a corollary and recited it to Hal.

"Do what you hope the one you love is doing."

"It's Suzy, isn't it?"

"Yes. It's Suzy. I love her. I always have."

"So, what are you going to do about it? Sit on your ass, get depressed and pass up opportunities that fall in your lap?"

I sat silent, feeling miserable at my unwillingness to be bad. In truth, I was tired of feeling guilt for things in my past. I needed to clean the slate, to ask God for forgiveness, and to decide to enjoy my life again. I looked at Hal. He looked at me with a *so what are you going to do?* expression. There was only one thing left to do, and I shared it with Hal.

"I'll call Suzy tonight."

7

FROM MY EARLY CHILDHOOD, AS I emerged from my toddler phase at two or three and began my memories, I loved two things—airplanes and women.

Many airplanes flew over our Oklahoma City house every day. Two aircraft were of most importance to me. First was the Beechcraft Bonanza. More than one flew over every morning when I went into the front yard to sit in the cool morning grass and look up to the west. The Bonanza, with its distinctive V-tail and colorful paint schemes, made me scream with delight. I couldn't pronounce the name, so I called it the *Beechcrap Banana.*

The other fascinating class of airplane was one I never saw and could only hear—the rolling waves of six-pusher radial engines that came from the awesome B-36 flying high overhead. Only later did I learn about engines out of sync in my twin jet T-37. Keeping six engines in agreement in exact revolutions per minute must have been a daunting task for a flight engineer or pilot. The waves of asynchrony were music to my ears. First, the sound would come, then some subtle asynchrony from high above would literally shake the ground in the most marvelous vibrations. I pictured myself flying both the B-36 and the *Beechcrap Banana.*

With like fascination, I became addicted to pretty women. I recall sitting on the couch with my father, looking at the television show, *Last of the Mohicans.* The Mohicans wore war paint with big circles and streaks on their chests and faces. I was fascinated. At a party for grownups, one of the wives had the most beautiful mahogany brown hair, voluptuous form, and the fullest, most luscious lips with bright red lipstick. Her lips were like a beacon in the night.

I didn't go to sleep at bedtime. I quietly slipped into the room where my mother kept her cold cream and red lipstick. Quietly I smeared lines and circles on my face, abdomen, and chest like a Mohican. Red was erotic to me, as were those luscious red lips. I looked at myself in the mirror, then stormed into our living room and announced myself with a war hoop.

I didn't impress anybody, least of all my mother. She took me in the bathroom, assayed the damage, and almost cried in laughter. She cleaned me up, using more cold cream to remove the red lipstick. I found that ironic.

"All clean!" she said. "Now off to bed, Little Rob."

I stayed in bed this time, embarrassed, but determined to do even better next time. That beautiful lady never visited our house again.

I did, however, start a habit beginning in kindergarten. From that first day until I graduated from college, I had a girlfriend each year. I never regretted dropping one and finding another throughout my first 29 years of life—until now.

Back in our room at the El Rancho, I went to our phone to call Suzy. I had her number memorized, which should have been a further clue to me. I read the long-distance calling instructions pasted to the base of the rotary dial instrument. I first had to dial eight to get a long-distance phone line. If I was lucky, I would get another dial tone, which then allowed me to dial zero for a long-distance operator. If I got her, I could ask to charge the call to my telephone number at home. The trick was getting a dial tone to dial the first number eight.

I dialed eight and got a busy signal. No problem. I hung up the phone, lifted the receiver once more and tried again. I got the hoped-for dial tone. Next, I dialed zero and got a busy signal, which meant I had to again start the complete process from the beginning. I had read in one of the hotel brochures that a big celebration in the City of Gallup was ramping up. That meant many people were competing for available phone lines throughout the system. I tried dialing eight a half dozen more times only to get busy signals. When I finally got a dial tone and dialed the long-distance operator, the familiar busy signal mocked me once more. That's when I gave up.

"Rob, maybe you should wait until later tonight when everyone's done their talking."

"The time zone's working against us." I was both frustrated, yet relieved. "I'll try again tomorrow. I'm too ticked off at Ma Bell to be on the telephone with Suzy."

"Fair enough, so what's the plan tomorrow?"

"No! No, we're not planning tomorrow. We never had any itinerary to begin with... by design."

"I guess you're right. Let's sleep on it and plan where we go based on the weather or maybe where we can go to kick the most ass."

"Where do you think we need to go to do some of this ass kicking you're so eager to do?" Hal used his best smart-aleck tone.

"Let's start with Ma Bell," I said.

8

THE NEXT MORNING, I CALLED Suzy again. Being an hour ahead in Mountain Time reassured me that I wouldn't wake her too early. Her little Sean most likely woke up before she did every morning. Unlike the night before, the telephone at Suzy's small quarters rang immediately and my heart started beating like a rabbit, like junior high school all over again. At the first sound of her voice, my eyes began to burn salty tears.

"Suzy? Is that you?"

"Oh, Rob." Her voice trembled both joy and sadness.

Neither of us said more for the next few seconds. When the silence ended, our voices were both higher in pitch and strained.

"Suzy, I called to hear from you that you're all right. Are you doing okay?"

"Well... I uh... I guess I am."

"I need to... I need to know for sure."

Another long silence prevailed. I waited her out. Then she spoke.

"Well... no. Not really."

"What's going on? You're near your parents. Can't they help."

"I'm lonely, Rob."

Her words shocked me. I was lonely, too, but I never had imagined she could be the same. She had her son to care for. Her parents were in the same house. She needed only to step from their backyard cabana to be with them.

"What can I do?"

"Where have you been?"

"I… I… had my own personal issues to deal with."

There was another long pause before she said, *"You, too, huh?"*

The greatest pain from suffering depression is when you realize you have fooled no one but yourself. Yes, I too was lonely, depressed, and silently begging for help. I had chosen Hal to help get me through this phase. Suzy had no one. Would helping Suzy help me?

"Yeah… me, too," I replied.

"Come home, Rob. It would be good for us to see each other."

"Yes, it would…." I hesitated to say more, but my regrets and guilt took over. "…I'm sorry things happened… like they did. Suzy, I'm so sorry."

Suzy's voice grew sterner. *"Come home, Rob. I need you to come home. Please?"*

In the background I could hear the babble of little Sean growing louder. Not yet at the level of crying, I knew my time was up.

"Soon. I'll be seeing you soon. Kiss Sean for me. I hear him."

"Yes, I better go. Sean is waiting for breakfast. Hurry back. Please."

We said our good-byes and hung up. Hal was beside me but said nothing. He was smart that way.

OVER COFFEE, EGGS, SAUSAGE, AND pancakes, we formulated our plans. We decided that, if all else failed, we could change our minds again. This was becoming man's greatest adventure—no plans, no aims, and no cares.

Our dinner companions, Elizabeth and Catalina, joined us for breakfast, looking just as happy and as attractive on this morning as they had looked last night. No one mentioned our polite rejection of their previous night's offer. They were still pleasant company, so we took the extra time to talk and compare notes about where each other's road trips were taking us. They ordered a much lighter breakfast than we meat and potatoes types had ordered. Their granola and fruit with juice and coffee wouldn't have fueled Hal and me for more than an hour on the road. They shared that they were headed to Santa Fe to shop—unless the weather got bad. They were fearless travelers, which I find to be an asset in a woman. Since we had both previously been to the South Rim, we knew it would still be a fine place to visit in winter.

The time to leave arrived for our lady friends, and we stood when they did. Catalina came up to Hal and placed a kiss on his cheek. Then she turned to me. I also expected a kiss but instead got a question.

"Are you two boys, eh…?"

"No," I said, for I knew what she was thinking. "We have girlfriends we dearly love and would never disappoint."

"See," Catalina said, turning to Elizabeth. "I was right."

Catalina turned back to me, kissed me lightly on the cheek saying, "Good for you… and thank you."

As they walked out of the hotel restaurant, Hal turned to me.

"Do I look gay to you?" His sarcasm was evident.

"Not usually. It sounds like you may have looked gay last night, though."

Hal laughed. "Let's get out of here so I can take you outside and knock your block off."

We didn't go outside. Hal didn't knock my block off. Instead, we sat back down at our table and calculated how long it would take using the quickest route to the Grand Canyon National Park. We estimated it to be about a five-and-a-half-hour drive if I followed the ridiculously slow federal speed limit. I would try to be quicker.

We packed up the Porsche, checked out of the El Rancho, and headed back onto I-40 west for Flagstaff. After only a few miles, we turned off on the outskirts of Gallup to buy gasoline at a Gulf filling station. The lines for gas had formed ahead of our arrival. We still had more than half a tank, but for some just waiting in line to get to a gas pump carried the risk of running out of gas before they got their turn. It turned out that the gasoline pumps had a ten-gallon maximum allowed. When it was finally our turn after 30 minutes, we joked that we got cheated because we only pumped a little more than nine gallons into our tank. We had trouble getting out of the way of other customers because there was a welding truck whose driver discourteously blocked the flow of cars out of the service station. We were stuck, with impatient drivers behind us.

Hal climbed out of the Porsche to politely request the truck driver move his equipment. The two men stood facing each other for a minute of talk. A few times the welder waved his hands in the air in animated gestures that became movements more strident with each successive gesticulation. Suddenly, the man chest butted Hal, placing his face into Hal's. As I guessed, it was a mistake on the man's part. To his surprise he crumpled to the ground at Hal's feet. Hal then walked into the station to pay cash for the exorbitant cost of nine gallons of gas. Returning to my car, Hal's sparring partner, halfway recovered, began hurling the standard curses and threats of the uneducated. Hal spoke urgently.

"Let's get the hell outta here."

"What did you say to him."

"I said, 'If I wanted any shit out of you, I'd rip off the top of your head and dip it out.'"

"And how did that work out?"

"You need to leave. *Now!*"

The welder climbed into his truck. I immediately assessed the situation. With little effort he could crush the front end of my Porsche with insignificant damage to the truck that he likely didn't even own. We were sitting ducks, and he was looking with furious eyes directly at Hal, sitting in my passenger seat. Behind me the nearest car driver waved his hands frantically for me to back up, which I did. It gave me a narrow window to pass around the truck by going onto the bedding plants that were about to be sacrificed for my safety. The Porsche performed admirably as I took advantage of the narrow escape route and squirmed around the welder's truck just before he hit reverse gear and backed up.

We got onto the service road to I-40 with ease and heaved a sigh of relief—or so we thought. Hal announced that Mr. Welder, as we now called him, was barreling toward us. This was bizarre. I was now in a Porsche we had proven could go at least 165 mph while being chased by a welding truck. If I ever had children, this would be an entertaining story to tell them.

We entered the interstate highway without delay, but so did Mr. Welder. Knowing the speed limit was 55 mph, I cranked it up to 60. In the rearview mirror, I calculated that at my speed, I would be dead in about 15 seconds. I shoved the Porsche up to 70, hoping that I wouldn't meet a trooper trying to make his early morning quota. My next calculation was that this welding truck must also race on the weekends. He was still gaining. I tried ramping up to 80 mph and got some spacing, but it was soon apparent that he was slowly closing the gap.

"If I get stopped at a hundred," I said, "it's a felony."

"Well, then, don't stop there." Hal's sound logic had merit. "Go a hundred and fifty if you need to. The crime is the same."

"Let's see if we can't tease him a little. What's he's willing to do."

"As long as you don't see a gun."

In my mirror, Mr. Welder moved to within three or four car lengths behind me. I inched up to 85 mph. Then 90. Next 95. Each time I did, his distance behind us remained the same. I was quite surprised he was able to reach our speed and maintain it. I cranked it this time to 105. I was tired of playing his game. Each time we had to go into the left lane to pass another car, I feared we would get stuck behind a vehicle and our pursuer would ram into us. It had to end, before we hurt someone. I decided it would not be we who caused an accident.

Even at 105 mph, Mr. Welder drew closer. I had no idea what his end game was, but then he didn't know mine either. I had no intention for my Porsche to get hurt. I turned to Hal.

"Make sure you're buckled up. Watch this."

I held on until my rearview mirror confirmed there were no cars behind me. Mr. Welder was within a car length behind me. I guessed correctly that he wanted to move over carefully to the left lane to get beside us. Now that he was in the other lane, I made my move.

With lightning speed, I slammed on the brakes of a car designed to brake or accelerate in equal measure. The truck zoomed past us at a true 105 miles per hour, not a stable speed for a laden commercial vehicle. Mr. Welder, apparently shocked by his sudden passing of his target, also hit his brakes hard. From the Porsche's windshield, Hal and I got a firsthand look at what happens when a welding truck tries to be a race car. At breakneck speed, the welding truck and its driver lost the grip on the road, turned front to back and rolled backwards briefly before rotating one more turn and rolling off the highway into a barbed wire fence.

"Do we pull over?" I asked.

"I see nothing we can save. I see no cars that could have witnessed it. We were the victims here. Drive on my friend."

"I'm pulling over." Hal's suggestion disagreed with my personal code. "We can't leave him to die."

I was already at the speed limit with Mr. Welder's wreck still ahead of us. I hit the brakes again and pulled onto the shoulder. To our shock as we egressed from the Porsche, a state trooper coming from the opposite direction pulled across the center median and came to a stop on the shoulder right in front of us. The trooper exploded from his patrol car. The urgency of his movements was enough to intimidate the hardiest of souls.

The trooper shouted. "Did you see the accident?"

"Yes," I replied. "He ran past us just before he flipped."

We started to approach the truck, but the trooper raised his hand to stop us. "Stay back!"

No problem for us. We watched as he put his head in the truck cab. "We have a dead body here."

We remained silent and waited while he checked for any other bodies. The tanks of oxygen and acetylene appeared intact, a great testament to the design and safety of the manufacturer. Returning to his patrol car he radioed for the appropriate help, which, because it took a long time, made us nervous. He eventually came back to us to get our statements.

"Tell me what you saw," he ordered.

I answered succinctly, using a few skills I picked up from Air Force Survival School and from life itself.

"We saw this truck pass us on the left," I said. "He had to be going at least a hundred miles an hour, and then he spun out right in front of us, angled to the right shoulder, and rolled. We drove up on it and pulled over."

"It sounds like he might have seen me and hit his brakes if he was going as fast as you say," the trooper said. He turned to Hal. "Tell me what you saw."

"I looked in the side mirror and saw him coming from far off," Hal began. "He kept getting closer faster than I liked. I was glad to see him pass us."

"So, he was in your lane at first?" the trooper asked.

"Yes, but I never saw when he moved over to pass us," Hal replied.

"You said 'he.'" The trooper challenged. "Did you know him?"

"I've never met a lady welder before," Hal replied. "I assumed it was a man."

"Good point. Anything else you can tell me?"

"That's about it," I said. "We were headed to the Grand Canyon today and hoping to see a sunset, so we were glad you showed up. Do you need us anymore?"

"Did you make contact with the vehicle?" the trooper asked.

"No."

"Then I thank you for stopping," he replied and pointed a finger westward. "You're free to go."

We made it to Flagstaff in record time.

9

FROM FLAGSTAFF IT WAS ABOUT a two-hour drive. After seeing the fatal accident, we were too nervous to enjoy the scenery along the way. We hardly spoke a word to each other on the remaining leg of I-40. We broke our silence with a bounty of questions.

"Did we just dodge a bullet?" Hal asked.

"At least we told the truth—just not the *whole* truth."

"So we didn't lie to that patrolman. We *did* stop to render aide."

"We did the right thing, Hal. But how lucky can we be that I hit the brakes when I did?"

"You live a charmed life, Rob. I'll say that."

"What could we have done if the patrol car hadn't arrived when it did?"

"What if I had decided to inch up to 110?"

"Did he note our car tag?"

"Could we be charged if a driver we both passed reports that both of us were going a hundred?"

The questions kept rolling off our tongues until we approached the lodges that ringed the entrance to the Grand Canyon National Park.

Before we got to the park gate, we found the Moche Lodge with a room available and booked it for three nights. With plenty of daylight left to get into the park and enjoy the view, we unloaded our packs, grabbed Hal's Nikon F2, and headed out in our car for the entrance. Both of us looked up at the same instance as an airplane flew overhead on its way toward the canyon rim.

"Is this in our genes?" Hal asked.

"What do you mean?"

"All pilots look up whenever an airplane of any type flies overhead. It must be genetic."

We kept our eyes in the sky until it passed on behind the trees. Hal identified it as a Piper Cherokee 6—a heavy hauler with an excellent safety record. "It looks like it's giving aerial tours. I just read about that last night."

Unlike most other national parks, the Grand Canyon had an entrance fee. It was a surprise when we drove up to the park ranger who asked us for money. We managed to pry our fat billfolds out of our Levi's hip pockets and share the payment rate for one carload. Parking was reasonably easy, compared to a visit in the summer months. Stopping first at the park's Visitor Center, we grabbed a few brochures to read. Approaching the information desk, two park rangers seemed eager to answer our questions.

"What's the best time to view the sunset," I asked.

"Today's sunset occurs at 6:10 p.m. Mountain Standard Time," the lady said and looked at her watch. "That gives you an hour to find a good spot to view our sunset or to take pictures."

Our sunset? It sounded like she owned it. These park rangers were really into this place. I had only been to the Grand Canyon once before when I was a child. For all my remaining youthful years I fantasized that the Grand Canyon sunset, being the most spectacular thing in the universe, would be number one on my list of places to see when I grew up. Ferde Grofé's classical symphonic masterpiece, The Grand Canyon Suite, that I played year after year was the icing on the cake. I was ready to own a bit of that sunset for myself this evening.

"You're lucky," the second park ranger told us. "The skies and the air should make for spectacular colors this evening."

"Where's the best place to go?" Hal asked.

"It's crowded sometimes," he replied, "but Yavapai Point is my favorite place to see it."

"We'll go there first, then," I said. "Thanks for the tips."

We headed out at a run. The setting sun filtered through the pine trees as we drove the short distance to our first view of the canyon. Through a gap in the trees, The canyon briefly appeared. Mr. cool and controlled Hal shouted out—a rare emotion from him in my experience. We parked with unexpected ease. Winter was turning out to be a wonderful time to visit away from the bustling crowds.

"I thought you had been here before," I said.

"No." His eyes were unusually expressive. "I've never in my life seen what I just saw."

We walked from the car to the Yavapai Point vista, with its guard rails and excitedly talking visitors. Hal started shooting pictures with his Nikon, as if Kodachrome slide film was free. The unique aspect of this view was the presence of the Tonto Plateau, a flat and green expanse of land at least a thousand feet below us that projected out from the rim of the canyon. In fact, it was only one of dozens of similarly green plateaus at the same elevation extending as far to the west as I could see. The sun, near its end for the day, illuminated the green growth on these plateaus. With each minute before sunset, we watched the greens change, just as the predominant reds of the rocks progressed. The sky was devoid of haze, which was good for Hal's Nikon shots, but sadly the sky did not turn the bright yellow and red that we hoped. At one point the Cherokee 6 flew past, then below the Tonto Plateau on its intimate flight well below the canyon's rim. We stayed there for over an hour watching the crowds thin, the colors darken, and stars brighten. The moon in its last quarter phase was only a third visible and nearly gone for the day. This would be a spectacular night to stargaze with a telescope. For the first time a chill was in the air. We had done nothing outside since lying supine on the Great Plains of New Mexico. Now we needed jackets.

"You want to hike down to the bottom tomorrow?" Hal asked.

"I don't know how far we can go, but sure."

I looked at Hal in the darkening sky as we walked back to the Porsche. Both of us dressed similarly in Levi's, a T-shirt under a buttoned collar sports shirt, and tennis shoes. We looked ill-prepared to be here in winter, having planned poorly. Fortunately, the facilities located on the South Rim were sure to sell us all the overpriced heavier clothing we would need.

We headed west and south along the road back to Grand Canyon Village to find a suitable place to eat on a Friday night. Our first stop was the Yavapai Lodge and Tavern, which we found suitable simply because it was there.

"You ever go on vacations with your parents," Hal asked, "and listen to them debate whether to keep on driving or settle for the first place they found?"

"You mean the kind of vacation where your dad says, 'this place looks great!' and mom says, 'I want to look further?'"

"Exactly!"

We both laughed, then I added the observation that summed up all men's thoughts throughout the world.

"Ours may be the greatest vacation I ever had."

The food turned out to be crappy, but we weren't there to have our palates sated. We were there to eat. I assume it was a lively place in the summer, but in February it was quite tame. That suited us fine, since we were still a tad nervous about the accident with Mr. Welder, God rest his soul. We had one more drink after our light fare of hamburgers, fries, and beer.

The time we shared together on the trip was working its magic for me. I had been in the depths of depression, which I suppose everyone but I knew. I needed to be bad just one more time before I became a full-fledged and responsible adult. With descriptions of depression being anger turned inward, I was now doing my best to turn that into reverse by turning my anger outward. When I asked Hal to come on a trip with me and kick some ass, I meant it. Yet, someone dying today did not satisfy. It made me angrier. People I met on this trip were hellbent to ruin their own lives, whether it be by searching for a one-night stand or by risking death on the highway to address some insult. Vietnam was dystopian enough. The real world didn't function much better.

As a child, I got angry a lot. I had my temper tantrums so often that my mother suggested I try a different approach.

"Rob, whenever you get angry, I want you to grab a hammer, go into the backyard, and beat that hammer into the ground as hard as you can, until you feel better."

I know my mother meant well, but it never worked. It only made it worse because it never solved the thing that caused the anger. I was now sitting in the Yavapai Tavern with my drink in hand thinking that kicking ass might not be the way to go.

10

THE NEXT MORNING, WE WERE awake well before the first hints of daylight, not because we wanted to see the Grand Canyon sunrise, but because we were military pilots. We were used to waking up early. At first, being young, it seemed torture. Just two years later it was exhilarating. Such was the case this Saturday morning.

We managed to find the Moche Café open and the staff chipper. A Moche Lodge brochure said this was an old Harvey House establishment. That was supposed to be good, and it was. The coffee, a pilot's staple drink while on duty, was perfection. We asked the waitress, a middle-aged and all-business sort of woman, what we should order that would best prepare us to hike down into the Grand Canyon this morning?

"First time?" she asked.

We both nodded our heads. She looked critically at our flimsy backpacks lying on the floor under our seats.

"Are you staying down there or is it a day trip?"

"Day trip," Hal replied. "Down to Indian Garden and back up."

"You like pancakes?"

"Yes, we do," I said. "Give us everything we need. Spare no expense."

"How do you like your eggs? And do you like orange juice?" she asked, never changing her expression.

We ended up with the same thing—three eggs scrambled, sausage patties, bacon, hash browns, English muffin, orange juice, coffee, and pancakes the size of plates. After this cornucopia plopped down before us, she gave us one more piece of advice.

"Before you go down, make sure you have lots of food and water. Get yourself a ton of trail mix and a gallon each of water. If you don't drink that much water, you'll regret it. And if you have any left, there's probably some idiot who will need it."

"We'll take your advice," I said.

"If you're here in the morning," she said with her first subdued smile, "you will be thanking me with a great big tip."

We ate like our lives depended upon it. The only issue was that it was cutting into our prospects of seeing the sunrise. It wasn't like we could wolf it down or eat it later. It took close to a half hour before we finished up and paid our tab with an extra percent or two in the tip.

Stepping outside, the stars were fading away, the sky was clearing with a million miles of visibility, and the clouds were turning the most marvelous pink and red to the east. We walked along the rim trail until we reached the view behind the classic Grand Canyon hotel, El Tovar. Now, many individuals and families surrounded us, none of whom were making any noise. Instead, the viewers seemed transfixed in a moment of divine reverence for God the Creator and this beauty He created. The colors of the rocks and plateaus were changing with each minute, waiting for the sun to make its first peek. Soon the reds on the horizon grew fiery, then glowed brighter, burning away the splendid reds and revealing a surprise layer of snow dusting the upper canyon surfaces. At 7:15 a.m. the canyon walls and the layers of sedimentary rocks catching the sunlight brought out a clearer three-dimensional perception of both the depth and distance of this morning's light show.

Hal and I stood side by side at the rim's edge, leaning on the stone wall that kept us safe from falling over the edge. I could understand how someone would occasionally fall into the canyon. They weren't looking at the ground.

I was struck also by the discovery that in my childhood mind, I had remembered the Grand Canyon as the biggest thing in the world. Yet, when I approached it yesterday, I was struck by the realization that my memory of the canyon's size fell way short of the truth. The Grand Canyon was so big, my own mind was unable to store an adequate memory of its vastness. I would need a bigger brain to encapsulate a more accurate memory.

"Big enough for you?" I asked Hal.

"I'm cold," he replied.

Fair enough. We voted to remain cold. Afterall, it would get warmer as the sun rose. And, too, if we hiked down into the canyon, it would get warmer. It was another great plan by the men on the greatest vacation of their lives. All decisions, dumb or otherwise, were great decisions.

We walked to a nearby gift shop.

"Did you bring a hat?" Hal asked.

"No, but I need one," I admitted, looking around for the hat aisle.

"I got one already," he said, then opened a button on the front of his shirt and pulled out a ball cap that I soon feared would cause us grief.

Hal placed on his head a black cap sporting the logo of the new organization, Red River Valley Fighter Pilots Association, with the emblem of the River Rats, in bamboo-like letters. This was an exclusive organization of men who flew aerial combat missions over North Vietnam and lived to tell about it. Hal had flown over 100 missions north of the Red River in an F-105 Thud. He had earned the right to wear the cap. Contrasting Hal to me, I also had flown missions north of the Red River, except my missions were crossing the *Oklahoma* Red River. Hal's Red River was a lot riskier.

"What do you think?" Hal asked.

"You're making me look like a slacker by contrast, but I'll defend your right to wear it."

"Yeah, I thought of that. I almost didn't bring it. But, hell, I'll wear it and see if anybody salutes."

"Don't let the hecklers get to you," I said. "I just hope we don't run into any."

"I don't plan on it."

"I'll check your six, but I need a ball cap that'll get people riled up, too."

After a brief grazing session, I bought a less-than-intimidating ball cap with *Grand Canyon National Park* emblazoned on the front.

"This should tick them off," I said.

We started to exit the gift shop when I spied a rack of postcards. I made Hal wait while I rifled through the offerings and picked out a view from our first stop at Yavapai Point. The colors on the photo were unlike our view of the day before. It further illustrated the diverse colors the canyon might reveal each day. I paid for the postcard and a six-cent stamp, borrowed an ink pen, and addressed it from memory. I quickly wrote.

Dear Suzy,

I'm at the Grand Canyon with Hal Freed. We're hoping to hike part way down later this morning. Vacation is good therapy to get my head on straight. I think I'm ready to become an adult again. This is a man's trip, so we don't know where we will go next. I should be back in OKC in about ten days. I'll call you when I get back.

Love to you and Little Sean,
Rob

"Can we go now?" Hal asked.

We walked down to the hotel lobby mailbox and dropped off the postcard.

"Let's sit down in these comfortable chairs and wait for it warm up," I said.

"I don't want to get bored."

"Well then, sit down and tell me about this girlfriend who's smarter than you. Lisa Anders, right?"

"Yeah, Lisa," he said, flashing a rare grin on his face. "I met her in Austin."

"What's her PhD in?"

"Wow, you remembered. She has a doctorate in political science. That's where we met."

"She's not your teacher, I hope."

"No, we were students together."

"You've been going to school in Austin?" I was amazed to think of Hal as a student.

"The Air Force is sending me. I already had my master's before I got hooked up with the military years ago. And with Laredo closing down, I was due for rotation, anyway, so I applied and got the slot. No big deal. It's great for career enhancement."

"When are you moving up to Austin?"

"It has to be fairly soon. I'm getting tired of the drive back and forth."

"Back to Lisa, is she one of those left-wing, hippie professor types?"

"She just got her doctorate in December. They'll let her teach there while I work to finish my dissertation. She's no hippie. She thinks Nixon is the greatest diplomat since John Quincy Adams."

"Why would Adams be the greatest?"

"Don't ask me. She could tell you."

"So, she's smarter than you, but is she dumb enough to marry you?"

Hal laughed. "She thinks I'm good looking, which means she's lost all sense of reason. So, yes. She's that dumb."

"You've made plans, haven't you?"

"If we make plans, it likely will be the same way we're planning this cluster foxtrot you call a vacation."

"Then I'd elope. Makes it quick and painless."

"How would you know?" Hal asked.

"The John and Suzy Alexander wedding. They both told me that when they next get married—they were tongue in cheek mind you—they would elope."

"I'm not much for elaborate ceremonies. That's what we'll do. Elope."

I laughed. "You know that I just manipulated you into confessing you were in love *and* getting hitched."

"Are we growing up, Rob? I mean, look at us. We're sitting here, too cheap to even buy a jacket to keep warm, because we don't have a woman in our midst to nag us into doing something sensible... and I miss that."

Hal and I looked at each other with self-deprecating disdain, got up from the large comfortable chairs, and walked back into the gift shop and each bought a jacket that our imaginary wives had just nagged us to buy. And we were happy they did.

11

WE BEGAN OUR TREK DOWN into the canyon from the Bright Angel Trailhead west from the El Tovar.

The salesman who sold us our jackets gave us a good suggestion. "Leave your car where it is and take the shuttle to the trailhead. When you get back up from your nine-mile round trip, you might appreciate a bus carrying you back, even if it is just one more mile."

This gave us a chance to meet other hikers aboard the shuttle, which meant we would not be alone on the trail. Once we began our hike at the trailhead, we found ourselves going through the first three or four switchbacks. It was clear that we would never be alone. There were hikers everywhere—going down, coming up, and standing still. After fifteen minutes, we shucked our jackets and stuffed them into our flimsy and already uncomfortable backpacks.

So much for the advice of our nagging imaginary wives.

The energy required for going downhill was oddly excessive. We first presumed that going down would be easy with gravity as our friend, but, with each step, it was evident that it was like putting the brakes on repeatedly. My left knee began protesting this new assault on its joint. We both had continued to work out routinely. Being in decent shape, we soon learned, was a fool's hope in the canyon. Nonetheless, we could descend much faster than many. Our other unexpected discovery was that the Bright Angel Trail was like a rollercoaster. There were many parts of the trail where we had to go up as many times as we went down.

The people we passed were interesting. Other people passed us. There were runners, often in pairs, who passed us at the speed of a marathoner. A fellow hiker told us to watch out for more runners. They were often running rim to rim for 23.9 miles.

"Those two who just passed us are descending about 4,500 feet to the Colorado River," he said, "but when they get to the ascent on the Kaibab Trail, the climb is much steeper than the Bright Angel and 6,000 feet back up. That's more than a mile. It's brutal."

"We'll walk," I replied and picked up our pace to pass the man.

Our next encounter was a mule team of packets and riders. We paused with our backs to the rock wall to let the animals brush past us. We again picked up the pace, now Hal taking the lead. The midmorning scenery was outstanding, but as we confessed to each other, our goal was the hike, not the view. We hardly slowed down as we passed by the Mile-and-a-Half Resthouse. Much to our surprise there was no drinking water available. We pressed on to the Three-Mile Resthouse and wondered if our water was adequate, remembering that our morning's waitress suggested we carry a gallon each. We were sweating, but it was so dry that we were not wet. The sweat left our bodies as vapor. How could we tell if we needed water? The answer was to drink water ahead of the need. As we rapidly approached the Three-Mile Resthouse, covering more switchbacks, we hoped to find water available. Upon our arrival, we found the same lack of water. A sign that told us water was available only from May to October.

Hal pulled out his Grand Canyon booklet.

"It says here that Indian Garden has water year-round."

"I guess that's why they call it a garden."

"Are you up for it? Another mile and a half? How much water do you have?"

"I've got half of it left."

"It'll be plenty hot down here when we start back up," Hal warned me, as he waved his booklet in the air. "This thing says it'll take twice the time to climb back up top."

"We better get going, then," I said, then asked. "Have you eaten anything?

"I had a little, but it made me thirsty."

"I forgot about mine, but now I'm shaking. I'm going to start eating as we head back."

"Okay, then, Indian Garden it is. There better be water."

"Hal." I paused for effect. "When I said we better get going, I meant back up."

"Back up?"

"Yeah. I'm tired, thirsty, and hungry."

"You're saying you want to go back up."

"That's what I said."

"Well, thank *God*."

Knowing we were going to have a different challenge on the return climb back to the South Rim trailhead, we consumed as much water as we wanted. The three miles up to the rim was much easier for us because now we used muscles to climb, rather than joints to descend. My knees did not hurt going up, but my muscles fatigued after some distance of climbing. We found ourselves frequently pausing for our legs to recover. It was much warmer now as well, but the sweat remained unseen, coming out as steam, not water. We continued to drink water and eat the trail mix that hikers called gorp while maintaining our relative snail's rate of climb. At one point I had to stop, out of breath. I told Hal an old fact we should have realized.

"You get winded at this altitude," I said. "I didn't plan for that on this hike."

"I thought I was in pretty good shape, but this... this is tougher than I guessed it would be."

As we hiked, our heads were down so that we could navigate the obstacles put in our path. Cross ties served as steps on the trail. They stabilized the path from erosion by rain, wind, or footsteps. We often stepped to avoid random road apples left by the countless mules we encountered on our climb. With such concentration on the trail, we took notice of few hikers. Then something changed. Ahead of us, someone spoke to Hal.

"Baby killer!"

Hal, sporting his River Rat ball cap, looked up just as the young man came abreast of him to bump his shoulder and knock off his cap. Hal stopped immediately and turned around to look at him as he passed. He was one of a group of four college age men, all with long stringy hair and hippie attire that we would never be caught wearing. The smirking antagonist who bumped Hal was still looking over his shoulder as he continued his hike away from us. Hal stared at him with the eye of an aggressor looking for a bogie. The three others with him let out some nervous laughter as they passed on, but none were turning around. They did not appear proud of being a party to the insult.

"Don't worry, Rob." Hal said, bending to retrieve his River Rat cap. "I just took a picture in my head of his pretty little face. When I see him again, I won't be this tired."

"I'll be with you all the way. I got a good look at him."

"This may be fun."

"It'll be like old times, eh, Hal?"

We resumed our trek switchbacking up the canyon wall, plodding one step at a time, and wondering if it would ever end. By the time we reached the Bright Angel Trailhead at the top of the South Rim, it was afternoon. We found our shuttle bus waiting by the trailhead for hikers. Our breakfast waitress was right. The mile ride back to our car was a true gift of mercy. We finished the hike of six miles dusty, hungry, and thirsty, which seemed appropriate for fine dining at the El Tovar Hotel restaurant, after a stop at their bar for more water.

12

WE SAT AT THE BAR dispelling the rumor that all fighter pilots drink alcohol like a fish. Early in our flying days we learned that it's not all glamor. The aircraft cockpit is cramped, sweaty, and exhausting. The last thing you wanted after a hot sweaty flight was booze. We asked the bartender for water, with the promise that in 30 minutes we would be ready to live up to the stereotype.

We sat down at a couple of their lounge chairs around a small round table and drank our water and watched the clock.

"I'm really tired," Hal said.

"You're dehydrated. After you rehydrate, you'll feel great, I promise."

"I should remember I'm not in my twenties anymore," he said. "Back in Thailand it was hotter than Hell outside of the cockpit. You then crawled into your Thud, lit the fires, and waited in line on the taxiway for takeoff. It was like waiting in a solar oven. I'd get back after another day of combat, make sure I got credit for the mission, and head to the bar."

"It was the same way at Laredo, as you know. I didn't think about that worry... getting too dried out."

"Are we growing up, Amity?"

"I'm afraid so. I don't even miss the strip clubs anymore. I'm embarrassed to say I had so much fun."

Hal chuckled, then paused with a smile. "If they had kept women out of pilot training, the girls would still be dancing. But that's progress."

"No more training films, either," I said.

"It will certainly ruin the comradery if guys have to raise hell with women—unless of course, they're performing on stage."

"I confess, Hal, that I do miss the *esprit de corps* we enjoyed as men. Remember that time when those three female captains joined us, when Honey and Boopsie were stripping. Honey stopped their act and demanded the ladies leave. It was an extremely uncomfortable moment. When they left, the whole male officer corps in attendance cheered."

"I can't believe you still remember the names of those strippers."

"They were memorable. That's all I can say."

"Then, are we just growing up or simply without opportunity?" Hal asked.

"I think we're growing up."

"Whether I've grown up may depend upon that little hippie twit who knocked my cap off. If he shows up here, all bets are off."

I waved my wristwatch into Hal's view. "It's time. A couple of drinks mixed with those hippies should answer your growing up question."

I hailed our barmaid and ordered a gin and tonic for me and Hal's Chivas Regal on the rocks. It was Saturday night, and the weekenders were beginning to filter in. Most were older people. Some were college kids here for their no-study weekend. An unexpected number of Japanese tourists filled the ranks. For Japanese, the cost of living and the value of our dollar made coming to America cheaper than vacationing in their own country. Hal got up and checked on reservations for dinner to get ahead of the throng of new arrivals. He had good news when he returned.

"We have dinner reservations at 1800 hours. That gives us over an hour to enjoy the bar."

Freed ordered another round for us, and we continued to enjoy doing nothing for the hour. An older gentleman came in with his wife. Their discussion culminated in her smiling at him affectionately and kissing him on the lips before walking away to do who knew what? He came in at a pace that belied his age. As he bellied up to the bar, his eyes scanned over the room, as if he was looking for someone. When he looked in our direction, he gave a nod of recognition to Hal.

Hal returned a nod of polite acknowledgement. The man made a beeline for our table.

"Hello gentlemen." He pointed at Hal's ballcap. "I couldn't help noticing your hat. You *are* a River Rat, I presume?"

"Yes, I am," Hal replied.

I had the good sense to keep quiet.

"May I sit down and join you for a moment? Can I buy you boys a drink?"

"No, thank you for now, but be my guest," Hal said. "Please sit and tell us what you know about the River Rats."

He sat down with his martini in his left hand, the excitement showing on his face. He had that look older people get when you know they want to share something, usually about their glory days. I was right.

"I flew P-47s in The War," he began, then turned to me. "I'm guessing you both are pilots."

"Yes, sir," I replied.

"Good for you boys," he said. "I don't get many chances to talk to other flyboys. I hope you don't mind."

"Are you kidding?" Hal said, doing his best to assure him. "I'm honored to find someone who likes us."

"Oh, surely not," he said.

"We had a detractor or two today on our hike," I said.

"Oh?"

"Nothing that a little spanking wouldn't fix," Hal said. "It was no big deal."

"It would be a big deal for me. My son was an F-4 pilot in Vietnam. He should be a River Rat, but on his second tour during Rolling Thunder, we lost him. Never found his body. It does my heart good to talk to you boys. God bless you for what you did."

"You mean what we tried to do, don't you?"

The man let out a sarcastic chuckle and shook his head. "Don't ever say that." He looked directly at Hal. "You be proud of what you did."

"Yes sir, I understand. And you're proud of your son, I'm sure."

"We grieve with you in your loss," I said.

"I'm proud of *all* of us," he said. "So, what did you boys fly?"

"I flew T-37 jets as an IP at Laredo Air Force Base," I replied. "I left the Air Force last year. Put in five interesting years."

"You still fly?"

"No, just drive fast cars."

"A Corvette or some sort of sports car, I bet."

I laughed. He knew his pilots of today's Air Force. At that time, lots of the astronauts were featured driving their hot cars.

"I have a fine little Porsche," I replied. "Hal here still flies. He's staying in until he becomes general."

"Driving a Kraut car. How about that?" He turned his head. "Hal? What do you fly?"

"Right now, I'm also flying T-37s. Before that I flew Thuds in Vietnam, probably about the time your son was there."

We were all silent for a moment as this gentleman took a moment to compose himself. He took a sip of his martini and looked down at his glass. Hal had told me of men who died fighting a war that none of our leaders had the guts to win. Then there was my own friend John Alexander who died stateside but was nonetheless a casualty of the Vietnam War. No one wants to die, but there was a greater sense of gratitude for those who died in combat. Other non-combat deaths were soon forgotten, not even a medal to commemorate their sacrifice. Those servicemen, who never served in Vietnam, were now being called draft dodgers by some. We, of the rear echelon like me, couldn't call ourselves Vietnam veterans. What were we? Dodgers? Slackers? No one had a name for us. We were nothing. Both ends of the spectrum maligned our veterans. I served, therefore I'm a baby killer by proxy, or I served, but I am a draft dodger for not going to fight in Vietnam. Veterans couldn't win, especially when it evolved into veteran against veteran.

"Tell us your story," Hal said to break the silence.

He perked up with an expression of gratitude for Hal's suggestion.

"Well," he said with a big smile. "I enlisted in the Army Air Corps in 1940 and soon got my chance as a cadet in flight school. Finished near the top of my class. My first airplane was the Bell P-39. The Airacobra. Great little airplane but not much armor on it. When Pearl Harbor got hit by the

Japs, I moved over to a Republic P-47 Thunderbolt. It was a monster of an airplane. Our government sent all the P-39s over to the Russians. By 1943 we were coming over to England to get ready for the invasion we all knew would happen sometime."

"Did you fly CAS or cover bombers?" Hal asked.

"CAS?" he asked, after taking another big sip of his martini.

"Close air support," Hal answered.

"Oh, of course. Back then, you did it all. We flew cover for the bombers, but with our short range, the Krauts just held back until we turned back. Then their fighters would jump our boys. After we turned back, we would go on the deck and strafe any target of opportunity we could find. It was great sport and dangerous as Hell. I think most of us who got shot up were on the deck at the time. The Krauts had flak towers everywhere, including the airdromes. We could strafe the towers, but they were incredibly fortified. We strafed the aircraft parked outside. German locomotives were interesting. Hitting their boilers was one goal. But the bastards would pack one of their cars. I think it was designed to explode upward to get us as we flew over the fireball. That's what we decided anyway. I had my youth stolen from me for six years, but now I see it as the most exciting time of my life. I had a hell of a good time. Not like those poor bastards on the ground or the sitting ducks who flew our bombers. I feel blessed. How about you boys?"

"We're getting there," Hal said, then added. "Sir, can we buy you a drink?"

"Hell, no," he said emphatically. "That's one advantage of getting old. It takes no time anymore to get a buzz on. One drink is more than adequate. So, I've had enough. How about you boys? You had enough?"

Hal lifted his glass in a symbolic toast. "Like I said, sir, we're getting there."

13

WE WERE FEELING NO PAIN by the time we grabbed our packs and checked in at the restaurant desk. The lady who took us to our table had a smile that was the best public relations a restaurant could hope for. Our waiter came by and asked if we needed anything from the bar. We declined but soon had our menu choices ready to order.

"I'll take your filet, baked potato with everything, and a house salad with ranch dressing," Hal said. "And cook that steak medium."

The waiter turned to me. "I'll take the exact same thing. Filet medium, loaded baked potato, house salad with ranch, and a Coke. That's it."

He thanked us for our order and promised my Coke would be coming up shortly. We looked around the dining room, surprised to see so many empty tables on a Saturday night. The bar, however, was packed. The staff was bustling in the back as if the few people in the room were the most important people on earth. So, with our third drink still in hand, we sat back to discuss any plans we had for Sunday. We were still in the negotiating phase of our planning when I looked at my watch. My Coke was not here, and it was already 8:20, a good twenty minutes since we sat down. We gave it another ten minutes before I called our waiter over to politely inquire.

"You forgot my Coke," I said.

"Oh, I'm terribly sorry, sir. I'll go get it right now."

Hal asked, "Are the steaks coming out soon?"

"Yes, sir. Right away. I'll bring your salads out first."

He was good for his word on salads. He had two at our table within the minute. Then Hal made a face.

"Does your salad have ranch dressing?"

I looked down at some suspicious lumps and took a bite. "Not ranch. This is bleu cheese."

"So is mine," Hal said with disappointment. "I'd complain but I'm hungry. So much for fine dining tonight. I hate bleu cheese, by the way."

He took another bite. So did I. In the scheme of things, this was one of those life goes on moments. No one was going to ruin our meal or our nice three-drink buzz. We downed our salads in short order and waited.

"Excuse me," I said to our waiter. "May I have that Coke I ordered."

"Oh, I'm sorry, sir, it will be right out. I do apologize."

It was now 8:40, but to my relief, he brought out my Coke in one hand and a steak dinner in the other. He set them both down in front of me, then looked up at Hal.

"Sir, I'll be right back with your steak."

Hal looked at me with a worried grin, nervously tapping his fingertips on the white tablecloth.

"Don't wait for me. Eat it while it's hot."

I was halfway through my baked potato when I looked up at Hal, now highly agitated. He waved again for our waiter who came up quickly.

"I had a steak coming. It was the same order as his. I would like to know where my steak is. Is it coming?"

"Sorry, sir, I know right where it is. I'll bring it right out."

Within thirty seconds he was back with Hal's dinner. It looked identical to mine, and Hal calmed down. He put a pat of butter on his baked potato and paused. He put a finger carefully on the side of his spud. Then he put a finger on his steak. He took a knife and fork and cut into the center of the steak. Placing a finger in the cut, he quickly looked up and waved to the waiter. As the man came forward, Hal asked me a quick question.

"Was your food hot?"

"Yes, and it's still pretty warm."

"Yes, sir," the waiter spoke calmly. "May I help?"

"Yes. I've been here for forty-five minutes waiting for a steak," Hal said, "and my steak is cold. I ordered it medium, and this one looks extremely rare. This baked potato should be able to melt a pat of butter. My house salad with ranch dressing came instead with bleu cheese. My friend here got the identical order ten or fifteen minutes before you brought me this cold plate. I want you to take this back and bring me what I ordered!"

"Excuse me, sir." Our waiter walked determinedly away.

We sat there for another five or ten minutes while I continued to eat my meal at the insistence of Hal. I looked up at him to see a rare vein on his temple pulsing rapidly.

"Hal," I said. "Let me handle this. You need to calm down. You look like you're about to have a stroke."

"I'm calm," he said, tightly gripping the tablecloth in both hands.

"Let go of the tablecloth." He obeyed.

I looked up to see a new man emerge from the back. From his dress I recognized him as the manager or *maître d'* of the restaurant. He approached our table not as a customer friendly helper but as an aggressor.

"Who here has a complaint with our waiter?"

"I do," Hal said and related once more the difficulties he had with getting a decent meal that was hot and prepared as requested. At this point, the *maître d'* interrupted.

"I talked to my waiter. He told me what transpired. I don't have to hear it again." He spoke with a sneer. "I will not allow anyone to treat my staff as you have treated this man. Do you understand me? I suggest that you can take your business somewhere else and never come back."

He spun around like the priggish little wimp that he was and strutted back to the kitchen. As I followed his departure, a face appeared around the corner. It was one of the chefs who looked familiar, even though wearing his *toque blanche* to hide his long hair.

"Did you see that guy?" I asked.

"What guy?" Hal was soaring higher in apoplexy.

"The chef behind the door. That's your buddy from this afternoon."

"I better eat this free meal then," Hal said, between heaving breaths of anger. "I'm gonna need the energy."

He ate enough of the cold steak and potato to satisfy his need for fuel and stood up. Our waiter came running out with the check. Hal looked at him with a keen eye before the light bulb in his brain lit up.

"Your boss told us to get out. He didn't say pay. You can keep your check and take it back to your boss and stick it wherever there is no sunshine." Hal paused, then added, "I know who you are. I know where you will be. Be careful."

We walked by the bar on the way out. Our bartender waved us over with the aid of our bar maid.

"Your *maître d'* is a jerk, but let him alone," our bartender said. "The other two will be leaving out the backdoor about 2200 hours. As one Marine to you two flyboys, thanks for the close air support that saved my life."

We thanked him profusely, asked a couple of further questions, and laid an extra few bills on the counter. After shaking his hand and hugging his barmaid, we left to regain our sanity.

14

"HOW WAS THE STEAK?" HAL asked. "Any good?"

"Oh, it sucked. You wouldn't have liked it."

"Is that why you ate it all in about two minutes?"

"Exactly. So, what do we do with those two pricks?"

"Let's do a little recon and determine where to drop the ordinance."

I followed him outside into a quickly cooling night. Even with entryway lights, the stars were more brilliant than I would see in Oklahoma.

"You understand that this is my battle, not yours?"

"The hell it is! This is a two-man operation. We do this together or not at all. Just remember that no one will pick on my friend ever again. You of all people should know that."

That Hal should be on his own was quite unthinkable. I invited him on this road trip so we could kick some ass. I never meant it for more than a metaphor, but this was the chance of a lifetime. I couldn't imagine he would ever not want to include me. We both stood there in the lobby licking our wounds for a minute. Hal spoke first.

"We did agree that it was the best vacation ever. There's no one to tell us we're wrong."

"We got an endorsement from the bar in there."

"But we can't touch the *maître d'*."

"I'd like to."

"But we can't."

"Okay, we won't, but we can sure make his work harder tomorrow."

"He needs more practice as a waiter and a cook."

We pulled our newly purchased jackets out of our packs, putting them on to keep the February night air away. We had seen the dusting of snow in the canyon at sunrise this morning. It could just as easily happen tonight. We stepped outside and around the lodge to the fenced off trash area. The gate was sturdy, but to our great fortune, its padlock was unlocked and hanging on the fence rail. The back door to the restaurant was to the right of the fence with a small porch of two steps to the ground and a single dim bug light off to the side.

"That should make it easy to catch them off balance, when they come off the steps," Hal said.

My watch read 9:20 p.m. We had an uncertain 40 minutes to wait for the two to leave. We discussed sorting out the dishwasher, waiters, and other innocents from the two targets. Having more than a half hour to wait, we started back around the lodge to return to the lobby when an innocent waiter came out the backdoor, going to his car.

"What do you plan to be doing to these guys?" I asked in a whisper.

"Relax. I won't leave anything permanent on them, but they will never mess with a veteran again."

"Okay, so what do I do?"

"Just stick with me. I'll need help with the garbage containers. And you check my six o'clock. Deal with those, while I hit the prime targets."

"Roger that."

The lady with the pretty smile was next to emerge. Our helpful barmaid was soon behind her, followed by the restaurant desk greeter who talked to them both as she came out. Fearing that we were late getting to our positions to grab the two perpetrators, we carefully moved around to where we could stand by the aromatic garbage fence but remain out of sight. We could pounce on them within five seconds. The waiters would likely emerge before the cooks, who had to clean up. The dishwasher might be next to last. Our priggish *maître d'* would be last.

Our luck came before we expected. The two of them, waiter and cook, exited the restaurant together, laughing and talking with glee about their little prank.

"You hold our waiter down while I work over my favorite?" Hal said. "It won't take long, I promise. I'm going to knock his hat off... and he isn't even wearing one."

The two young men stood on the first step, oblivious to our presence. I bolted forward first as our waiter took his first step off the porch. I pegged him with an upright block that slammed his back against the logs of the outside wall. With him briefly stunned, I reached down for a double leg take down, a trick I learned living in the jock dorm on the wrestlers' floor. It took him by so much surprise that the only sound he made was the exhale of his lungs upon impact. To my left Hal stepped up to his target and delivered a single side kick to the groin that leveled his victim with an agonizing groan of pain. From the look of Hal's movements, I was partnered with some type of ninja warrior. He grabbed our cook by the collar and rotated. In the near darkness the cook sailed over Hal's shoulder and landed on his back. With lightning speed Hal tied him up into what looked like a pretzel hold. At that point there was no movement from either of them. Why my waiter was not moving I could not discern, until I realized he had knocked himself silly on the first porch step when I executed my take down, like a real badass. I quickly put his lights out.

"You okay?" Hal asked.

"Mine's out like a light."

"Over here, quick."

I left my man crumpled on the ground and at Hal's direction grabbed our cook's legs. We carried his limp body inside the fence to the trash bin. We let him down to the ground, while Hal lifted the lid of the bin, then we again picked up our pal the cook and dumped him inside.

"Leave the lid up," Hal said. "Let's go get your guy."

We raced over to the waiter and carried him the same way through the gate and to the garbage bin. The back door squeaked open for another male worker, who stopped on the stoop, stretching his arms high with an audible yawn. He soon walked out of sight.

"Okay. Help me lift him up."

"Do we need to, Hal? He's not the main culprit."

"Did you check your Coke he brought you before you drank it?"

"No!" I replied. "You think he did that? Spit in it? You sure?"

Hal was nodding his head, light from the back of the building filtering though the fence.

"Then let's dump the SOB!"

We struggled to lift the second body into the bin, but we laid him gently next to his partner. Hal them reached for the padlock to the gate.

"Do they have any bears that come around here at night?" I asked.

"Oh, let's hope so."

"Have we considered how they might get hurt if one showed up."

"No problem. Lower that top quietly," he said. "I'm going to lock the lid."

"No, we're not," I said. I was aghast. "We're not trying to kill them. We want them found and humiliated."

"Okay, so what do we do?"

With a wave of my hand, I led him out through the gate, leaving the bin's lid open. I quietly stepped up to the porch and hooked the padlock on the outside doorknob. Our restaurant manager was sure to find it and check inside the gate. That tempered any guilt we might have. To my relief, the two bin occupants began to curse up a storm.

"We better get outta here," I said.

"Not yet," he replied.

He reached into his pocket and pulled out a River Rat challenge coin. He laid it on the stoop of the porch for all to see. Quietly, we made our exit into the dark.

15

BREAKFAST CAME EARLY AT THE Moche Lodge. We could hardly get out of bed, get dressed, and walk to the Moche Café because of our sore muscles. We both were suffering the Grand Canyon's most challenging aspect—the day after. Even our simplest movements were agonizing. Our muscles screamed in pain. Each step triggered muffled cries of agony. We decided that the Grand Canyon was too rife with risks to our bodies and to our reputations. Hal made me take a vow that we would never do this again. Making it worse, we kept looking over our shoulders for someone with handcuffs. Kicking ass was now all out of our system, and we wanted to go home.

"I said it before, but I'll say it again." Hal sipped his coffee and contradicted everything he said about hiking. "This is the best road trip ever!"

"When did you learn karate?" I asked. "Last night you looked like you might know some things I was unaware of."

"I wouldn't call it karate," he replied, "but I learned martial arts from a Vietnamese soldier. What else did we have to do while waiting for our missions?"

We looked up to see our waitress who gave us so much good advice the morning before.

"You made it back," she said in her all-business voice.

"Yes, we did," Hal said.

"Just barely," I replied. "It was brutal, just like you said."

"So, I'm waiting," she said.

"Oh," Hal said, after an absent-minded pause. "I admit that your advice was spot on. Thank you."

"Thank you," I said over Hal's last word.

"Is the coffee good?" she asked.

Hal and I looked at each other and laughed. "It's the best," I said truthfully. "It's really good."

"Yes, it is," she agreed. "Now, what can I get you boys for breakfast? You hiking again?"

"No ma'am," I replied with emphasis. "Hiking almost three miles down was enough for me for one day."

"For a lifetime," Hal said.

"So, what you gonna have?" she asked, again all business.

We ordered our food with fewer items this time. We were not hiking. Instead, we were at leisure and had the time to plan our day.

I looked Hal in the eye. "And you know, I remember yesterday's hike as an exciting experience, where I did things right and cheated death by using my good skills and training. But I would never want to go through that again. And Hal. About yesterday. I never want to kick ass like that ever again."

Because of her own suggestion from yesterday morning, we gave our all-business waitress a generous breakfast tip of forty percent. She was the perfect example of how being of good service can earn a person some serious cash. It got me to thinking about the kind of job I could do. The oil industry was growing again because of the oil embargo. Price per barrel was spiking, which made for a Black Gold Rush in its infant stages. It appeared that we were out of oil—and then we were not.

I could be of service to oil field workers.

16

WE CANCELLED OUR THIRD night at the Moche Lodge. Climbing into the Porsche, we chose to head for Amarillo on I-40. It was a long drive, but there was plenty of talk still in us.

"Okay, tell me how you managed to steal this car." Hal's question was more of a demand.

"Okay, but first you have to tell me more about who and what this woman named Lisa is doing in your life."

We took the Desert View Drive east on Arizona Highway 64 and south on US Highway 89 down the western edge of the Hopi Reservation, where the prototype for Indian culture and religion began. From Flagstaff we headed west on I-40 before Hal began to speak.

"Her name is Lisa Anders, and she is a Texas girl," he began. "Like I said, she has her PhD in political science, and she loves Nixon. I'd like Nixon a lot more if he had kept up the Christmas bombing over Hanoi for a day or two longer. We would have had our airmen back home instead of doing close air support for the South Vietnamese Army. But I digress. She's the most attractive woman in the entire world… except for that one snaggle tooth on top and a big jagged scar on her cheek… but you get used to it."

"Prove it, Hal. I know you have a picture. Pull it out."

Hal dutifully lifted his left hip to pull out his wallet. He opened it up and pulled out a clear photo folder with a portrait of Lisa. I looked it over. She was pure blonde with luscious red lips and a milky white face. Photographed in winter, she sported a bulky turtleneck of burnt orange in a heavy weave. She was stunningly attractive and without the heavy eye makeup and the big hair so popular in Texas. Her smile was beautiful and genuine.

"So, how old is Scarface?"

"To tell the truth, I don't know." He ignored the nickname I gave her. "I don't think she's thirty yet."

I thumbed through the photos carefully one at a time as I drove down the interstate. Each one was of Lisa. Each shot gave me a sense of her happiness and her comfort in front of a camera.

"Beautiful girl, Lisa. With the name Anders, she must be Scandinavian by heritage. Nobody under thirty has hair that white."

"No, she's totally blonde, I guarantee, and with the most hauntingly blue eyes. When she looks at you, it's almost like watching the movie *Children of the Damned*."

"There you go again."

"When you meet her, you'll see what I mean. I promise she'll dazzle you."

We drove on for several minutes at our legal 55 mph before Hal spoke up again. "Why don't you let me drive this monster of a car while you tell me how it came into your possession?"

I pulled onto the shoulder at the first safe opportunity. We traded seats after a few stretches. After squeezing himself into the driver's seat, I gave him a quick tutorial before letting him lose. He didn't need any tutorial. His control of this 911 was like a pro. His shifting was a marvel to watch. We got back on the highway well above the 55 mph speed limit in three heart beats.

"When did you learn to drive like that?" I asked.

"You're kidding me, right?" Hal laughed. "Every kid in America drives like this."

We made much better time with Hal at the wheel. I looked over to see 85 mph on the speedometer. He was following a semi loaded with oil field pipe, which was the tail end of a truck convoy. It was usually the point on the convoy that got the ticket. Being at the back seemed a safe bet, so I stopped worrying.

"Okay, you want to know how I stole this Porsche? The truth is as crazy as it sounds."

I described how I traded my worn out 240-Z for this nearly new rare Porsche, using the dealer Mike's guilt and love for his son to swing the deal of a lifetime. Hal scoffed at first when I told him how a newly rich oilman had swapped his brand-new Porsche for a Rambler American with automatic transmission so he could get home on time. The oil patch was a crazy place. The deal was a three-way break-even trade. Everybody won.

"Hal, I have concluded you have to believe three things. First, everyone at some point in their life has a weak moment. Second, Mike's guilt was for real, and I became his therapist. Lastly, sometimes you have to ask for the impossible for a miracle to happen. That's what I did, and this Porsche is what I got."

"Yep, you really did steal it, didn't you?"

"Now you get it, don't you?"

"So now we can talk about Suzy?" Hal's comment took me by surprise. "Why don't you use those skills on her and steal her away?"

17

WE DROVE INTO AMARILLO WELL after sunset. Hal parked my car at a Holiday Inn located on the west side of town, the newest area of growth. We locked the car, shouldered our packs, and stumbled into the hotel lobby hoping to find an available room. We lucked into two twin beds for the night. Better yet, the Holiday Inn was serving a free breakfast in the morning—a perk we were hearing about for the first time. We checked out our spartan room, dropped our backpacks on the floor, and hurried down to sit in the lobby.

"Where's your car, anyway? I never thought to ask when I picked you up."

"Where do you think?"

"I would guess Austin."

"Since I'll be stationed at Bergstrom while I'm going to UT on Uncle Sam's dime, I got me a decent apartment ahead of time."

"You want me to drive you down there? It would be fun to meet Lisa."

"I want you to get home to Oklahoma City and get together with Suzy. You can drop me off at the airport there. Or Tinker... if I can line up a hop to Bergstrom."

"I hate having to make you do that."

"You need to get your business done, son. Call her tonight and tell her you are on your way."

After leaving the Air Force, I believed that no one could ever tell me what to do again. No more orders. No more pulling rank. No more pushing me to call Suzy. But I needed the push. Like a thirteen-year-old kid calling a prospective date to invite her to the junior high dance, I had call reluctance. Hal was giving me a kick to commit.

"Excuse me, Hal. I'm going to the room to make a call."

I climbed the stairs two steps at a time to get to the third floor. Our room was at the far end, which seemed to be miles away when you are carrying luggage or planning to make an important telephone call.

Once in our room, I sat down at the writing desk and began the laborious dialing process. Eight for a long-distance line. Zero for a long-distance operator. It worked the first time. I gave the operator my home phone number to bill me for a station-to-station long distance charge. She dialed Suzy's number. I waited. Two rings and Suzy's voice greeted me enthusiastically.

"Suzy, this is Rob." I listened for a response that did not come. Her phone shuffled so that my ear was filled with clicks and scrapes. I said nothing more, only hoping for her response.

"I'm so relieved. Please, say you're okay. It's early. You said ten days."

"I need to see you."

"Where are you? I want to see you, too. Oh, Rob, I've missed you. I wish I could have called you first. I'm sorry."

"Have we both been bad? I thought it was my fault. I'm sorry, Suzy."

"Where are you? I want to see you."

"Amarillo for tonight, but I'm coming home."

"I don't even know where you live."

I stopped, unable to speak. Waves of uncertainty collided with my emotions. Dare I say what I felt? *"I don't know where I live."*

"Have you had a place to stay?"

"Yes, but calling Hal Freed for a road trip was a good idea. It did me good to get away, but I want to come home again. It hasn't even been a week."

"You need to come by and see me first thing, please."

"I... just feel alone. I don't want to be alone anymore."

"Did you call your parents?"

"No."

"You need to call your parents."

"I only want to see you... for now."

The uncertainty of the following silence brought me to panic. Was this call a mistake? Had I said too much? Did I sound needy? Real men don't sound needy. I wanted her to need me, too.

"Are you coming back tomorrow?"

"Tomorrow? Yes."

"Please promise me you will come here first, okay?"

"I will."

"Do you know where I live?"

"Have you moved?"

"No."

"Then, I know where you are. I'll hurry up Hal. I have to drop him off at Tinker so he can catch a hop to Bergstrom."

"Then come straight here."

"I promise."

"Rob, I've missed you."

"Yes, I've...."

"Hurry home, okay? I'm waiting. I better say goodbye."

My words would not come out. Sensing it, Suzy again whispered, *"Hurry... goodbye."*

I held the receiver in the palms of my two hands, not wanting to let her go, trying to hold the warmth of her being for only a few more seconds. I laid it in the cradle, a mournful sigh coming from the depths of my yearning soul. I sat in silence, a hand still atop the phone, unable to move. I pictured in my mind her beautiful smile and willowy outline. Heartache overwhelmed me with an added feeling unfamiliar to me. For the first time in my life, there was a person I could not live without. Sleeping alone tonight overwhelmed me with fear. Could I wait, or would heartache take me tonight. A yearning-like depression took hold, except I hoped the pain would go away forever when we came together.

18

"I FORGOT TO ASK ABOUT the baby."

Hal's grin faced me from his perch on our room's windowsill. "It sounds like that wasn't the priority of either one of you."

I laughed. He was correct. Suzy may have a child to take care of, but I wanted to be near her, not her baby. This is how men get turned into parents. First, desire. Next, parenthood.

Hal spoke up. "Right now, *my* priority is to eat. We need to find some place that is open this late at night."

We drove I-40 to the east side of Amarillo, where we found a Denny's open 24 hours a day. For this late at night, it was a busy place for truckers and travelers of all types. We stood in a line of a dozen people, all tired and silent, waiting to be seated.

A waitress soon seated us and stared at us patiently while we looked at our menus. Remembering the great Air Force midnight breakfasts back in training, I ordered a Slam Breakfast of eggs and bacon and a whole lot more with all the standard sides for a bit of nostalgia. Hal, in the true spirit of truck drivers everywhere, ordered Chicken Fried Steak, potatoes, and gravy with two fried eggs on top.

"Is this like our last meal? Here we are, two bachelors, eating stuff that's bad for us, and no woman to tell us we are going to kill ourselves."

"Still angry?"

"Maybe until tomorrow."

"You better get me to Tinker, then. While you were talking to Suzy, I was downstairs getting set up with a tanker headed to Bergstrom tomorrow at noon. Lisa'll pick me up. It's working out perfect."

"That means we'll need to leave in the morning at zero dark thirty."

"Roger that."

"You sure we don't need a beer?"

"I thought we were finally growing up here. Suzy will *not* be impressed if I have a hangover. I couldn't drive, either."

"Okay, here's what we're going to do. On the way back to our Holiday Inn luxury penthouse suite, I'm going to get a six-pack of anything, except Pearl beer. I'll have two or three, you can drink your coffee, and I'll tell you a story I've not told anyone."

We finished our nighttime breakfasts, paid, and exited the Denny's. Stopping at a 7-Eleven, Hal purchased his required six-pack of Miller's, before spilling his guts back in our room—a rare treat.

19

I WATCHED HAL PULL OFF the tab on his first can of Miller's and put it on his finger like a ring. He sat on the only upholstered chair in the room. At his feet rested the remaining six pack. He took a swig before speaking.

"Old habit from Vietnam." He waved his finger with the pull tab. "One night we had a rocket attack in Da Nang. One of the men ran out of his hooch in his skivvies, tripped in the doorway, and fell on a beer tab, probably his own. He cut himself fairly good. The idiot put in for a Purple Heart. We practically ostracized him."

I waited for him to collect his thoughts. "Surely, that's not the story you wanted to tell me."

"No, it's not, but you've heard the rumors the past three years about me?" He popped open another can and put a second beer tab on his same finger.

It was rumored Hal decked a full colonel in a bar in Okinawa on his way back to the states after his hundred plus combat missions over North Vietnam. Having lost a few friends in the air battles over the north, Hal was in no mood to have another officer order him out of the bar.

"I know you've never admitted that you slugged that colonel returning from a B-52 bombing mission. But we all assumed you did. Are you finally going to confess?"

Hal took a long draw from his second beer and exhaled in a satisfying sigh. "No confession needed. I've ridden that rumor successfully for three years. I didn't deck a colonel." He laughed. "I decked the captain who was ordered to kick me out."

He downed the second can and arched it expertly into the waste basket. The reticent Hal was already second guessing his decision to clarify his mystique. I pressed on.

"What happened to you?"

"Nothing. The captain got up from the floor and held back the others coming toward me. He was a gutsy guy. About my height. He was no push over, either. I just got in a lucky shot. Obviously, he could take a hit. As he came up to me again, to my surprise, he offered to buy me a drink. Taking me over to the far corner of the bar, we sat down. In the meantime, the entire crew compliment of BUFFs poured into the bar. We talked for a few minutes. He apologized for having to ask me to leave. 'It's the Old Man's policy. When we return from each mission, the bar is off limits to everybody else.' He asked me what I flew in Vietnam. When I told him the long and short of it, he bought me another round. I wanted to get home, so I agreed to leave voluntarily with my drink in hand. Nothing officially was ever done. The captain even gave me his name and address back home."

He was through volunteering information. He was not through drowning in beer.

"Did you ever make contact with him again?"

"I did… right after Linebacker II. He was already back home standing alert in SAC. He regretted that he missed the chance to fly over Hanoi, but he said something funny. 'The boys, after they came back, sure wished you had done a better job of taking out SAM sites.' He was an okay guy. In the end, I guess we're all the same. We do what we are ordered to do. Some get the milk runs. Others get the glory."

Hal remained seated in his comfortable chair and popped open number four. We turned off all the lights. The window curtains stayed open, and the lights of Amarillo put a glow to the room's inside. I closed my eyes and tried unsuccessfully to fall quickly asleep. To pass the time I began to think of many things. Mr. Welder's rage and death. Young hippies getting their just desserts. Hal's insistence that we cut our road trip short. Lying on our backs in the Great Plains to see nothing but sky. Suzy was the one last piece of the puzzle to bring me blue skies. Her absence was the reason for my road trip. My trip should have started with her.

Hal, in the glow from the window, still sat in his comfortable chair at 1:45 a.m., holding one last can of beer. I raised my head to focus, and he chuckled.

"Don't worry about me. I'm just over here having deep thoughts. Did you know you snore?"

Hal stood up from his easy chair, pulled six beer tabs off his finger, and tossed them and his remaining empty cans in the waste basket.

"Six dead soldiers laid to rest."

"So, what deep thoughts did you have with your six-pack?"

"That I'm tired of doing stupid stuff. It doesn't have the thrill is used to. Getting chased by that welder? That made me uncomfortable. Getting back at those young men and putting them in the dumpster? I don't want to do that anymore. It just wasn't fun to do. I think I've grown up. I don't want to take stupid risks anymore. I'm too old for such nonsense."

"You know what we're doing? Can you remember the day you woke up and discovered that your toys were not fun anymore? The shock of it depressed me. But then I found other things to drive my passion. We lost interest in toys but discovered girls. Then we discovered our freedom as pilots. We've discovered something else. Love."

"And nothing has ever been this good."

"Hal, we're going to Hell, aren't we?"

"If so, Suzy and Lisa are Hell's Angels."

20

ZERO-DARK-THIRTY CAME LATER than usual next morning. I went down for a free breakfast while Hal remained in our room sleeping off his six-pack. I called my mom and dad to inform them that I was coming back home and might stop by late in the afternoon. They were curious as to why I was cutting my road trip short. Later today, I would be answering a lot of questions.

Once Hal was awake and had his breakfast, he looked at me impatiently. "I checked us out of our room already, so we're set. Let's go."

AFTER FILLING THE GAS TANK at exorbitant prices at the nearest gas station, we headed eastbound on Interstate 40 and Route 66 for the city.

"You need a radio for this car," Hal said.

"But the purr of the engine is music enough."

"I think you've used that line already."

"You are growing up, Hal. You sound like my dad."

"Okay then, if I'm sounding like Dad, when are you going to get a job, son?"

"I'm sure Suzy's dad will be asking that."

"If I were Suzy, I'd be asking that, also."

"I've used the GI Bill for one semester. They've paid me some, and I still have a good stash in my savings."

"You always were cheapskate, a bit of a Scrooge."

"And now it's paying off. With what I can invest while this oil embargo goes on, I think I can make a killing selling the oil fields what they need."

"Are you needing an investment partner?"

"You want to lose a friend? Go into business with me."

"So how are you going to execute this plan."

"First thing, I'm taking some business courses on the GI Bill to learn how to work smart. I don't care about a degree. I care about learning to run a business. Then I'll learn what people need. Maybe more importantly, discover what the workers need but are not getting."

"That's what it was like in Vietnam and in Thailand. When I was in country, the people were amazing. Once they found out what GIs wanted, every corner in every village in Southeast Asia became a store selling something. I could buy anything in the world if I would pay the price. With so many entrepreneurs, the prices gradually went down, and they still made a killing in sales."

"Then you get it. I plan on making a killing and plowing my profit into more investments, until the infant oil boom grows up and dies again. I've read my history. Oklahoma has had incredible boom and bust cycles in oil. I know it will end, but I'll still have my profits. That's the plan, man."

"Then you'll get a job."

"Then I'll get a job."

With visions of dollar bills flying my way, we flew east on the interstate, finally hooking up with a big rig convoy rolling at 90 mph.

21

WE APPROACHED A REST STOP just short of McLean and pulled over to switch drivers. We stretched our legs at first, looked around, and grumbled about the lack of a restroom. The wind and the chill of the winter air was incentive to make our stop brief. Hal rounded the front of the Porsche when he looked up to see at least two dozen bikers pulling into the area. Filing in one and two at a time, the rumble of their Harleys was inspirational. No sound on earth is like a Harley's. By the time two dozen of them gathered, the thrill was beyond my limit. I looked at Hal again only to find him with a big grin on his face.

"Rob, are you aware that we are surrounded by Hells Angels."

I turned to inspect the logos on the men's jackets and bristled at the realization. This was not good. Hal was smiling. Why?

"Hey!" the lead biker said. "Where did you get the car? That's a fine piece of German shit!"

The men were all dressed for the chilly weather. A temperature of 45 degrees is cold but add a windchill on a 70 mph bike. The men were all in heavy round-toed boots, heavy leather gloves, dirty jeans, and club jackets. I assumed they carried something forbidden underneath their outfits. Many sported heavy dark beards, but a few were greying.

Hal shouted back. "It's a '73 Porsche Carrera RSR 3.0, and it doesn't ride as good as a Harley, but it'll outrun any trooper in Texas."

The man was walking over to us. To my surprise, he was friendly. Clean shaven and thinner than most of the others, it was clear that if he stayed on our side, we would be okay. "That is one hell of a rare car. They only made like a hundred of them."

"You're right," I replied.

"I know my Porsches. So, how did you get hold of this beauty?"

Hal pointed at me and said, "He stole it."

"He stole it, you say? That's just wrong. This yours?" He was looking at me.

"It was a steal all right," I said. "The previous owner was one of those crazy get rich oilies."

"You guys with the Red and White?" Hal asked.

"When we do right, nobody remembers."

"When we do wrong, nobody forgets," Hal replied.

"Ooh! The man knows his stuff. You a one-percenter?"

"No, but I know my Hells Angels. I know that the first members were American Army Air Force pilots out of WW2. We're both Air Force pilots ourselves, and you guys have that link with us. No greater motto could you have than yours. 'When we do right, nobody remembers. When we do wrong, nobody forgets.' It applies to us, too. Hell, we're practically brothers."

Other bikers began to gather near us, listening to the conversation. The rough bunch of men were surprisingly polite, as their leader responded to what we were saying about their club.

"You guys are both shit hot fighter pilots, then?"

I pointed at Hal. "He is. I'm only a has been."

"We're both rated fighter pilots," Hal said.

"Hell, then. You're into wreaking havoc, just like us. We're brothers." He gave each of us an animated salute, which we returned.

Hal was on a roll. "You guys should see us in a bar fight."

"I hope you've put a few of those peacenik hippie pussies on the floor in your bars."

Hal and I looked at each other and chuckled. I lowered my head as Hal, I feared, was going to reveal something he shouldn't.

"If we did that, we'd never tell. Would you?"

"Well, I hope you do something to those bastards."

"If we ever did something like that, I can assure you it feels mighty good."

The leader laughed, as did the other bikers lingering within earshot. "Hell, you jet jocks are all right." He gave us another half-hearted salute. "Go about your business. I gotta take a piss." He turned and walked away, followed by his other biker pals.

Hal motioned with his finger to get in the car. We closed our doors. Hal put keys to ignition, threw the Porsche in gear, and gave them a show of raw sportscar acceleration out of harm's way and onto the highway. We joined another 85 mph convoy heading east. I pondered our encounter after fleeing over five miles from our friendly bikers.

"Where in the devil did you learn to socialize with the Hells Angels?" He laughed at my question.

"Identify with your new acquaintances. Didn't you know the connection of the Angels to military aviation?"

"No."

"Look at the Harley-Davidson logo for crying out loud. It's a set of Army Air Corps wings with the words *Harley-Davidson Motorcycles* planted over the shield."

"The first Hells Angels were pilots from The War?"

"Exactly. Must have held one hell of a grudge against life and civil society."

"You asked if he was with the red and white. What was that all about?"

"That's the colors on their patches. They have logos, too, just like any other club."

"Okay. He asked if you were a one-percenter, and you knew what that meant. too?"

"Answering that question wrong could have gotten us into a real jam. A one-percenter is a term for any biker gang member, not just a Hells Angel. They call themselves that because only one percent of motorcycle riders are bad."

"How does that question get us in trouble?"

"You sure as hell need to make it clear that you're a one-percenter with the Hells Angels and not with a rival gang—or better yet, that you're not in any gang. It was a little dicey for us when he asked that question. He knew I had some knowledge of their group. I could have been a cop, FBI, or anything they didn't like. That's why I gave them a history lesson."

"I got a history lesson, too."

"Everybody's a winner," Hal said, giving a short answer that I was more used to hearing.

"So how did you learn how to talk to the biker boss?"

"I read a lot, for one thing. You must understand that these guys don't ride around with the sole motive to whip your ass when they park next to you. They're like all of us. There's only so much whoop-ass they can stand. Look at us. We're finished with our ass kicking after less than a week."

"Did you ever think we would see the day when educated people called us baby killers and the Hells Angels sang our praises?"

Hal looked at me, then back to the road. "I'm motivated to get home to our women before we get the snot beat out of us."

"Said the steely-eyed killer."

"Keeping your cool is always the best answer."

Hal was still playing the role I valued above all. He was my mentor.

He drove us through the gates at Tinker AFB in early afternoon, going first to the BX to buy cheap government premium gas for my Porsche, then to the Officers' Club for a quick lunch.

I dropped him off at the flightline. He grabbed his pack from the front trunk of my car and waved. I waved back with a sigh of regret. It was great that we had one more chance to spend some man-to-man time together. I would see him again someday, but both our lives were about to change forever.

22

AS A THIRTEEN-YEAR-OLD boy in seventh grade, I called my first girl on the telephone, since going through the change. I had called girls before in grade school, but it was an enormous change at thirteen. I asked my mother what to say. She was a superb coach in etiquette. My father had a more direct approach. No advice gave me the courage necessary to complete the call. I dialed our telephone to ask a girl named Elizabeth to go with me to the Seventh Grade Fall Dance. I would dial six numbers, then hang up. I would dial all seven numbers and hang up before her phone would ring. After a half-an-hour of vacillation, it would be my father who would inform me he needed to use the phone. Only years later did I realize that he didn't need to use the phone. He was pushing me to fish or cut bait.

I called Elizabeth, and to my shock, she said yes. That was easy. From then on, I had less fear of calling. But just in case, I started jotting down topics to discuss, whenever I called a girl, just in case there was a lull in the telephone conversation. It was my first checklist, just like in my jet airplane.

I was driving into Nichols Hills, where the speed limit, even on the main streets, was 25 mph. Their police were strict, as many of my friends from high school knew. I went through my mental checklist of what to say to Suzy, what to say to her toddler son, Sean, and most importantly, what to say to Suzy's parents who lived in the big house. Suzy and Sean were staying temporarily in the spacious pool cabana, situated in the back corner of the two-acre estate that made up her parents' home. Pulling into the driveway of Suzy's parents, I had to marvel at how some hard-working people chose to live. It was my style. I exited from my car, feeling like I had come back home.

I walked up confidently to the porch of their house. Unlike in seventh grade with my telephone, I rang their doorbell on the first attempt. While waiting, I looked around the familiar house. I knew it well, since I had dated Suzy up until college when we split up for all my wrong reasons. The immense circular cobblestone driveway was diminished in proportion by the house set back from Wilshire Boulevard that allowed a deeply splendid, manicured lawn, peppered with matured and finely maintained red oak trees. The landscape added to the home's 12,000 square feet of three-story grandeur. A fountain, centered facing the home's entryway, rested on the inside of the circle drive. The home consisted of stacked white limestone capped by an enormous mansard roof with many dormer windows, which allowed for a ballroom on the third floor. Large windows allowed for wonderful indirect light to brighten the north facing home in all months of the year. This was no slouch of the house, and I was only seeing the front of it. I knew it to be more spectacular in the back. Suzy's view from her guest cabana would be hard to give up. This was all the result of oil money. This was where my new career would begin.

Through the diamond cut glass panes of the massive and high double doors, a woman approached. My heart began to pound, and I forgot what my mental checklist told me to say. If this was Suzy, my plans were dashed. I was void of words. Doors opened. Arms came out. The woman enveloped me in her arms in an embrace wholly unexpected. She wouldn't let go for the longest time, until a gentleman appeared behind her.

"Missus Jensen, it's so good to see you." I then took my free right hand and shook the hand of a man I knew well. "And Mister Jensen...." I became mute from fear and emotion.

The three of us looked at each other, still holding an arm around Suzy's mother and grasping the hand of her husband. I was paralyzed. Then, Suzy's father pulled me off his wife and hooked his left arm behind me in a warm and welcoming embrace. I managed to keep my true emotions wrapped up. My heart, though, was quickly unwrapped, reassured in a rush of relief and overwhelming joy.

23

THE JENSENS DRAGGED ME FROM their elegantly decorated entryway, still wrapping a hand around each arm. They seemed genuinely happy to see me again, possibly because they had received warning from Suzy that something was afoot. They had always been gracious to me, with none of the affected and condescending speech of some parents toward their children's friends. The Jensens were upfront with their observations and treated us like the full-grown adults we wanted to become someday. After flying for five years in the Air Force, and one abbreviated road trip, I approached them as one grown up to another.

"What a pleasant surprise to be greeted so warmly."

"Well, we certainly are happy to see you again. How long has it been?" Mr. Jensen asked.

"It must have been Suzy and John's wedding. A lot has happened since then, but you two haven't changed."

Mr. Jensen smiled. "Oh, my hair and sideburns are longer. They add about five pounds to me, too."

"Oh, what a cute little car," she said. "What is that?"

"That car is not cute, Dear. That's a Porsche." Mr. Jensen then turned to me. "What in the world are you doing with a car like that?"

"It's a long story, but just to let you know, I didn't steal it."

Mrs. Jensen continued to hold onto my arm, rubbing my wrist and hand like a doting mother. If I hadn't known them for so long, I may have been taken aback by their affections. This was how they had always been, which was why Suzy was such a catch. They never pretended to be anything but what they were—people who enjoyed the presence of others in their lives.

"I bet you are tired," she said. "Come and sit down."

"Dear, he's been sitting since Amarillo. You want to walk around awhile?"

"I'm fine for now. I must go see my parents in a bit, so I can't stay long. Is Suzy here?"

Their expressions revealed their disappointment. "Rob, Suzy went out for a minute. She promised to be back soon," her father said. "She didn't expect you to arrive this early. You will wait for her, won't you?"

"Of course, I will." My face surely showed my disappointment. "May I sit down with you while I wait?"

Mrs. Jensen suddenly broke into a broad smile and said, "I want to show you something before we sit down. Could you wait right there for a minute?"

"Of course."

She turned and hurriedly went down the hallway to my left and disappeared in the distant shadows. I turned to Mr. Jensen.

"How is she doing?"

"Who? Suzy?" I nodded.

"She's restless. Feels isolated. Once you get married and move into your own place, drastic changes that follow can be a downer."

"I understand that, sir."

"She lives here, but I know how she feels. This is not her home anymore. She left it before... on purpose. What makes us happy will not make her happy. She needs to get on with her own life."

"I hope I can cheer her up."

"I know you will, son."

"It'll cheer me up, too."

"I know it will, son. So, tell me how you have been getting along. You have had a hell of a twelve months yourself."

"Okay, I suppose. I went to Central State and took a few courses on the GI Bill. I spent a lot of time at the Veteran's Hospital. I decided to fire them, after I land a job and get civilian insurance."

"The VA did great work for me years ago. What's the problem?"

"You knew I got medically grounded?" He nodded his head. "Every time I went to the VA, I was surrounded by men smoking in the waiting area. They were bringing cartons of cigarettes with them, not just a pack. You wait two, sometimes three hours. I was grounded from flying because of my cigarette smoke sensitivity. It didn't make me get better going to the VA. It made me worse."

"I'm sorry that happened. I quit that habit shortly after I returned from Europe. The doctors told me it would make my frost bite worse. I nearly froze to death in Belgium."

"I'd like the hear the details of that someday, but first tell me how your grandson is doing?"

"Well, you can see for yourself. Turn around."

I did just that. Mrs. Jensen's surprise turned out to be little Sean himself, hanging onto her arm as tightly as her grandmother had recently been hanging on to mine. The young boy greeted me with a happy smile. With a hint of a tooth, a predictable drool, and two fingers in his mouth, little Sean could not conceal that he was the perfect likeness of his father, John Alexander. Joy came over me, seeing my late friend smile at me through his only son's eyes.

"Isn't he beautiful?" she asked.

"I like to think he is handsome, Dear."

"He looks manly," I replied. "He looks like a miniature John."

The baby boy and I stared at each other momentarily, like two kids trying to size each other up. I put the back of my finger against his puffy cheek to feel the warm soft flesh. I had not done that since soon after he was born back in Laredo, Texas. It was my way to get reacquainted.

"Would you like to hold him?" she asked.

Without waiting for a reply, she plopped the boy into my arms. I took hold of him awkwardly at first, but with some coaching from both grandparents, I found a comfortable way to hold him that met with their approval. He had grown enormously in the nine months since our last meeting. I no longer had to hold his head for him. He looked at me briefly, smiled, then twisted around to see his grandmother. After a couple of whimpers, he extended his arms and nearly leaned himself free of my inexperienced grasp.

"That's it," she said. "Come to your grandmama."

She rescued Sean from me and me from Sean. Who knew for sure? She led the three males into her spacious living room to sit and wait for Suzy's return. We shared idle chatter, catching up on such topics as the weather, places travelled, church gatherings, and the latest aches and pains from growing older.

The Jensen's living room was adorned with beautiful objects of art from all over the world. Two floor-to-ceiling windows looked out to the fountain and elevated front lawn, which blocked views of the street. The eclectic décor painted a splendid picture of a life lived on a grand scale. Absent in the room were televisions, telephones, radios, or anything else electronic except for the lamps that illuminated each table near a plush chair or love seat. This was a room for parties, quiet gatherings, or reading.

For the first time I took notice of Mrs. Jensen's attire. Since I first met her, she had projected an image of the woman we used to see in commercials, wearing a freshly ironed flowing dress, high heels, perfect hair, with a dust cloth in her hands. She would winsomely twirl around in her dress, happily dusting the house. That was Mrs. Jensen for real. Mr. Jensen was truly a lucky man. His wife remained surprisingly attractive for a woman still in her late forties. Only twenty years separated Suzy and her mother. I imagined that what Mrs. Jensen looked like back then had to rival the prettiest of girls. Of course, money can sometimes do that. I could hear it now. *How does your wife stay so beautiful?* The answer? *Oil.*

When I looked at Mr. Jensen, he was not quite as impressive. A product of World War II, he was content when not at work to wear the no longer popular jumpsuits that were the rage in the early 1960s.

I came to a sudden conclusion. How could I have overlooked it? What was he doing home? He was a hard charging relentless oilman, known for his work ethic and take-no-prisoners approach to competition. Why was he home on a Monday? The answer was clear to me. I was coming to see his daughter, and that was more important than anything else he would confront at work. His daughter and I were more important than money.

24

"WHO OWNS THE PORSCHE?" A female voice asked as the Jensen's front door opened. The four of us still sat comfortably in their living room, Sean in the affectionate arms of his grandmother.

I stood up, my heart instantly pounding from excitement and dread. Excitement for Suzy but dread for the fear of failure. Was I assuming too much? I was about to find out.

Suzy walked curiously into where her mother called out to her. She focused on Sean, who quickly held out his arms and squealed in delight. She dropped her coat on the nearest armchair, revealing blue slacks and a simple white sweater—a stunning beauty as always.

"Whose car?" she asked again.

Her mother started to speak, then caught herself, just as Suzy turned around. She looked with surprise as she realized that it was my car. Her mouth opened in shock. My checklist went out the window. Hers did, too. She stood still briefly, no smile on her face. Everyone remained silent. Then Suzy lifted her two hands to her face and began to cry.

The Jensens did not move or speak. Her father looked at me with a forceful nod in her direction, ordering me to go to her. I approached carefully, reaching out a hand to her cheek to wipe away a tear. At the soft touch to her cheek, she opened her eyes to see me in the flesh and wrapped her arms tightly around me in a powerfully strong embrace. My fears disappeared, and I confidently put my arms around her in response. We held each other tightly for way too long before releasing our grip to look at each other for the first time in nine months. Tears came from both of us, making it hard to see the other. She grabbed my two hands in hers.

"I've missed you."

"Oh Suzy. I have missed you, as well."

I glanced through my tears toward Suzy's father, who knew instinctively what to do next.

"Mama and I are going to let you two alone, so you can be in private."

As Suzy's parents, with Sean, exited the room, I grew embarrassed, like I was still in high school and worried they would think we were up to something forbidden. We sat down in one of the nearby love seats. She kept her hands clasped tightly in mine, looking overjoyed to see me.

"What are we doing here, Suzy?"

"I don't know. You tell me."

"I haven't thought about much else the last few weeks, except about you."

"Meaning what?"

"I'm in love with you. I always have been. Even after you got married. I never wished or dreamed that I would have a second chance."

"You are the only other man I have ever deeply loved."

"Okay."

"You hurt me when you dumped me for that hussy."

I couldn't help laughing at her description. "She was worse than that, wasn't she?"

"How much can I trust you now, Rob? I want you to tell me."

The insinuation cut me to the quick. It hurt me because I knew it was a legitimate question. *How much can you trust me?* Totally now, but how was I to convince her of that? Would she trust my words alone? I wouldn't trust me in her shoes. I knew the monkey was on my back to show her I had grown up.

"You have every right to ask me that. And I know the burden of proof is in what I do from now on, not what I say. Talk is cheap, right?"

She did not reply, she only held my hands still and looked into my eyes with sadness.

"I'm lonely, Rob. I was not meant to be a single mother. We got you in trouble by seeing each other too much after John died. It was all so innocent. The three of us were such good friends."

"I don't care anymore. We're adults... and I'm lonely, too... for you."

"It's too early for that. John only died a year ago."

"I thought of that myself. Why do you think you haven't heard from me? I was afraid of what I might say to you. I would've violated John's trust in me—and he's dead."

"It *has* been a year almost."

It was an appropriate time to lighten the atmosphere in the living room. "What would Sean say?"

Suzy reacted the opposite of what I intended. She welled up with tears and took a tissue from her purse to dry them. "Sean needs a daddy."

"So, I'll ask again. What are we doing here?"

"You tell me." Suzy looked up, giving me an impish grin.

I let out a muted chuckle. "I need to see my parents. I'll call you when I get to my apartment. In the meantime, we're going out to eat some night when you're free, with or without Sean. Better yet, with Sean. You pick the restaurant and time. We both need a good night's sleep to think about it with a level head."

"Okay, I agree."

I stood up from the love seat, reminding Suzy that I needed to go. She walked me to the door. Her parents were hiding out somewhere, good to their word not to interrupt our private conversation. I stepped out on the porch. Suzy followed. I turned to face her.

"Are we making some assumptions here?"

"What do you mean, assumptions?"

"Are you going to marry me if I don't ruin it this time?"

"That was bold."

"Isn't that what you liked about me?"

"Yep."

"Yep what?"

"Yep, I'll marry you."

I reached my shaking hands to her shoulders and kissed her ever so ten-tatively on her lips. She responded with a closer hug than I dared to try. As she held me, the warmth of our bodies drawing us closer, she let me savor the form of her breasts and the muscles of her legs as she stretched up to fit into my form. With her head now buried on my chest below my throat, she looked up, the warmth of her sweet breath against my skin. I melted into her arms, gave her one last hug, and let her loose. She held on.

"I'll call you tonight."

"Okay."

"I won't let you down this time."

"I know." She grabbed my hands again and squeezed them. "I love you, Robert Amity. I need you."

"You have to know… I never stopped loving you. Never."

I leaned down to kiss her one last time. This time she pressed her slightly parted lips against mine. We lingered for one last moment of tenderness, then she pulled away. Without another word, I stepped to my car, glanced once more in her direction, then drove away.

25

I WAS AS GIDDY AS a Christmas morning Scrooge. Everything I dreaded vanished into a promising vision of tomorrow. I carefully drove my Porsche at 25 mph west past the watchful eyes of the Nichols Hills patrol cars and entered Oklahoma City a mile later. I headed north on May Avenue, known in high school as the two to three mile stretch of road where all the action was. I crossed Britton Road and noticed a new business on my left in the shapes of a railroad caboose and several boxcars assembled in a jumble. It was a new restaurant placed where a vacant lot existed my whole time in high school. Looking to my right stood the remains of Twilight Gardens Drive-in, closed only two years before in 1972. I had many memories flash by as I looked at the now crumbling screen. The speaker poles were still in semicircular rows, with many of the speakers missing or off the hook dangling by their cords. When I looked to my left, I simultaneously passed the old and repurposed Wiley Post Airport Hangar still there, but without a runway. The landing strip where Wiley Post and Will Rogers sometimes landed was now an extensive housing addition. I turned left just past the hangar and drove to the house where all my mostly good, but sometimes bad, high school memories still resided.

I pulled into the driveway. To the west, a new home sat in front of the lake that I grew up with. Built the year before, this house blocked my view of Lake Hefner. My parents could no longer enjoy from their front porch the spectacular Oklahoma sunsets reflecting off the large three-mile diameter reservoir. On a windless day, the dark and brilliant reds would rival any other wonder of nature. Like every visit to my parents, a tinge of melancholy hit me as I stepped onto their porch. I found change involving my boyhood home to be a problem.

Because we had promised to be courteous to each other, I didn't use my door key, but rang the doorbell. My mother must have sprinted to answer it because she opened the door before the bell's ring had quieted. As usual, her open arms enveloped me. The excitement in her voice, that I once believed was made up, was in her blood. My mother made all visitors feel welcome and loved. Her delight was real. That was just the way Mom was.

"Oh, Rob. You got a haircut. You look so much better."

I entered my moderate-sized teenage home and headed to my favorite room in the house. The den was a place of happy times as a teenager with parties, television, music, and dating. I glanced over to the wall where rested a dark red sofa, the sight of all my necking sessions with each year's new girlfriend. My parents had built our house so that I could entertain my dates without their intrusion. I had earned their trust. I was good at following their rules of conduct in their house. Besides, Lake Hefner was less than a quarter mile from the house. Lots of necking went on there. Fortunately, I never had to go to the lake. My parents were modern, but I was traditional.

Mom looked at me with curious eyes. "Well?"

I gave her another hug. "Where's Dad? I'll tell you both."

"At least give me a hint. Did you do anything interesting on your trip?"

"Most of the interesting part has happened today, actually."

"Oh, dear," Mom said. *Oh, dear* was her favorite phrase, which was a catchall for *oh my, oh no, ah-oh, or what have you done now?*

"Let's wait for Dad. I think you will like what I have to say. Where is Dad, by the way?"

"He's out back in his shop, trying not to cut his fingers off. You might go out there and save him. I'm dying to hear what you're up to."

We walked through the kitchen and out the back door. I realized that it was cold. Temperatures had obviously dropped. In my giddiness I had not noticed. Mom stayed behind. I ran to Dad's heated workspace at the back of the yard. Air compressors and impact drills competed to damage my ears as I stepped inside of the overly warm workshop. At first, he didn't notice my entering. He looked to his left, then back to his task. Laying down his drill, he lifted his shop glasses onto the top of his head and pulled his Micky Mouse ears down around his neck.

"Rob, my man. How are you... and why are you here?" He laughed at his joke as he stepped over to grip my hand in a vice. "I hope everything's all right."

"It is, Dad. Hal and I decided that we were getting too old to be acting like those guys on Route 66." I stepped closer. "Now don't tell Mom, but we got in a little tussle more than once. Those Vietnam protesters are everywhere we went. Dad, I fear I'm turning into you."

"It's about damn time, son." He laughed.

"We went to the Grand Canyon. Did a little hiking. Then some of those preppies, you know, the ones who don't think theirs stinks? They tried some thumping on us in the canyon after they found out Hal was a River Rat, which we ignored. Then they continued their harassment back up top. We got 'em good. We may get arrested, yet."

"Reminds me of when I removed the teeth of another soldier one night in Manilla. You're old enough. Had you ever heard that story?"

"Not until now."

"Never futz around with a GI. That's all I'm going to say."

"I feel better already."

"Now you're in the club. Is Mom waiting for us to come in?" My father carefully put away his tools, all in their proper place. He turned off his compressor, laid his safety glasses and Micky Mouse ears on their proper hooks, and turned off the lights. We stepped outside. I waited while Dad locked the door to his shop. It was colder still. Obviously, a cold front was already way south of the city. The wind chill bit into my thin emergency dress up clothes. I followed him into the main house in the kitchen.

"We've got a norther here. Step outside and feel that."

"You can tell me about it. I'm not going out there."

They both laughed at their little inside humor. All couples had little jokes that were their secret one-liners that no one else would understand. Since I grew up with them, I was privy to most. Their sexual innuendos I still was not privy to, but I guessed there were several. As I watched them laugh together, it was a change in their marriage, not evident the year before when I came back to bury John Alexander. The tension evidenced then seemed gone. This was yet another event among many today that made me Christmas Scrooge giddy.

26

"DIDN'T YOU CANCEL YOUR APARTMENT lease?" Dad asked.

"Yes, like a fool. I'll try to get my lease back tomorrow. I still have it for the rest of this month."

We were eating dinner, a ritual that Mom had insisted would continue in the finest fashion, until she pushed up the daisies. She was a wonderful cook in her day, but as she aged, her cooking fell into a simpler practice. Her cooking style evolved into two settings. OFF or HI. Everything was well done—meat, potatoes, vegetables. Any risk of a pathogenic organism was boiled to death well before the cooking ended. By contrast, items that should be refrigerated after opening were not. Ketchup, parmesan cheese, salad dressing. It didn't matter. They were all put in the cupboards. Dad hadn't died, yet. He seemed resigned to ignoring my pleadings for better food storage. The survival of his marriage probably depended upon it. Mom, having grown up using an icebox, was unmoved. Then there was the can of bacon grease under the stove. I remember her instructions as a child when she told me how to fry chicken. "Be sure to scoop just the top layer of bacon grease into your spoon. If you go deeper, it's rancid."

"Have you already moved your furniture out?" Mom asked.

"I never had much. I've been living kind of spartan. I have a bed, table and chair, and one set of silverware, one plate, one glass, one… well, you get it."

"Oh, dear."

She passed the food around our kitchen table, the site of every family meal I ever had in the house. The dining room table was reserved for I never knew what. I evaluated each item passed to me, based upon my careful reconnaissance while talking to her in the kitchen. Everything tonight passed inspection. Was she turning over another new leaf? Both her cooking and her marriage seemed to be improving.

"Will you stay here tonight?" Dad asked. "I know Mom would like that."

"I'll go to my apartment first. I still have a key. If anything is wrong, I'll come back here. I appreciate the offer."

"So, what's the news your mother is so hot to trot about?"

Mom noticeably perked up as I relayed all the adventures Hal and I had. I referenced our feeling that we were growing up. We both found that what we liked to do was changing and that we joked about it by saying we had gotten to the age that our toys weren't fun anymore.

"Speaking of toys, did you see my new car?"

Mom chimed in. "I *did* see that. What a cute little car?"

I chuckled and gave her my favorite new one-liner. "Mom, real men don't drive cute cars."

"I was out back in the shop. What did you get, son?"

I told my story about talking to the owner of the dealership when he was in a giving mood.

"It sounds like you could deal in anything. A Porsche 911 in an even trade. Your other car certainly wasn't worth that much."

"It was the deal of a lifetime."

I told them about my joining up with Hal in Big Spring, Texas, and our drive to the Grand Canyon. I mentioned the welding truck and the men who harassed us on our canyon hike and beyond. They were amused by our encounter with the Hells Angels. I left out what happened to the welder, our preppie anti-Vietnam harassers, and the Gallop girls. I told them I stopped by to see Suzy and her parents but no more details than those.

I looked at Dad after mentioning Suzy. "That's it? You just talked?"

"This is *not* the boy I raised," Mom said.

"Come on. Spill the beans."

"That's all I'm going to say."

"I knew it," she said.

"Knew what?"

"We'll learn more soon enough." Dad was looking at his wife with that stare of silence.

"Well to change the subject, can I tell you what I'm going to do for a job?"

Dad laughed and added, "The way you bought that car, I hope you picked sales. I like conversations where my son says he's getting a job."

"With the oil industry at the beginning of a boom, I'm going to invest in things the oilfield needs and sell it to them. I'm not investing in oil wells. I'm into supporting those who are drilling. I figured I might use Mister Jensen's expertise to advise me."

"You sure better be on good terms with his daughter," she said.

"I think that is an excellent idea, Rob," he said. "Jensen has certainly been right for a long time. The times I have met him, he seemed like a straight shooter. Don't expect him to sugarcoat things for you. It's rough and tumble out there these days."

"I think the Air Force was a perfect warmup for me to tackle this. I just need to learn what people want."

"Now, son. You know that it takes money to make money. Do you have the money to invest?"

"Yes, I do, but I've already heard advice to never use your own money for a business adventure. I might borrow some money to get started."

"Talk to Jensen. See what he says."

"And, Honey? Don't let him loan you the money."

"I know not to do that. Too many things could go both right and wrong with that arrangement. I can't afford to mess it up if I want long term success."

27

THE NEXT MORNING THERE WERE clear skies before the sun appeared over the horizon. That meant a cold start to the day. I was in my apartment office asking for my cancellation letter. The lady was hesitant. She was already getting people lined up to move into other apartments in the complex. The oil industry was spiraling upwards with too few apartments to fill the need. I talked her into keeping me, after convincing her that I had been a good and reliable tenant and that, if I left later, the lengthy list of people waiting would guarantee a quick new lease.

After leaving my parent's house, I had spent the night in my bleak residence. Looking around at the spartan surroundings next morning, I decided to best fight my returning melancholy by making my home livable. I would start my new quest for riches by buying more furniture and stocking my kitchen. Why had I been saving every penny if not for this moment?

Having salvaged my apartment lease, I called Suzy's father at his office. I asked him if he could advise me about my plan to start a business to service the oil industry. He practically ordered me to drop everything I was doing and see him. I did not yet have a suit or sport coat. I put on the best pair of slacks I owned and ironed a previously worn shirt I pulled out of the closet. After finding some old Air Force black socks and slipping into some well-polished loafers, I headed to his office. I decided to add updated clothing to my home shopping list.

It was nearly ten o'clock when I arrived at the new twin eight story buildings near Baptist Hospital on the Northwest Expressway. After entering the west tower, I checked to see the proper floor to select for the elevator. I remember correctly that he was on the top floor. Having ridden the slow elevator to eight, my heart began to race. This was a call, not only about seeking advice, but also about selling myself to Suzy's father. There were so many ways I could foul it up.

I entered the small dark oak-paneled lobby of this successful and stable enterprise, first meeting the receptionist, an attractive lady in her 50s, who greeted me with a smile that every business needed for success. On her ornate black-lacquered desk, a nameplate read Mrs. Stone. She had a telephone to her left. A pen and pencil holder lay behind her nameplate, with an IN-OUT basket to her right. Her desktop was devoid of anything else. Behind her, against a wide floor length window, was a bureau with a handful of family pictures of her husband, her children, and her dogs. Outside her window was a marvelous view of Lake Hefner looking north.

"Good morning," I said. "I'm Robert Amity. Mister Jensen asked me to stop by."

"Yes, Mister Amity. He's waiting for you, so please come this way."

She led me a short few steps down the pink marble hallway to my left, knocked on a heavy and ornately carved oak door, and opened it without waiting for a reply.

"Mister Jensen, I have Robert Amity to see you."

"Rob! Come in here and take a seat. Thank you, Missus Stone." She closed the door behind me.

For a split second, my eyes marveled at the sumptuous décor of his office that screamed success. The walls were covered in myriad pieces of Southwest art ranging from local native watercolors and oils to older examples of ledger art. Native blankets hung from the high office ceiling. Built-in shelves held pottery of many forms. Two large Kachina Dolls rested on opposite corners of the room. Navajo rugs added a softness to the marble floor. Mr. Jensen's furnishings were right out of the National Park playbook of lodge lobbies with two heavily upholstered oak chairs, a matching sofa, and a small conference table in the corner. Windows met in the corner of the office, giving the man a full 270-degree view of the city south, west, and north. This was what success looked like. It occurred to me that the Jensen house was not like this at all. This was his own little taste of independence, where only his rules applied.

With his hand, Mr. Jensen motioned for me to sit in the first large chair facing his desk. He then came from behind his desk and joined me in the other matching chair. He dressed casually in slacks of a small houndstooth pattern of black and white. He wore a black mock turtleneck and a yellow dress shirt. His tan corduroy sport coat hung on a coat tree standing behind his desk.

"Rob, I'm flattered that you called me for advice."

"Well, sir. I think I need it. I knew you would have some sound advice for me."

"I *do* have some good advice." He paused for a moment, gathering his mental notes. "First, can I get you something to drink. Coffee? A Coke? Water?"

"No, thank you, I'm fine."

"Rule number one. Never turn down an offer from a client. It's a peace offering. Even if you don't really drink it, accept it. They are giving you a gift."

"Okay. A Coke would be wonderful, thank you."

He stood up and leaned over his equally uncluttered desk to page his receptionist. When she responded, he asked for two Cokes. Within 30 seconds she was through the door with a cart with ice, soft drinks, and glasses. She put ice in each glass and gave each of us an open can, all while her boss continued to talk to me. She slipped out again before I noticed.

"Were your parents all right yesterday?"

"They are. They seemed happy to see me. They also seemed happy in each other's company. It was a fun day."

"Are you staying with them, or do you have a residence still?"

"I just got my apartment back. I cancelled the lease last week, thinking I would wander aimlessly for a while, until I got my future figured out. It turns out, it took little time before I was ready to make a difference and go to work."

"Well, it was nice of you to stop by and see Suzy. She's a lonely mother and needs a boost in morale. She was a lot more cheerful after you left. I admit to you that I worry about her. Staying with her parents is not a good long-term strategy for any of us."

It was hard to keep my feelings to myself, but I knew that even my private conversation yesterday with Suzy was not a sure thing. Did we love each other, or were we merely lonely? Were we just friends, or did we dare express the passion necessary before we got serious enough to join in marriage? Our confessions that we loved each other were not enough reasons to dive madly into matrimony. There were repercussions to any decision we made.

"Tell me first, Rob. What exactly do you want to do?"

"I don't want to find oil. I want to supply the needs of the ones who find the oil."

"That's smart. Are you talking big things like housing, pipe, mud, etcetera, or are you talking small things like food, beer, clothing, and so on?"

"Since I don't know the drilling industry well enough, I thought the small things that keep the workers working would be better suited to me."

"That probably means that you set up a mobile franchise that follows the workers as they move to new wells in the oil patch."

"I need to learn how they do that. I hear they'll buy anything on paydays."

Jensen paused a moment. I stayed silent as he considered. "What you need to do first, to learn what goes on and to hear what the guys want, is to get a job for a month or two. Listen to the lingo. Learn what the boys are needing, what gripes they have. I guarantee you there are items or services that are going unfulfilled right now because no one has asked them what it is that they need but can't find. It can be as simple as selling them a shirt a day. You watch. Those boys go through a shirt a day and throw it away. It is impossible to wash. Multiply that by a hundred and you'll have a promising idea of how many things they need just to make it to work."

"I like that idea. It would be like one of my college jobs. I learned a lot in three months, doing manual labor." I paused, with a question that was a rethinking of my original plan. "Do I need to take some more business courses before I try this? I've got the GI Bill."

"It's a good idea in the long term, but in this atmosphere, you may lose your best opportunity. It's fast growing in the oil industry. Now's your time to get in, not in a year."

"I think I have fairly good instincts."

"You go to school now and you'll learn all about how not to do things. That information might be valuable in a stable market, but this is not that sort of marketplace."

"Take advantage of the crazies?"

"You will certainly learn what the real world is like." We both chuckled. "Which brings up something important to stress with you. You must go into this knowing that it is the wild west out there. The oil patch is like the combination of the end of the cattle trail in Dodge City with the California Gold Rush. There are murderers, thieves, liars, drunks, gamblers, you name it. And if you cross them, they attempt to beat you to death. Go in with your eyes wide open."

"Are there any good people in the oil patch?"

"Oh, sure. Lots of people are good folks. Most are not too smart when it comes to money. That's where you can help them. Be fair. Be helpful. Be moral. Listen to them. They will reward you in return. Now, here's what not to do. Don't over promise. If they ask for hookers, kickbacks, any of the finer things in life, say no, N-O."

That would not be a problem, but responding to him seemed a bad idea, considering the subject. I simply nodded in agreement and moved the conversation elsewhere.

"Where do I go to work in the oil patch?"

"I don't want you to work in the oil patch unless you are just determined to learn the business. That's dangerous work, both on and off the rig. Instead, I want to send you to one of my friends, who supplies lots of the stuff the rigs and their workers need. His name is Stanton BigHeart. The company is A-to-Z Oilfield Services. At my request, Stanton will hire you, but you will be working night and day for a while. It's the best education you will find anywhere."

"I'm fine with that. When can I call on him?"

Mr. Jensen stood up from his comfortable chair, walked around to his desk, picked up the phone, and speed dialed his friend as I sat waiting. A minute later he hung up the phone and said an interview for me was scheduled for Friday at 11:00 AM.

"Will that work for you?"

"Of course, it will. Thank you."

"So, I've given you some pointers. You can mull them over at lunch. Will you let me buy you lunch?"

I laughed. "Wasn't that the first rule you told me? Never say no when a client offers food or drink."

Mr. Jensen walked to the door of his office and opened it. "I have a wonderful place in mind you will love. And you're taking me in your car."

28

THE GREAT AMERICAN RAILROAD WAS a new restaurant at the most important intersection in my growing up years at the southwest corner of Britton Road and May Avenue. Located on the corner opposite the Twilight Gardens Drive-In Theater, it was the location of too many happy memories to count. Mr. Jensen directed me to the same location that I had driven by and noticed with interest the night before. He was suitably impressed with his ride in the Porsche and to his credit asked me no more questions. He was aware that it was a rare and expensive addition to the racing-mad Porsche corporation. I turned into the parking lot to find it already showed signs of success if the few places to park was an indicator. When we parked and climbed out of the car, I was surprised to see the difficulty my passenger had trying to egress gracefully. It was no car for old men.

As we walked in, I was greeted by a familiar voice. "Rob Amity. What are you doing in these parts?"

I looked up in surprise to see the constantly smiling face of Brad Kilty, the man obsessed with flying and, as it turned out, this new restaurant's manager. A grade school and high school friend, Brad had learned his trade at the Oklahoma State University School of Hotel and Restaurant Management. And unlike me, he learned his art of flying from high motivation, mighty effort, and a lot of money. He did it the hard way. I did it with stressful work and a million-dollar donation from Uncle Sam.

"What a surprise! Come in here," Brad said. His excitement was contagious. "Where do you want to sit?"

I looked around and realized there weren't many options for seating. The place was already packed at peak lunchtime.

"Anyplace is fine. How have you been, anyway?"

"Great now. This is my first gig as manager of a restaurant. You're going to love this place. Follow me."

He walked us up some steps to a part of the building that from the outside was the caboose. The interior gave all indications of being the headquarters of a freight conductor. Brad seated us, placed a menu before each of us, and slapped me on the back.

"It's good to see you. I'll be back when I have time to talk. I want to know how the Air Force is managing. You're still in, I hope?"

"We'll tell you all the scoop when you get back."

Without another word, only a nod to both of us, he was whisked away by a waiter in need.

"Interesting place. When did this get started?"

"It's brand new. Just opened last month. Too bad they weren't open at Christmas. They would have made a killing. This is a boy's paradise."

I looked around the interior of our caboose to see model trains perched high atop shelves along the length of a wall. It brought back memories of my own childhood and my fascination with Lionel trains. I had even run past my brand-new Schwinn Corvette bicycle on Christmas morning as a nine-year-old to get to the Lionel train and train board my parents had so carefully kept secret. It was an hour before they made me turn around to find my bicycle. It was the Christmas I will most vividly remember.

"Do they have any trains that are running?" I asked. The kid was coming out in me. I was embarrassed to admit that my childhood enthusiasm had returned.

"You've got a bigger toy now in that Porsche." We laughed together.

I knew what he meant. We were never too old to enjoy a toy or two. Then it dawned on me. Mr. Jensen had no son to play with. Was this why he wanted to help me out? Was he hoping to finally get a son? My own father loved to help me play with trains, play catch with baseballs, fish, and share the joys of his own exciting boyhood. Did this man sitting across from me miss that joy of fatherhood with a son? Perhaps.

"What did your father say about your car purchase?"

"He was amused. I guess proud of my persuasive hutzpah. He said he hoped I got a job in sales."

"Is that what you want to do?"

"For now. When I started college, I wanted to go into veterinary medicine. That's why I went to OSU, to be in their program. I got to do something else."

"Any regrets?"

"About vet school? No. Your son-in-law dying in a plane crash? Yes."

"I'm sorry. That was a poorly thought-out question."

"That's okay. I have a joke I know I have overused, but I tell people that I had a goal to be a vet. I achieved it. Just the wrong kind of vet."

"That's a new one to me. I like it."

"No, I don't regret how my life has travelled in directions I never expected. I have a clean slate now. I learned that everything I have unexpectedly been given to pursue has been fun to do."

"You've had a varied experience ever since you had your summer jobs."

"You're right. In my experience, I've learned that a new path is not to be feared. I believe we are all lucky, but only a few of us are aware of it when luck falls in our laps. With your advice, sir, I feel like my luck is just starting."

Our waiter stepped up to take our orders. The lunch menu was a standard fare of hamburgers, sandwiches, soups, and salads. As much as I wanted a beer, I ordered a Dr. Pepper, instead. Dr. Pepper had been a staple of my diet on the flightline the year before, but this was my first one since departing from active duty. Our food came quickly. We were both hungry, putting a quash on any meaningful conversation. It was comfortable being around this gentleman.

"How's your food?"

We both looked up from our comfortable silence to see my boyhood friend, Brad.

"Good!" I said. "I think you'll have a job for a while."

"Great to hear. The owners are top notch. They are opening more restaurants soon, and I'll be moving to those as their startup manager."

"If you have time, Brad, sit down and join us." I turned around. "This is Mister Jensen. He's now my official oil industry advisor. Brad is a childhood friend of mine and a fellow OSU Cowboy."

They shook hands cordially. "You must be Suzy Jensen's father. I knew Suzy when she and Rob dated in college."

"That's my girl."

"Rob, are you still flying in the Air Force?"

"I got out about nine months ago."

"Don't tell me that." Brad looked bothered by the news. "Does that mean you're in the reserves?"

"I'm out totally. I got medicaled out of flying. Had a few issues too involved to explain today."

"Now, Suzy married John Alexander. Is he still flying?"

We paused a moment. Mr. Jensen spoke first. "John was killed in a military accident a year ago."

"Oh, sir, please forgive me. I had no idea. I'm so sorry. John was a nice man. He was a good match for your daughter. I hope she is coping all right now."

"She lives nearby," I replied. "She and John had a son. She's doing fine. I've started checking on her. Seeing how she's doing."

Brad looked over his shoulders, like someone hoping for his name to be called so he could escape the table. I tried to put him at ease.

"Surely you're still flying your Cessna 172."

"Every Saturday and Sunday. I fly every day at sunrise if the weather is good. I'm working on my CFI now." He looked at Mr. Jensen. "That stands for certified flight instructor. I have close to 800 hours of flight time logged. I hope someday to fly full time. Rob, you going back to try vet school again?"

"That's in my past," I said. "I'm looking for opportunities during this oil boom. You know. Get in on it while you can. Get out of it when you can't."

"That too risky for me," Brad said, "but you wouldn't believe what it's done for the service industry. Look around at this crowd. That's oil money you hear talking. The growth of customers is unbelievable. It's a profitable time to be doing what you see around you."

"I'll tell you what," I said. "Give me your address and telephone number. I want to go see your airplane. Then I'll tell you my story."

Brad pulled out his business card, wrote his home address and phone number on the back, and handed me the card. "Good to see the both of you. Tell Suzy hello for me. I wish her the best, and, Rob, call me. Now, I gotta go."

Brad was gone before I could reply. The place was busy. Mr. Jensen looked at me. "You see why this is a valuable time for you. Because of oil everybody, inside or outside of the patch, needs lots of something. We just need to uncover for you what that is."

29

I ARRIVED FOR MY 11:00 A.M. interview 15 minutes early, which in the military would be considered just barely on time. The location was in an industrial part of Oklahoma City a quarter mile east of the now deserted downtown. The old brick warehouse buildings scattered throughout a quarter section of land were mostly abandoned manufacturing facilities of a bygone era of the city's more prosperous days. With the growing price of crude oil, the smart money was taking advantage of cheap rental properties to make a profit without the insane overhead incurred by those with new money. The old money knew not to get too fancy. Crude oil was the same price, whether your offices were brick or marble.

I stepped through the door into the offices of A-to-Z Oilfield Services. An attractive bleach blonde twenty-year-old gave me a big smile as I stepped into the plain but efficient waiting room. She sat behind a desk, typing what looked like a small-sized invoice. A stack of envelopes rested behind her typewriter along with a nameplate with her name, Mary. Each time her head bent down to type, her black roots distracted from what was otherwise a libidinously pleasant visage. Dressed casually, she could not hide her magnificent profile, more than adequate to melt the hearts of young men.

"Good morning, Mary," I said. "My name is Robert Amity, and I have an eleven o'clock interview with Mister Stanton BigHeart."

"Yes, Mister Amity. You are early. That is good. I think Mister BigHeart can see you now. Let me check."

She got on her desk phone and paged into his private office the message of my arrival. In a matter of seconds, a man of enormous size stepped through his doorway in the short hallway. He wore old blue jeans, cowboy boots, and a dark western shirt. His only decoration was an ornate bola tie with a slide of a huge turquoise anchored in silver. In curt fashion, he waved me to come to his office. I quickly came down the hall to greet him. The military teaches us to wait for a superior officer to offer his hand to shake. I waited in vain for Mr. BigHeart. Lowering his head, he preceded me into his office and again wordlessly offered me a folding chair. A quick look around the office confirmed my first guess. With his size and the few hints on his office desk, plus friends of my parents named BigHeart, he had to be Osage. Historically, they were feared so much that Indian tribes came to the U.S. Army begging for help in fighting them. I wondered if the fierce warrior heritage of the Osage would pass down to one Mr. Stanton BigHeart.

He sat down at his disheveled desk and mercifully finally spoke. "I got a call from Mister Jensen. He's a man I trust. He asked me to talk to you and let you learn my trade."

Was there a question here? I couldn't tell. He wasn't continuing. I decided this was a man who wasted no time in small talk. This was not new. The military style was the same.

"I'm interested in learning what needs the oil field workers have and figuring out how to get them what others have failed to get them."

"I already do that."

"Have you ever asked them what they are not getting?"

"No."

"We could find a gold mine from supplying them what no one else will."

"I'm busy enough already."

"Mister Jensen suggested I could work for you for a month or two and learn the trade. Rather than compete with you, I want to discover what you don't want to bother with and go off on my own to sell that. If I learn well enough, perhaps we could team up and refer to each other when the workers or the bosses ask for something."

"Why would I hire you for two months and have you take what you learned and compete with me?"

"Because you are already busy enough, and all I want to learn is what you don't sell. I want the business they tell me they don't get."

"Are you military?"

"Yes, sir."

"Pilot?"

"Yes, sir."

"How do you feel, killing all those innocent women and children?"

The conversation stopped. I looked at him with growing contempt. Was this a trick question or a sincere statement? Was it a reference to the Osage atrocities committed over headrights in the early 1900s?

"I find that offensive." I paused both for effect and to collect my thoughts. I was now seething. "I served my country with pride. No one calls me a baby killer. This interview is over."

I stood up and walked urgently out of his office and into his front waiting area. I looked at the young blonde with the black stripe down the middle of her head.

"It was nice to meet you, Mary."

I stepped through the door to the parking lot and got into my car where I sat for the next five minutes trying to calm my nerves. It was not only offensive, but it hurt me deeply. None of us in the military, with any honor in our being, ever intended to harm innocent women and children. We were all drafted against our will, but we served loyally. Being accused of this atrocity was to carry forever my contempt.

I started up the Porsche, giving it an inappropriate dose of RPMs leaving the parking space. I was too angry to drive until I settled down. I paused a moment. *Don't drive stupid. What would Mr. Jensen say? What would Suzy say?* I collected my thoughts and judiciously drove away. To my surprise, in my rearview mirror Stanton BigHeart stood on the front step waving his arms.

30

"WHAT DID HE ASK YOU?"

I was on the phone with Mr. Jensen, trying my best to sound calm.

I was failing.

"He implied I was a baby killer."

"Tell me again exactly what Stanton said."

"Well, sir, he asked me, 'How do you feel, killing all those innocent women and children?'"

"How did you answer?"

"I didn't answer. I told him the question was offensive and that our interview was over."

"Is that all you said. Did you insult him?"

"No! I only told him I had pride in serving. I may have told him something like 'no one would dare call me that.'"

"What he asked is unacceptable, I agree."

"Sir, what is society coming to? Are we all going to get this constantly? I didn't even get a chance to fight in Vietnam. We all get the same insults."

"Anything else you want to tell me?"

"The interview went well until he popped his question. It came out of the blue. He was interested in my idea. The only thing that made me wonder what was going on was that he came outside and waved to me as I drove off. I wasn't about to stop."

"Okay, Rob. Here's what I'm going to do. I'm going to call him and ask what in the world he was thinking?"

"Why bother?"

"Because he is a genuinely nice man and honest as they come. I don't know what he was thinking. He's an Army veteran. He saw combat in Korea. I want to know what he was doing following you outside."

"I didn't want a fight in the parking lot."

"I understand, but you drove away, instead of beating him to a pulp. That's in your favor."

"I doubt if I could have. He's a big man."

"True, but let's pause a moment. Let me make a call. I'll be the heavy on this. You sit tight."

"Yes, sir."

We hung up, and I chose to wait in my apartment until he called back. I switched on my cheap BX-purchased black and white 12-inch television to watch anything I could find on my four channels that was cheerful. In previous days on CBS News, Walter Cronkite reported several events that were often depressing. Of interest to me was the inaugural flight of a new fighter jet, the F-16 Fighting Falcon. Where did they come up with these cumbersome names for airplanes? I knew about it from classified briefings I received two years before. Oil rationing was still a worldwide problem, with even the West German Autobahn reducing max speed to 100-kph. The Irish were still bombing the Brits. Patty Hearst, granddaughter of William Randolph Hearst, was kidnapped by one of those lunatic groups in California. The world had its first close view of Venus, thanks to Mariner 10 photos. The movie *Blazing Saddles* was all the rage. Just as nutty, an Army private buzzed the White House with a helicopter. Israeli forces were leaving Egypt's western Suez. It was the news guaranteed to put me in a mental slump.

The worst news of all was the start of impeachment proceedings for my Commander in Chief, Richard Nixon. President Nixon filled me with pride when he sent our massive military might over North Vietnam and forced a peace treaty on the communists. Now two years later, peace was unravelling, and Congress was out for the kill. The two were unrelated except that both made me uncomfortable. It seemed like the whole country was turning to a collective of sore losers, who were now bitterly turning on each other.

The phone rang to shake me out of my daydreaming. I turned off the television and picked up the receiver.

"Rob, its Victor Jensen. I just talked to Stanton."

"Yes sir... so, what's the story?"

"He told me he made a big mistake. He knew it the moment he asked the question. He knows it is unforgivable what he said."

"I agree with him on that point. What was he thinking?"

"I'm going to let him tell you himself."

"I don't think so."

"Yes, you will. This man is your best shot here, Rob. He's a good man. We all make mistakes, son. It's just that most mistakes we make are never heard about. I believe in redemption. He's going to make it up to you in a big way. Give him that chance to redeem himself. Do it for me. Promise me, Rob."

I was silent, trying to keep my hurt and anger at bay. Jensen was patiently waiting in silence. He waited a long time. Discomfort in the silence got to me first.

"That will be hard for me to do."

"I know it will, but man up, son. You think it's tough on you? Try being him. You two are both mad at the same person—Stanton BigHeart."

"I might want to kill him first."

"I know, but you won't if you meet him in my office. How soon are you going to get here?"

"He's there with you?"

"How soon will you be here?"

Another silent standoff ensued, which I knew he would win. "Give me 15 minutes."

31

I TOOK A DEEP BREATH, then knocked on Victor Jensen's private office door. With my heart racing and my lungs nervously breathing, Jensen opened the heavy door and looked me straight in the eye. He said nothing but motioned me to step inside. By the big window behind his desk, Stanton BigHeart stood looking out at the wide view of Lake Hefner to the north.

"Rob, take a seat." Jensen pointed to his small conference table.

Turning to Stanton BigHeart, Jensen spoke to him with the same tone and the same directions. Once BigHeart sat down opposite me, he unexpectedly looked straight at me. As uncomfortable as it was, I stared right back.

"All right gentlemen, you know the rules. When you sort things out between you two, come out and get me."

He walked out of his office, shutting the door behind him.

And so, the unplanned standoff began. We both seemed surprised to be left alone. As we continued to stare, I revisited our earlier encounter—how he was short for words. He was no nonsense, a proud Osage with a heritage of dominance over other tribes and fierce defenders of their lands. I knew from hearing my grandmother talk that when she was younger the Osage had been murdered for being oil rich. I knew right away that he would not talk first. I pondered how to begin. I could stand it no more.

"I was hurt by your question."

"I know."

"Why would you ask me about killing babies?"

"I didn't think."

"I've heard those words too many times before. Coming from a veteran. I still don't understand why?"

"I'm sorry."

"Why would you ask that of me? How do you feel killing…? I've never killed anybody."

"I wanted to see if you were a hot head." BigHeart paused, now his eyes looking down. "I didn't know your story. I asked the wrong question."

"What would be the right question?"

"There's not one."

"Ever hire anyone where that question was good to ask?"

"A month ago."

"Really?"

"I hired a guy, a real antiwar nut case."

"Would that question ever be appropriate?"

"For him, yes."

"Tell me why."

"He was militant. Insulted customers. He dodged the draft and bragged about it. He used the term 'baby killer' when talking to a site manager at a rig. The guy reacted like you did. I couldn't have my customers insulted by some antiwar hippie. I fired him in less than a week."

"So, you had me next up."

"Yes."

"Why ask about baby killers?"

"I only wanted to know who might be on the extreme side, either way."

"Well, you got one."

"Not really. You had the right answer."

"Which is?"

"You walked out on me. You didn't hit me or break things. You left. That's what I wanted to see."

"So, I passed your test."

"You did. *I* didn't."

The man who faced me was contrite. I looked back on the dumb things I had done. There were many. The mistakes I made were often handled by acts of forgiveness and tolerance, others with confrontation and vindictiveness. I was more inclined to ask forgiveness born of tolerance, never from reprisal. Was there such a thing as redemption? There had to be. Otherwise, no one, whether perpetrator or victim, could ever get on with their lives. I softened. If we were ever to end this nightmare of antiwar hatred against veterans of the Vietnam war, it had to be through the embrace of forgiveness.

"So, where do we go from here?"

He looked at me. This time his eyes spoke differently. "We could start over."

"Mister Jensen would like that."

"I let him down."

"I take it he has made you a good living."

"We have been two honest men in a vast wasteland of shady men. I never want to let down a good man like Victor Jensen."

"Let's start over then. I want to learn from you."

"I've learned a lot today myself." We laughed together for the first time. "You, Mister Amity, are a principled man. I want to reward you with success, if you will let me teach you."

"I need it, sir. And I accept your apology."

"Then we call back Victor. Yes?"

I stood up and extended my hand to Stanton BigHeart. He clasped my hand with his enormous grip, and we made a deal. Stepping out of his office together, we walked to Mrs. Stone's front desk. Mr. Jensen, sitting in the lobby like an eager salesman, stood up to welcome us from the arena.

"Who won?" Jensen asked.

"We did," we said together.

"I think I underestimated what a tough man Rob is," said BigHeart. "He is well suited for the oil patch. He doesn't take crap from anybody. He gave up a chance to work for me on principle. I admire that."

"I understand now. I think I can learn a lot and make you both happy."

For the next two months, Stanton BigHeart was destined to be my new best friend.

32

TWO MONTHS LATER IN APRIL, Stanton BigHeart turned me loose to work as an independent contractor. The oil market was quickly outgrowing supply, and the prices for everything skyrocketed to unheard of levels. BigHeart, now my good friend, had no time for me. Time was money. Any delay cost drillers millions of dollars. Even the simplest of items could save a thousand times their cost. Because I was so successful, he offered me a partnership in A-to-Z Oilfield Services to sell everything he was not interested in selling himself. He loaned me the money for a buy in, which I soon learned was easier to pay back than I expected with the exponential growth we had. For both Stanton and me as co-equal partners, the money started rolling in at a level we never dreamed possible. Our dual relationship with customers created a synergy we could not explain but were smart enough to exploit.

The two months had been exhausting training with little time for leisure. The frenzy in the oil patch itself had to be worse than what I was going through. I spent most of my time traveling around the western half of Oklahoma in my A-to-Z Oilfield Services Chevy truck, inquiring of the workers their needs. Stanton connected me with the companies that manufactured what we sought. As others came into the business, quick response and absolute integrity became the most important commodities in the oil patch.

There were the scallywags who made it difficult for us, but we passed them off to customers who paid us less reliably. We had so much business that we found it easy to pass up many questionable opportunities.

There was temptation, however. I was working up north of Elk City, where the hottest activity of the oil industry was going strong at some of the deepest wells ever drilled. In 1972, one well in the Anadarko Basin drilled down 30,000 feet. The intensity of the competition went both ways. A driller with a sordid reputation approached me one afternoon. He let me know that he could order enough supplies from me over the next year to make me a millionaire. He had a stipulation. I had to provide a half dozen high class prostitutes to some of his potential investors.

"You get them-there hookers, and you have a deal. If I need more later, you will arrange it. You'll get all my business from now on."

I responded with an emphatic no. I turned away a million dollars without thinking a second. The driller threatened me with all kinds of empty warnings, both financial and physical to no avail. The market was too volatile to make his threats possible. I did find another seller who made that deal and supplied the investors with the required entertainment. He drilled the well. The well was a dry hole. The investors lost their shirts. The driller lost to his bank and couldn't pay his supplier. The supplier moved on to another sleazy driller in hopes of striking it rich again. Integrity to Stanton and me was worth every dollar we lost. The irony was that we made so much money on the up and up that we made more money based on our reputation than we would have if we had tried to accommodate the darker side of the industry.

Early in April I picked up a copy of the *Oklahoma City Times* to read about Hank Aaron's 715th home run. Finally, a player had exceeded the insurmountable record of career home runs set by Babe Ruth. It was inspiration for me to keep up my success for a while longer. Like Hank Aaron, who was coming to the end of a lengthy career, the oil patch would someday get old, tired, and collapsed. I used home runs as my inspirational metaphor to keep going while the opportunity still availed.

Furthering the chaos in the world were myriad Muslim fundamentalists in the Middle East, the societal misfits of the Red Brigade in Italy, and the Symbionese Liberation Army in America. The void left by the ending of

America's involvement in Vietnam was being quickly filled by the counter chaos of America's haters. I decided it was time to get a radio to put in my Porsche, so I could keep up with the music and events in the world, as I was doing while I drove the Chevy truck in the oil patch. The local Porsche dealer was happy to install one for me at an exorbitant price. I didn't care. I had the money.

I had neglected Suzy for the most part since I came back from my road trip with Hal. I had phoned her on occasion to reassure her that I was starting a job that required a length of time to learn the trade. Nonetheless, Suzy's loneliness was not improving in my absence. I knew that I needed to check on her more frequently than I was able to. Stanton by now was fully aware of my story. We had spent many late-night sessions in his office sharing stories over a Pabst Blue Ribbon or a Budweiser. He urged me to spend more time outside of work and to go on some dates with Suzy.

His story was much different than mine, starting with his strong cultural ties to his Osage tribe. The Osage Nation had a unique story. In signing their treaty with the United States, the tribe elected to own mineral rights in common. That meant that each member of the Osage tribe as it existed at the time of the treaty had a headright to an equal share of any minerals in the reservation. That meant little until oil was discovered in Osage County. Congress by 1921 decided the Osage needed their help and passed a law requiring every Osage with a headright be appointed a guardian, until the person could prove they were competent to manage their own affairs. By 1923 the Osages were the richest people on earth. Then, the jackals came in. Guardians robbed the individual Indians of their royalties and kept them in ignorance of their chicanery. Osage women married white men, only to be murdered. Their headright transferred from the deceased Osage wife to the white man husband. Some even murdered whole families to inherit a whole line of deceased family headrights. Murderous conspirators killed sixty Osage during this thirteen-year *Reign of Terror*. The mastermind for the whole tragic episode was a man named William Hale, King of the Osage, a title given him after years of assisting the Osage in order to gain their trust—then their lives and headrights.

Stanton's grandparents survived those years of terror and burned the memories into his conscience. I understood much better why he addressed the killing of innocents with me on our first interview. His family had lived through it. Fortunately for his family, their appointed family guardian was a kind man who had the best interests of the Osage on his agenda. There were other mindful caretakers of Osage headrights but not enough of them. This white man, Mr. Stanton, took great care and declared them competent early in the Osage oil boom. The family continued to seek his wise counsel and later named a grandson after him.

33

SUZY LOOKED AT ME WITH a worried eye. I sat across from her at the Magic Pan, a French restaurant in the new 16-story office tower, 50 Penn Place, notable for its four red neon piggy banks facing each direction of the compass atop the building. What should have been a pleasant dinner together had turned into a dressing down.

"It is not fair that you have spent all your time working and have ignored me," Suzy said. "Daddy and Mother are asking questions about what's going on."

I looked down sheepishly but still resolute. "You have to give me time to get this business started."

"Even your own parents are calling me. Hal called and wondered where you were."

"I'll call them."

"It's embarrassing."

"I said, I'll call them."

"You should want to call them, not just because I tell you to call them."

"Can we just order, please?"

Near our table rotated the iconic contraption that made crepes, a series of eight pans upside down by their handles and turning like a merry-go-round, the crepe batter cooking on the bottoms of the pans by a gas flame. It was a welcome distraction from my not so pleasant confrontation. How did I end up with this? Shouldn't she be thrilled that I took her to dinner after two months of being busy?

Suzy sat silent and frustrated, looking vacuously at her menu. It was evident that she had made a point to look her best. Her model's figure and her fine taste in clothes made Suzy a head turner. I knew she had worked hard for my sake. Being the Monday after Easter, she had unleashed her spring wardrobe in a beautiful pastel yellow quarter sleeve above the knee dress, tied with a wide white bow at her empire waist. She had her hair combed back in a ponytail. A large gold pendant hung from her neck between her décolletage. She wore little makeup and subtle red lipstick. Compared to her, I looked like a slob. We ordered the same thing, chicken divan and crepe suzette for dessert.

"Maybe we should order strawberries and cream, too," Suzy said. "It would be a fitting end."

The reference cut me to the quick. On our last date in college, before I dumped Suzy for another girl, we watched the movie, *Elvira Madigan.* In the movie, two destitute lovers, the man being a deserter from the army, eat a last meal of strawberries and cream before ending their lives. I sat in silence, looking at her beautiful face. A tear fell down my cheek. It was not fair to bring up our past. We had never done that before. The sting of past mistakes she brought up was how many relationships ended.

It cut so sharply that Suzy instantly expressed her regret without saying a word. She reached out for my hand which simply said, *"I miss you."*

She continued to hold on to me across the table, a look of anxiety in her eyes. "I need you in my life. You are the only other man I ever loved, and I'm glad you are back."

"Me, too. I don't want to be without you, either."

"I hardly heard from you after we both left Laredo last year. Then you show up. It was obvious we missed each other. The absence worked in our favor. But now, we cannot be apart like this. First, nine months and now another two months. Decide if you want me."

"I *do* want you, Suzy, but what can I do? The time to build up a nest egg is now. I can't just stop this job. It's too important to our future."

"For how long, Rob?" Her eyes reflected my own hurt expression.

"Two or three more years and we'll be multimillionaires."

"I won't give you that much time, and I don't care if you're a millionaire."

"I can't just dump my partner. He needs me."

"I don't need you?"

"That's not what I meant. I'm not working hard to make him happy, but I can't just dump him."

I looked at Suzy and immediately regretted my choice of words. I had dumped her before—back in college. "Don't say it, Suzy. I just dug my own grave. I'm sorry."

"Perhaps you should pay the waiter and take me home before you dig it any deeper."

We paid our bill. Had I paid for strawberries and cream? Like Elvira Madigan, the end seemed near. I drove her home to the guest abode behind her parent's plush home. I walked her to the back. The sun had only set minutes before, and the western skies were glowing yellows and rich oranges across a wide swath of the horizon. We kissed goodnight, but her lips evinced no passion, only cold indifference. I left only after assuring that she was safely inside.

Back inside my car, I watched as Suzy exited her house to reclaim Sean from his grandparents. She had a great deal of responsibility being a mother. I knew that, but she needed more empathy from me. I had no idea what burden she was under. I assumed the Jensens suffered for her. There were too many pressures on all of us to address someone else's needs. She needed to understand that I was focused upon the future, not the here and now. It was clear that Suzy was not looking at the big picture. What was wrong with her? What part of my common sense did she not understand?

I assumed Suzy would be sharing her frustration at this moment with her parents. Would Mr. Jensen understand my point of view? Surely, he would. We were both grown men. I was eager for success. He had already achieved success. Mrs. Jensen was open about her happiness. That would not have come without the financial security their arduous work produced. I imagined the two lecturing Suzy about her responsibility to support my efforts.

Without doubt, I expected a phone call and a better optimistic attitude from her by tomorrow.

I got home to my apartment, wondering if I could sleep. The stark bareness of my surroundings began to take its toll. The contrast of the Jensen's home, with their works of art and meaningful knick-knacks, began to weigh upon my optimism. Until now, I had little sense of why things can be so important to a home's warmth and comfort. There was nothing in my apartment I could find that brought me contentment. I undressed for bed and tried the whole night to rest up for tomorrow. Instead, I lay awake thinking for over six hours in wretched misery.

34

MY TELEPHONE BEGAN RINGING PROMPTLY at 6:00 a.m. Already dressed and ready to head for the office, I picked it up to the crisp deliberate and stern voice of Mr. Jensen. *"What in blazes were you thinking last night?"*

"Sir?" I could tell I was in for a beating.

"You disappoint my daughter with indifference like that and we will have a problem. I helped you get a job with BigHeart, but I didn't expect that you would marry it."

"I don't understand."

"Suzy came home last night crying because you are wedded to your job. She feels abandoned. Has money become your new mistress?"

"No, sir."

"Don't be so quick to answer that. You've been to our house only twice now in nearly a year. She thought you were committed to her. Decide whether that's true. If not, leave my daughter alone."

He hung up the phone without further words. I stood stunned, holding the receiver in silence. What was wrong with everybody? Did they not know that I was taking advantage of an opportunity that wouldn't last forever? I was desperate to talk to someone who would understand, so I called my father and arranged to meet him for coffee before he went to work.

I showered and dressed in my customary Levi's and polo shirt, with a light jacket to stave off the morning's chill. After battling my lengthening hair with a comb, I stepped outside to drive to the Denny's on Northwest Expressway. I listened to Bob Riggins on my new car radio, tuned to KTOK 1000 AM. The unflappable DJ and talk show host informed me of spring storms coming into the Oklahoma City area from the west with a line of storms running northeast up the line of a cold front. He hinted of possible strong winds, hail, and tornados during the day. I worried more about my Porsche than I worried about myself or any human. Oklahoma was so used to tornados that it seemed routine to anticipate them. We knew when to go to our safe place or 'fraidy hole, or better yet, when to run outside and take photographs. The clouds were already darkening along the entire western half of the horizon.

I parked next to Dad's car. Stepping inside Denny's, the aroma of their special blend of coffee gave me a warm feeling. I had never been much of a coffee drinker until I had my first Denny's cup. I became hooked. Denny's staff never would tell me what the secret ingredient was. They sold bags of Denny's coffee, but they were always out when I came to buy it.

I looked around and found my father sitting next to the window facing the street and our two cars. He was drinking a cup of the special coffee that he enjoyed as much as his son. A man with a calming nature, he was a perfect complement to my mother's more volatile personality.

As I sat down across from him, an attentive waitress served me coffee. I nodded my thank you to her as she warmed up Dad's cup as well.

"This is Janie," Dad said. "She does an outstanding job for me every time I come here."

She smiled at me and asked, "Cream and sugar?"

"Cream only, please, and Janie, could I see a menu?"

She was efficient. In seconds she was back with both. Dad and I began an idle chat as I mixed the cream into my hot coffee cup.

"Your mother has me scheduled for all sorts of duties this week. I was glad for your call, so I can have a moment of no responsibility."

"What's your job at home?"

"Your mom is planting spring flowers—an unlimited supply of flowers according to me. I dig. She plants."

"Your yard always looks spectacular, Dad. I give you half credit."

"Yes," he said. He paused to take another sip of this coffee nectar of the gods. "She's a slave driver, though. She says it gives us something to do together. Now mind you, I love your mother, but I wish we could do something together that doesn't make my back hurt."

"Outside it looks like we might get stuck here for a while. Mom going to freak out?"

"I don't think so. Not anymore. Age has a way of making us calm down a bit about the weather."

We sipped our coffee while checking the morning storms moving in, each in our own thoughts.

"You see much of Suzy?"

"No, and I think I'm in trouble because of it."

"Well, Mom has been complaining, too. We spend the first twenty years preparing you to leave the house, then when you don't come around, we get a little fidgety."

"It sounds like you're both complaining."

"I suppose."

"Well, Suzy is *more* than fidgety. She just doesn't seem to understand how hard I'm working."

Dad took another pensive sip of coffee, motioned his favorite waitress, Janie, over for a refill, and savored another sip of warmed up brew.

"Do you plan to marry her, son?"

"Maybe." His question startled me. The word *marry* was not yet part of my vocabulary.

"You said 'maybe' to her?"

"Sort of."

Dad looked at me with aggravated amazement. "What the hell does that mean, sort of maybe?"

He didn't wait for my response but went into a full-blown diatribe that rivalled my telephone conversation with Mr. Jensen.

"I've said a lot of things to you in your growing up, but if I had had a daughter, I would have given her this advice. The nicest thing you can do when a boy asks you on a date is say 'yes' or say 'no.' If you want to be mean to the boy, say the word 'maybe.'"

"But I'm not a girl. What's your point?"

"You told Suzy maybe, then apparently ignored her for months. Do I need to clap a couple of bricks together to get your attention?"

"No."

"Do you love her?"

"I guess I do."

"Do you *love* her?"

"Of course, I do. I love her." I knew I was sounding wishy-washy.

"Get used to saying it then."

"I will."

"And another thing. You better like her, not just have the hots for her. Do you understand?"

"I understand."

"If I didn't like your mother, I wouldn't be digging those damn holes for her flowers."

"I like her a lot, Dad."

"So, why are you ignoring her then?"

"I've been depressed since I left the Air Force. I'm afraid if I hang around her too much, I'll chase her away."

"You want to get over your depression and fear of losing her?"

"What?" I said it in sarcasm, not as a question. "What are you saying?"

"Man up!" he said. He continued with a directive, not a kindly suggestion. "Act like a man, son. No woman wants a depressive wimp for a husband. Stand in her shoes. Would you tolerate a whiney and needy wife for your whole life?"

"No."

"Then man up. Go see her. Tell her yes or no and quit torturing the girl."

We ordered breakfast with few words. When my scrambled eggs, sausage patties, and hash brown potatoes came, we said little beyond "pass the salt and pepper." I sat there steaming mad at my father. He hadn't said a word about what I needed, only about Suzy. He didn't get it at all. To call me wimpy and to order me to man up was inexcusable. I had done my part to serve our country. I had gotten a job in the oil patch and was making tons of money. I was man enough. Looking at my father, calmly eating his breakfast, I resented all the advice he gave me.

Dad soon enough said that he had to go to work. As much as it angered me, I thanked him for his advice. We shook hands, and he gave me a bear hug that I hadn't had in years. I stepped inside my car, buckled up, and hit the steering wheel with my fist. My anger caused me to realize that I had indeed wimped out. I had thanked him for making me mad at him. A real man would have told him off. I, instead, wimped out. I was the very person he described me to be.

35

IT WAS ALMOST 9:00 A.M. when I arrived at the A-to-Z Oilfield Services office. Stanton, agitated at my late entrance, didn't take long to sense my own seething anger.

"Okay, Amity. We're both aggravated about something. You first. What's going on?"

"You wouldn't understand. Just tell me why you're so bent out of shape."

"You're late. We have things to do. Now, your turn."

I hated his man-of-few-words trait. He stood there, staring at me—waiting. He sat down on one of our old beat-up chairs in his office we now shared. Continuing to stare, he propped his feet on our shared desk. Then Stanton pointed a hand to the chair behind the desk, inviting me to take a seat. I sat down, not saying a word. We stared at each other.

"Oh, for goodness' sake! Spit it out! I don't have time for this junior high school stuff."

There it was again. Another reference to my immaturity.

"Suzy."

"Suzy? That's it?"

"She's mad at me."

"So am I, but I'll get over it. So will she. What's the big deal?"

"She wants me to quit working so hard."

"Not a bad idea."

"I can't afford to stop working."

"Can you afford to lose her?"

"She won't understand that I'm working furiously for her benefit."

"What's got her riled?"

"She thinks I work too much. I haven't seen her often enough since I joined you."

"How many times are we talking about? You've been here two months. You've worked your ass off. How often are you two together?"

"Last night was the first time."

Stanton began to laugh—not a laugh of hilarity but a cringe worthy laugh. "You're joking, right?"

"No. I've been busy."

"What kind of bonehead are you? One date in two months and you wonder why she's the slightest bit miffed. Are you nuts?"

"Nobody will understand what I'm trying to do."

"You want to get hitched?"

"Yes." My dad's spirit was in the room, waiting for me to say, 'sort of maybe.' Then he asked me something that kicked me in the gut.

"Are you getting hitched to Suzy or to money? I'm sure she wants to know."

"I'd have to slow down here."

"So what? You not making enough money already?"

"I'll need it in the future."

"Why? You planning to retire in the next two years?"

"No."

"Then decide how much is enough." Stanton paused for a moment. He was trying to say something but had to search for the right words. "Why don't you take today off and figure out your priorities. You're thinking like you're working a temporary summer job. You've got time for rest and recreation. We call it vacation in the civilian world. There's a reason for it."

"So, what will you do if I'm not here?"

"We might start by hiring more people to help us out. You want to have a board meeting, or do you want to vote to do it right now?"

"Okay. Do it. Just don't ask them about killing anyone."

"I won't," he replied. It was too harsh a joke.

"My father told me to man up. Is he right?"

"We Osage value our elders. Listen to them and learn wisdom."

I thanked my friend for sharing his wisdom and left the office after giving our receptionist a smile on the way out. Mary knew everything in this office.

"Go get her, Mister Amity. There's still time."

I laughed and thanked her. Stepping into my car, I knew I needed another perspective on what I was finally realizing was the biggest boneheaded action I had ever taken, since nearly killing by accident the meanest man in the Air Force. The one opinion I needed, before I did anything more, was from the person I had been closer to than anyone in the world, my mother who gave me life from her womb.

36

IT WAS A YEAR NOW since I had left the Air Force. In looking back at those five years, it was a heady experience. The thrill of taking off and landing my airplane filled my heart with a longing for one more chance to do it again. Did I leave the service for the right reasons? All my friends were still in the Air Force. Only now was I making new friends and reaching out to old ones. I spent seven months isolated, depressed, and embarrassingly nonproductive. Now, I was getting reality kicked back into my head. I had ignored my parents, my military friends, my old school friends, and worst of all, Suzy. Trying to remember what I had done during that time, failed me. The black dog of my depression had cut over a half of a year from my life. Then I tried to come out of it, only to replace depression with manic work. I had not seen combat. God only knew what combatants leaving the service were going through.

I pulled the Porsche over at a 7-Eleven when I spotted a pay phone. I searched my pockets for two dimes. Dropping them in caused the familiar dings, then a dial tone. I turned the rotary dial to call my old home. The automated voice shocked me.

"I'm sorry. The number you have dialed is no longer in service. Please...."

I hung up the phone and waited for my two dimes to drop into the coin return. Old habits die slowly. Only recently Ma Bell had changed every customer's telephone number. I had dialed the new number when I called Dad, but in my frustration, I dialed the old number out of habit. I tried my two dimes with the new number. It didn't help my depression knowing that nothing was the same when I came home from serving my country. I dialed the new number, and the telephone began to ring.

"Hello, Mom."

"Rob? Is that you?"

"Mom, are you around the house for a while? I need to come by and talk."

"I'm here. Did you want to see me now?"

"Yes."

"Have you eaten?"

I looked at my watch. It was just past ten o'clock. Nurturing seems ingrained in mothers. Today, it was a welcome offer.

"An early lunch would be wonderful, Mom."

"Great! I'll leave the front door open for you. You've made my day."

"Mine, too, Mom. I'll see you about eleven."

Driving through the middle of downtown Oklahoma City, before turning north to Mom's house, many abandoned shops and offices that I had visited as a child came into view. Few people walked on the sidewalks. There were fewer cars than in the past. Urban renewal, a product of President Kennedy's plan to revitalize the city's downtown district, was a total disaster. Buildings were gone, leaving vacant lot eyesores everywhere. The dream of rebirth in the downtown sector was a sham. Once again, knowing how nothing to me was the same only five years later added further to my melancholy.

I drove north on Classen Boulevard then crossed over to Western Avenue, passing the old worn out shops that still thrived on the west edge of urban renewal decimation. Traveling north past homes of increasing size and curb appeal, then past the magnificent gothic First Presbyterian Church, things began to look familiar. It instantly elevated my mood. Homes near the affluent Nichols Hills suburb grew bigger to the west but were diminishing in size on the east side of Western Avenue. When I reached Britton Road, and the community of Britton, I turned west. This led me through the vestiges of Britton, long since incorporated into the city of Oklahoma City. I passed the largest and most expensive private school in town. Casady School was an Episcopal school where many of my high school friends went for a much tougher education. That brought me into The Village, my own home suburb since I was 12 years old. Not much had changed here.

I turned off May Avenue, soon reaching my old home. Parking in the driveway, I emerged from my car to see Mom standing at the front door to greet me. With a smile, she opened the door and once inside grabbed me warmly in a hug.

"My baby!" Kissing me on the cheek, she said, "I know you're a grown man, but you'll always be my baby."

"I feel like a big baby today, Mom."

"What's wrong?"

"I've messed up bad. I need your advice and counseling."

"Suzy?"

"Suzy."

"Well it's about time. Come in here and sit down. I have a little snack waiting for you."

A snack to a mother is a banquet. She didn't know if I wanted breakfast or lunch. At the kitchen table were both options. I made a bold decision not to inquire as to the dating on the food set before me. In perfect Southern Belle fashion, the table was set with a crisp white linen tablecloth, silverware placed in the exact proper order around our two plates. There was a drinking glass to the right, a bread plate to the left. Never forgetting where I sat for meals, my place was prepared as if I was at the finest restaurant—and with a real napkin.

If I ever waited for my mother to sit down, we would never eat. Standing until the lady is seated was the one bit for protocol Dad and I tried to skip. I sat down at my traditional seat and my devoted server went at it.

"Okay, Rob. What can I pour you? We have orange juice. I have coffee. I can get you milk if you like. I can make some tang. Would you prefer some of Daddy's beer?" She stood still and awaited my command. The older I got, the more uncomfortable this ritual of my mother's grew.

"Milk will be fine." I really wanted her to sit down. When she returned from the refrigerator and poured me a glass, I spoke to her as she placed the milk back in its proper place.

"Mom, I need you to sit down for a minute if you can."

She asked me again, "What's wrong?"

"I need your advice about the other mother in my life. Or at least a mother no longer in my life."

"I don't believe that for a minute." She sat down at her chair and unfolded a napkin onto her lap. "You tell me what's going on."

"I've been a fool staying away from everybody. I'm so unhappy. I think I made a mistake leaving the Air Force. I hated it. I wanted out. Then I had a change of heart."

"You know what they say. 'The grass is always greener on the other side of the fence.'"

"I didn't expect it to happen like this. When Suzy lost John, she became a further complication in my life. I have an interest in Suzy, but I feel so guilty. My best friend died and here I go after his wife. I don't see any good answers."

"Have you talked to your father?"

"We had breakfast this morning at Denny's. That was a disaster."

"What do you mean? I can't imagine how talking to your father would be a disaster."

I related how I got my 6:00 a.m. telephone call from Suzy's father. I continued with a recap of the conversation and "man up" comments with my dad. I related how Stanton BigHeart told me I was working too hard and sent me home for R & R.

"They told me the same thing. Why have I been so dense? The last two months seemed like about a week, then everyone turned on me, complaining that I had ignored them completely. I thought they understood. I think I'm the only one who had his head up and locked."

"I don't know what that 'up and locked' means, but I can give you some good advice. Your family has recognized that you're not yourself. I know because we've talked—all of us. So, we decided we needed to get your attention." Mom paused a moment, a tear welling up in her eye. "Suzy's terribly upset. She thinks you've abandoned her, especially after what you two talked about."

"I think I understand. It's been tough this morning. Everyone I respect has beat me up about this... even Suzy."

"I want to remind you of a word of wisdom from your father. Do you remember it?"

"You'll have to remind me." I looked her in the eye, having truly forgotten what she was to say.

Mom looked at me with a smile. "Sometimes it's not until you turn on the lights that you learn you're the only one still left in the dark."

I looked at her. We smiled to each other, and I remembered. "I finally see the light."

"Yes."

"And I have to do it myself."

"I think you already have. Now what are you going to do?"

"I may need to get some of your womanly wisdom for step two."

"Not until you eat something." She pointed at my empty plate, then at the banquet of choices which lay untouched by either of us.

She let me make my own sandwich. That was a minor triumph for me. We had a choice of ham or turkey, mustard or mayonnaise, and bread or croissant. There on a separate plate lay cheese slices, pickles, lettuce, and tomatoes. She had even cut out each individual wedge of a half grapefruit, just in case I needed breakfast.

With my sandwich constructed to my specifications, she pulled the grapefruit in front of her and ate each precut wedge of grapefruit with a grapefruit spoon. Only a Southern Belle would think to do that.

I was, of course, still full of Denny's breakfast, but I wasn't going to spoil the mood and insult my mother by not eating. Between mouthfuls, I finally had the chance to ask her a question.

"Would you share with me something? Have you talked to Suzy?"

"I have."

"What did she say?"

"We ladies speak in confidence."

"Okay, what can you share?"

"She's hurt. She's lonely. She feels abandoned."

"What did you tell her?"

"You don't want me to tell you what I told her."

"Yes, I do."

She stared at me, a conflicted expression shown on her face. Putting her vestigial grapefruit spoon on her dish, she sighed in exasperation.

"If you must know, I told her you were still too immature for marriage but, if she could train you properly, you might make a decent husband."

"Too *immature?*" Dad's words, "man up," came to mind, and I blushed.

"Rob, Suzy needs someone to cheer her up. Do you really think you are the only one here who is depressed and isolated?"

"You think she's like me?"

"Of course, she is! Suzy lost her husband. The Air Force made her move out and away from supportive friends. She had a baby with no income except what the Air Force paid her in life insurance. Now she's living with her parents and has no time for cultivating a life outside of that pool house she lives in."

"And I've been working away for all this time, only sympathetic to my own problems."

"Something like that, yes."

"So, what do I do? She's upset with me already."

My mother looked at me with a hint of frustration. "You boys need our help, don't you?"

"What do I do? Tell me."

"Go to her. That alone would probably do it. But tell her you're sorry. Have you told her you love her, need her, or want to be a father to little Sean?"

"I guess I need to do all these things."

"Do me one favor, Rob. Change your work habits. Spend every day with Suzy. Speak humbly to Suzy's parents. You've upset them, too."

"Okay. Anything else?"

"A little of the caveman wouldn't hurt. Let her know she's desirable." An afterthought caused her to pause for the right words. "Pick up that precious little boy and show him some love."

"Okay."

"Suzy needs to know you desire her—and her baby boy, too."

"I hope it works."

"She'll melt if you do."

"I would like that."

"Finish your sandwich, then, go to her. Now!"

37

I BOLTED DOWN THE LAST of my sandwich, hugged Mom with the sincerity of a man who had received a most precious gift, and hurried to my car. Mom stood at her front door, waving at me as I backed out of her driveway. I drove to the main road leading to Suzy's lonely home with the same words chanting in my head. *Man up! Caveman! Love the child! Tell her of your desire!* Then the words became jumbled as I recalled the mistakes I had made and the effects I had caused in my family and hers. *Wimp. Work. Immaturity. Depression. Abandonment.* Then new words came into my head—those from listening to myself. *Embarrassment. Shame. Selfishness.* Then *Redemption* and *I am a Man!*

I am a Man! fixated in my head. The same chant repeated, until I finally parked and walked to the back of the big house and knocked on her borrowed quarters. I waited for a response at the door. I concluded she was either not there or not interested in seeing me. The doorknob made noise before I could turn to leave. My heart kicked into high gear as the door began to open. With adrenaline pouring into my brain, my breathing increased to a level that made vocalizations difficult. Suzy stepped through her doorway, still primping her hair with one hand while straightening with the other the thin straps at the shoulders of her lavender sundress. She stood still, unable or unwilling to speak. I garnered my wits and my breathing to speak first.

"Suzy, would you forgive me. I was wrong, and I promise to never be absent from you and Sean as long as I live."

"Well, that's quite a difference."

"I've decided to finally grow up."

"Uh-huh." She didn't move. Her expression remained unreadable.

"Would you give me a second chance?"

"Why should I?"

"Because I think we are both equally lonely, depressed, and in love with each other."

Suzy looked at me for the longest time I could endure.

"I would agree with that."

"I love you, Suzy. Will you ever love me back?"

"I do believe I will." She stood still briefly, then stepped forward, with arms wrapped around me, and planted the most powerfully enthusiastic, moist kiss we had ever shared.

The kiss lingered. It shocked me. I was not expecting this response, which caused me to wish I could ask my mother another question or two. She eventually let go of me. I caught my breath long enough to be able to talk again.

"I love you, Suzy."

"I love you, Rob." Then she punched me lightly in the stomach. "That's for not being here."

She next grabbed my arm and pulled me inside the doorway. Closing the door behind us, she turned to me again to plant one more lingering kiss on me.

"I need to do my part, too, to make sure you won't leave me again." She spoke the words without her lips leaving mine. Her breath was an elixir of passion and delight, certainly not what I expected. I pulled away simply to get more air.

"I've been talking to people all day about what a bonehead I've been. I get it now."

She grabbed me again, placing her cheek against mine and her lips at my ear. "I should have been nicer to you. I didn't make it clear I missed you. Let me make it clear." She moved her lips once more to me and made it abundantly clear.

I was at a crossroads of indecision. My reverence for her and my respect for the memory of her husband John weighed heavily on my proper way to respond. She continued to kiss me. I kissed her back just as passionately. Finally breaking free from my enveloping arms, she stepped back enough distance that we could focus on each other comfortably. Without saying a word, she carefully reached up with her hands and grasped the thin spaghetti straps of her dress. She looked straight into my eyes and dropped the straps to each side. Then, placing her hands on her hips, she pulled down on her lavender sundress until it fell at her feet.

I had never seen Suzy naked. The beauty of her figure before me made my whole body respond in the shivering fits. The unexpected had already filled my entire day, but this topped them all. Any naked woman is a thing of beauty, but this was the body of the woman I loved. The way she stood was so inviting. Her mature and taut breasts were perfect. Her still firm and subtle hourglass figure was any man's dream. The well-maintained V, where her thighs came together drew me down to the beauty of her legs and ankles. I looked up quickly, half in awe, half in embarrassment for my being caught looking at her with such desire. I was unable to speak. I asked her a question with my face alone. Suzy answered me in soft tones.

"If you want this, Rob, I am yours. First, you must show me by your actions that you are committed to us. I love you, Robert Amity. What you see is waiting for you but not before."

She reached down, lifted her lavender sundress back to her shoulders, and stepped forward to kiss me lightly one more time.

38

SUZY EXCUSED HERSELF, TELLING ME that she was cold and wanted to put on something warmer. I couldn't disagree with her assessment. I sat down on her loveseat, even now suffering from the shivering fits. It had been back in high school, since my last bout of this young man's malady. It would culminate in an uncomfortable walk to the car, the pain only subsiding after a night's sleep. Suzy had punished me for my stupidity in the kindest and most clever way. I had to give her an A for creativity and effectiveness. The pain I suffered had all been worth it.

Suzy, I was certain, had also sought out someone to share her troubles. Who would have suggested that last move? She was quite effective. It told me that she was determined to win me back, even though I had no earthly clue that I had run away. I knew now how much Suzy wanted me. It was a risk, presenting herself naked for my inspection. She opened herself to me out of love. From our years of dating, I knew her well. This was her two bricks to my head gesture. Guilt and shame filled my soul because I had forced her to forsake everything that she believed about the sacred nature of modesty outside of marriage. What would John say about his widow's actions? What would he think of me? Even in death, I would not disappoint him.

When Suzy came back into her small living room, she wore the same lavender sundress, but this time with all required undergarments. Sitting down next to me, she took my hand and held it against her sternum.

"Robert Amity, I don't want to lose you. If that was what it takes, I won't regret it."

"Would you always keep that dress? From this day on, it will mean something to me. You loved me that much." I looked into her green eyes. She still clasped my hand in hers, holding them between her breasts. "I know you love me. I needed you to love me. I've always loved you."

"Then we agree."

She kept her grip on my hand, as if waiting for something to break the spell. My gaze moved down. My eyes closed. I formed my words in fear they would sound as awkward as I felt.

"Suzy, if we keep this up, we're going to have to get married."

She laughed aloud, but differently than usual.

"Now don't laugh at me. I mean it. We must get married."

"I'm not laughing at you, Rob. What you said makes me happy."

"Are you sure?"

"Yes!" She dropped our hands down to her thighs, grabbed my other hand, and turned to face me. "I want to marry you."

"But I'm on probation."

"I don't think for long."

Another wave of shame passed over me. "We haven't really talked to each other since we left Laredo. It's been almost a year. Are you sure you won't find me less appealing after we share our feelings together? A lot has changed."

"It will be interesting. You and John shared the same interests, so I think I know you already."

"Yeah, we shared an interest in you."

Suzy laughed. "Yes, and you were a good boy around me—just like John always was."

We were a rollercoaster of emotions. It had been this way for both of us since our dinner at The Magic Pan last night. With today's busy schedule of discussions starting at 6:00 a.m., my half day was more like a week than only nine hours. Suzy knew I was exhausted.

"Would you stay and have dinner with Sean and me?"

"I forgot about Sean."

"You better get used to him. He's napping longer than I expected."

"I don't know if eating with your parents is a good idea."

"I heard what Daddy said to you this morning. He's mad at you." After a theatrical pause she giggled.

"Maybe I should take you to dinner."

"No, silly. I can cook. We're eating here. Please, say yes."

"Yes, I'll stay. Will this bother your father?"

"Oh, I don't think so. What I love about you is that I feel perfectly safe with you."

Her efforts were warming my sense of welcome. "The way to a man's heart is through his stomach" may be hackneyed, but it is true when a man is lonely. I suppose the other trite phrase that would apply in reverse would be "the way to a woman's heart is through her feelings of love and security." I laughed to myself. If she feels safe with me, is that a compliment or an insult?

"You know you are over the hill when all the women in your life say they feel perfectly safe with you," I said. I couldn't hide the smile prompted by my own cleverness.

Suzy walked closer to me and reached out a hand to my cheek. "Oh, I feel safe with you, but you may be in danger with me, once we are married." She kissed me ever so lightly.

"I guess I will have to take up flying again, to overcome my premature midlife crisis."

"I thought you were grounded. Can you do that again?"

"Probably not. I wish I could."

"Don't you have a friend who flies a lot and owns an airplane?"

"Yeah, Brad Kilty. I saw him a couple of months ago. He manages the new Great American Railroad restaurant."

"You should talk him into taking you flying. Maybe civilian airplanes would be okay for you."

"Would you ever fly with me?"

"Sure, I'd love to go fly. I've never flown before in anything but an airliner."

The vocalizations of a one-year-old boy, happy to be awake, interrupted our conversation. Unlike us, Sean was unworried about everything. Suzy soon had little Sean up and prepared to see me. In he came, walking on his own, but still holding onto his mother's hand for support. She broke his grip on her hand and stepped behind him. Sean stopped walking and stood there, unsteady, and staring at me with cautious curiosity. As he wobbled back and forth, he started to smile then turned to look at Suzy. The rotation of his head caused a loss of balance and he fell to his knees. The toddler looked at his mother for a clue. Since there was no shock or concern from her, he started to laugh rather than to cry. This was one tough and happy baby.

Standing behind her baby boy, Suzy lifted him up. Walking over to me, she sat him down in my lap. I held him under his little arms at half arm's length, instinctively bouncing him on my knees.

"It's time you met our son properly. You will be adopting him." It was not a question.

Sean smiled back at me. A special dollop of drool wet my jeans. Suzy was already gone to the kitchen, preparing an evening meal. We looked at each other, not saying a word. This sweet child had the lifeblood of his beautiful mother. He had the core of my late friend, John. What was there not to love in this beautiful child? I had an instant bond with Sean. I was not marrying Suzy alone. I was marrying this child, as well.

39

SUZY WORKED AN HOUR PREPARING a meal for us. Sean remained in my lap, content to amuse himself at my expense. I talked gently to him, asking him questions and receiving no reply but for the smiles, drools, and giggles he constantly produced. I was taken aback by the constant activity the toddler exhibited. It became exhausting, but it was an eye opener, too. So, this was what Suzy did every day. With Sean around, I would never be lonely again.

Suzy came to join me briefly. "Can I call myself Dad now?" I asked.

"No. I stated the rules," and there she paused to carefully say her words, "but you may practice saying Daddy when you are over here with Sean. Let him get used to you first."

Dinner was later than I expected, which was good for me. I had already eaten two other meals while eating crow at the same time. At least this evening I would be more relaxed than at my breakfast and lunch with my parents. Sean was on the floor now, rid of the confines of my clutch. I was not used to such rebellion. He defied every order I gave him. My own childhood was a great tale of how much I learned when no one was stopping me. He roamed all over the living room, stopping occasionally to pick up a spec of something off the floor. This went on for ten minutes before Sean wobbled up to me with a cricket leg hanging out of his mouth.

"Dinner's ready," Suzy said. "Give me Sean, and I will put him in his highchair." She started to walk over, but I stopped her.

"Let me try to put him in his chair." I picked up our boy, turned his back to his mother, and innocently removed what was left of the insect from his mouth. "I better start learning how to do this now."

I lifted him high above his highchair, only to have him spread his legs wider than the chair. His feet continued to take their own path, regardless of my inputs. Suzy watched with amusement as I struggled with an uncooperative child. At last, I figured out the complicated puzzle, when I completed the one leg at a time method of child seating. First, the left leg went into the leg opening of the seat, then, with the aid of my other hand, I practically bent the boy's leg into the other opening. He seemed happy. Suzy clapped her hands. I sighed in relief.

My bride-to-be turned out to be a fantastic cook. She first served Sean little pieces of our meal. He quickly demanded a jar of Gerber's that to me looked wholly unappetizing. For the first time in my life, I ate fresh vegetables that were not boiled to death, ala my mother's technique. They were surprisingly good. I had to eat them, of course. I would have eaten sand for dinner if she had prepared it for me. We had the most delicious creamy mashed potatoes with chicken gravy. Suzy prepared the tenderest chicken breasts, cooked I don't know how with wine somehow included. I was no cook. I hadn't watched what she did to prepare our meal. I was too busy with Sean. It was a fantastic meal, topped off with an unusual and wonderful bottle of Christian Brothers Piesporter Riesling. As the three of us ate, Suzy began asking questions.

"Okay, Rob. Let's compare notes. First question. Do you approve of the civil rights movement?"

"Of course."

"Me, too. Next, are you a hawk or a dove on Vietnam?"

"I used to be a dove, but now I'm a conditional hawk. If we are going to war, we need to fight to win."

"I'm a dove. Completely. Next question. Do you support a woman's right to an abortion?"

"No. Look at Sean. How could I be?"

"I say sometimes. Next...."

"That means yes."

"Okay, next question. Women's liberation. Do you support it?"

"Do I support men haters? No. Do I love women who are successful and independent? Sure."

"We agree. Next, is Nixon a good or bad president?"

"Nixon is a good president. He ended the war using the massive force Johnson should have used."

"Both are bad. Next up. Did you cry on the day when Martin Luther King was assassinated?"

"Yes."

"Yes. Next, what is the most important job a woman can do?"

"Stay home and care for our son, Sean."

"We agree. Next, would you go to a movie starring Jane Fonda?"

"Never ever in a billion years. The mere mention of her name makes me upset. She should be in jail, not in a movie. She's a traitor."

"You're supposed to give me short answers. Next, what—"

"Then it's best not to bring her up."

"That's a bit harsh, don't you think?"

"No, it's not. There are things in life that are significant to me. What she did with our enemy, if it had been World War Two, would have gotten her a firing squad. That's an absolute. No more discussion."

"Okay. I'll ask the next one. What do you think of men who did not serve in Vietnam?"

"*I* didn't serve in Vietnam."

"I'm sorry. You're right. I'll reword it. What do you think of men who did not serve on active duty during the Vietnam War?"

I looked over at Sean and pondered her question. My mind was reeling with mixed opinions, both anger and sympathy for every man involved.

"I'm sorry if this is longer than you want."

"That's okay."

"I honor everyone who served. I detest those who weaseled out of service and chose to harass those of us who had no choice. I wasn't drafted, but I would have been had I not volunteered. I took my chances, like everybody else, of ending up in Southeast Asia. I'm happy things worked out for me the way they did. To me the worst men are those who lord their service over others. That's what is so sad about Vietnam. It ended up pitting brother against brother, friend against friend, and father against son. Some people ridicule the men who joined the guard or reserves. I envy them. That's where I tried to go but failed. They, too, served. Enough said."

"Whew! I will be careful what I ask," Suzy replied. "I'm willing to go along with what you say. The war did not bring people closer."

"It did us."

"It did us. Some good came of it. Okay, next question. Do you like hippies?"

I laughed aloud. I startled Sean and interrupted his eating bits of our food on his large tray. He looked at me with interest, then began pushing his food around again.

"Hippies? Not my favorite, although in high school I wanted to be one, you know, all that free love and stuff. But now that I've gone through my transition in the Air Force, I see those men as draft dodging long-haired dirty worthless pussies."

"I agree. Next question. Do you support Israel?"

"Absolutely."

"So do I. Do you like Secretariat?"

"Of course. Does this mean we must buy a horse?"

"I like horses, especially Secretariat, but no, we don't need a horse. What about travelling?"

"My next getaway must be with you. Have you heard? I'll be taking days off now."

"Sounds exciting. What kind of house do you want?"

"Something with an American flavor, a ranch style perhaps. I'll know it when I see it. You are definitely in charge of interior design."

"I haven't even been in your apartment. Is it pretty?"

"It has no furniture in abundance, just a bed, a table and chair, and some stuff I just bought."

"You'll love living with me then. I want to live in the lap of luxury. After living in base housing for those early years, I want classy surroundings."

"Looking in your parents' house always lifts my spirits. Interior décor is important to me, also."

"Guys don't say that very often."

"Let me ask you a question," I said. "Are we going to join a church?"

"I hadn't thought about that. Do you want to?"

"If you ask that question, I know that you're ambivalent about it."

"Yes, but we have to think about Sean. He needs to have a choice. Where did you start church?"

"I grew up a Presbyterian. You?" I was careful to observe her expressions throughout our religious conversation. She was devoid of enthusiasm when she spoke.

"Southern Baptist. I confess I haven't gone in years."

"Sounds like we need to compromise."

"I'd go to the Methodist Church. That's where Mother and Daddy go now."

"I would, too," I said. "I don't have any bad stories about the Methodists."

"We'll have to talk about it some more, won't we?"

I was no fool. Her answer was like saying maybe. In other words, hell no!

"Suzy, I'm exhausted answering all these questions. Can we just sit and say sweet nothings to each other for a while?"

"Let's clean up the table first, then we can see what's on television."

We cleared and cleaned the dishes together as Sean sat contented to keep nibbling his remaining dinner of peas and carrots that he had smeared on his tray. There was something pleasant about working together on such a mundane evening chore. We compared and joked about how to thoroughly clean dishes in our dishwasher. I wasn't about to strongly volunteer my opinions about that. I stole glances at her, admiring the concentration she put into every item she cleared or put aside for hand washing. At certain angles, my glance revealed a face seemingly too young to be of marrying age. Other glances, especially when she turned toward Sean, revealed a magical look of joy, caring, and experience that only comes with maturity. Beauty and experience. What a wonderful combination in the one I loved.

Suzy lifted Sean expertly from his highchair and wiped clean his face and hands. After changing his diaper, she brought him out to play near us in his playpen. He was having none of that. For the first half hour he sat in his mother's lap and pestered her for attention. When I tried to rescue her, he would push me away. I had a lot to learn.

I didn't care what television show we watched. All I needed was to be near her and feel her hand in mine. Sean eventually got tired of separating us and contented himself with the nine or ten toys and stuffed animals in his playpen.

Suzy tuned into the new television show *M*A*S*H,* which I watched with mixed opinions. It was irreverent, which I enjoyed like any veteran. But occasionally, it cut too close to home. I had seen the movie earlier when I was still flying. Everyone in the squadron had liked it, except for one conservative Christian, who objected to the Last Supper scene. He walked out of the theater. The television show was quite different. Only the character Radar was the original member of the movie cast. My favorite memory of the whole series was Radar's successful theft of a Jeep, sending home one part each week. Hawkeye X-rayed a box to reveal a steering wheel, plus other obvious Jeep parts. It was funny with an element of truth to it.

Suzy and I watched the show together, sitting close, holding hands, and savoring a long overdue moment of serenity together. It was nearly ten o'clock when we woke up. Somewhere between *M*A*S*H* and another mindless show, we passed out, still holding hands. When we looked up to check on Sean, who had played well in his playpen, he lay on the cloth-covered pad sound asleep. We three humans had found, at last, contentment. I kissed Suzy goodbye. As a last gesture, I stooped down to lay a gentle hand on sleeping little Sean's head. I had to leave my soon-to-be-family for now, but I was going to be back every day, until I didn't have to leave.

40

THE NEXT MORNING, I ARRIVED at our A-to-Z office before 7:00 a.m. to find Stanton already at his desk making calls. He waved me over as he listened to a customer drone on. I looked at a single sheet of paper he handed me. It was a letter pertaining to orders at issue. He was claiming non-delivery of some expensive items in Stanton's area of expertise. The tone was demanding, bordering on hostile. I waited until he could shake off the caller and explain it to me. Eventually the marathon call ended, and he set the phone down in frustration.

"I will never figure out these guys, who always tell me they are pressed for time, but then won't hang up the phone."

"I learn more about human nature every day," I said.

"Well, learn this. If they have time to chat, they are poor prospects for buying anything."

I held up the letter. "What is this?"

"The letter is from the biggest blowhard I must deal with—and there are a lot of blowhards out there. He's trying to screw us again. The guy's a moron if he thinks we will fall for it. Just another white man trying to steal from an Indian."

"I sense you showed me this for a reason. It's out of my area of experience."

"I think he needs another white man to straighten him out this time."

"So, tell me about this." I looked for the name of the man. "Mister Helmut Reihert."

"You may be able to let him down easy. He's a former Air Force pilot. He keeps bragging about being in Vietnam. He insults the infantry. He doesn't pay us but demands more equipment."

"You think he'll be nicer to one of his own?"

"That's what I hope."

"Career Air Force?"

"No. He keeps talking about three years flying some airplane over in North Vietnam. He got shot down. Was a POW for a year or two. I don't know all the details. You figure him out."

"Sure. I'll see him. I owe you, anyway."

"You owe me?"

"I spent the entire day talking to my family and Suzy last night. The day off was much appreciated. Suzy and I are going to be okay."

"Good to hear."

"I'll take you up on your offer of getting some help, so I can have some time off. I promised Suzy I would stop by to see her and her son every evening from now on."

"Love beats money, right?"

"Yeah, I suppose it does."

"I already hired us each an assistant at 6:30 this morning."

"That was fast."

"Rob, your presence and skills have already brought me more business than I ever expected. You make A-to-Z seem friendlier. The oil patch likes you and tolerates me."

"So, who are these boys you hired?"

"You'll love this. For me I hired a tough looking broad by the name of, get this, Lily White. Lily White! I'm not kidding. I've seen her work out in the patch. No man out there would dare mess with her. She's a go getter."

"Lily White, huh? I can't wait to hear who you hired as my assistant."

"You'll get used to the name. Luther Muttencherry. He's about your age but bigger than both of us. He knows both sides of our business. Like Lily, he's been out in the real world and knows all the lingo, slang, and so on. He's a good old boy who will have your back in a scrap. Known him for years."

"Why do they want to join us?"

"They're tired of getting their hands dirty. One more degree of separation. Is that what everybody says? It didn't hurt that they think they may make a ton of money helping us."

"They're coming in today?"

"Next Monday. They are good people and wanted to give some notice where they work. The boss will probably fire them today anyway."

"Tell me about this Helmut Reihert schmuck, and I'll go see him today."

Listening to Stanton describe this oil field boss was familiar behavior to me. The captain that I utterly detested in my flying days must have been reincarnated as this Okie. The northwest quadrant of the state had a large German immigrant population beginning early in the 20th century. Mennonites had a large presence. Their old ways and their quaint dress code had not changed in nearly a hundred years. They were wonderful to deal with.

Helmut Reihert was not one of them. My experience in dealing with difficult officers would make the encounter fun. I had nothing to lose, since Stanton was encouraging me to tell him to get another supplier.

41

SHORTLY I WAS ON THE US Highway 81 north, heading to Kingfisher, going through two-lane roads to Watonga, then Fairview. During the whole drive it was easy to spot the farms of German Americans. The fence rows would single them out. While half the farmers realized that a pretty fence didn't contain cattle any better than a well-built ugly barbed wire fence, German farmers would maintain a pristine fence row. They used the sturdiest posts to anchor their barbed wire. Other farmers used whatever wood they found nearby. Although tall grass and hedges of Osage Orange or *bois d' arc* would envelope many fences along the drive, the German farmers kept theirs looking like well-manicured lawns. It would be interesting to learn how well manicured this Helmut Reihert really was.

I reached the location of the drilling site at ten in the morning. It would be an easy trip to get the truck back to the office and see Suzy in the evening. This part of Oklahoma was well suited for filming a good Western. The land was arid and craggy. Few crops grew except in spotty regions nearby. It was relatively desolate, except for the oil field equipment that occasionally rumbled by. At least one county bridge was out, because trucks ignored the weight restrictions posted on signs placed there 50 years before. Companies often decided incorrectly that time was money, so not taking the longer route over a proper bridge was worth the risk.

I drove down the temporary dirt road to the boss's shack and parked the truck with its A-to-Z letters plain to see from inside. I looked to the northwest to find a towering cumulonimbus exploding skyward. Absent only a minute before, it reminded me that spring in this part of the country could often be exciting. Rain, flooding, lightning, hail, and tornadoes were consistently on April's menu of weather. I had not planted my second foot on the ground before the office door flew open and a man rushed out yelling obscenities, already reminding me of every foul word I knew that was not allowed in a dictionary. He came right up to the truck door, grabbed it, then stopped his rant abruptly.

"Who in the hell are you?"

"Who in hell are you?" I replied.

"Where's that big fat Indian you have? BigHeart. Why isn't he here?"

"Well, because you're a pain in the ass, that's why."

"You want my business, then show some respect."

He flavored every sentence with unnecessary and undefined words. I tactfully ignored his bluster.

"I understand you're an Air Force flyboy. You look about my age. What did you fly?"

"Who wants to know?"

"Rob Amity, Class 70-03, Laredo Air Force Base." I extended my clean hand to shake his. He grabbed my hand, leaving me with a great desire to wash the unctuous feeling away. I might as well have shaken the hand of Uriah Heep.

"Helmut Reihert," he said.

"Where did you train?"

"Sheppard."

"What year?"

"Sixty-eight, I think. How in hell should I know? That's in the past."

"What did you fly? Back then nearly everyone got a fighter."

"F-105." Reihert looked at me warily. "Why in hell do you ask me so many questions? What do you want?"

"I don't meet many other Vietnam War veterans. We have something in common. Let's talk about this letter you sent us." I pulled the letter out of my shirt pocket and handed it to him. "One fly boy to another."

Reihert looked at me with piercing, irritated eyes. He motioned with his hand and turned away, walking to his shack of an office. His hand motion either meant follow me or get out. It didn't matter to me. I followed him inside. He let the door close behind him. When I opened it and stepped inside, he turned to me with uncertain intentions. Again, I didn't hesitate to proceed with my business intentions.

The room was stifling—warm and humid. It had the odor of stale breath and cigars, with a touch of petrochemicals to make it more toxic. His desk was a mess, as I anticipated. Papers, oilfield parts, assorted gloves, hats, and coveralls lay everywhere. Any place to sit was certain to cause permanent oil stains to my clothing. A wall featured a current Snap-On Tools 1974 calendar, with its beautiful, scantily clad women. Unfortunately, they were the most tasteful pictures of women in Reihert's shack. At least a dozen other pictures adorned the interior with disgusting poses that caused me to blush. There was nothing sexy about them.

"You owe us money," I said. He stepped quickly into my face. I fought my instinct to back off a step.

"You owe me an order from a week ago," he replied. Again, his message was peppered with words with no suitable definition, coupled with the foul odor of his breath in my face.

"That's not how it works," I said. "This is your last chance, or we drop you. Simple as that."

"I don't have to answer to you. BigHeart is the only one I talk to."

"Then you're SOL and up the creek without a paddle. Whatever you want to say. I'm your only hope of getting your order—one jet jock to another."

One of the foremen entered the shack and interrupted our confrontation only to be met with a barrage of undefinable verbal abuse concerning their drilling operation. I peered outside through a dirty window to note again the presence of the towering clouds that soon would darken into the storm that customarily gained life in the high plains of Colorado, Kansas, and New Mexico. It was now raking the ground of the Texas Panhandle and gaining energy for a push into western Oklahoma. Meanwhile, the storm brewing inside the shack with Reihert and his foreman gained momentum. I watched how the foreman handled this tyrant. He was no pushover. The foreman let him rant on, absorbing all the verbal abuse and intimidating body language. When Reihert ran out of steam, the foreman simply made his point again and got a grudging okay. This kraut was all bluff.

"Back to the money you owe us," I said, watching the foreman step outside.

Reihert's second withering verbal fusillade at me soon ran out of ammunition. There were only so many ways you could use the same four words repeatedly in a sentence.

"Before we cut a deal, let me ask you. I hear you were a POW."

"I was." Stanton was right. He was ready to brag.

"God bless you, sir. You've paid your dues. When were you shot down?"

"It was 1972... Linebacker. I was leading an element of four F-105s into a target."

"I forget. Were your Thuds single seat, or did you have a GIB?"

"Single seat. Like I said, I took a SAM strike and bailed out. The Viet Cong captured me. The next thing I knew I was in the Hanoi Hilton."

"So, you were a Weasel?"

"Yeah, I guess so. We were targeting missile sites. We were taking them out as fast as they were bringing them back on line back then."

"You may know a friend of mine. He's another F-105 driver and Wild Weasel. He was in Nam a little before you. Saw combat in Rolling Thunder. Ever heard of Hal Freed?"

"Was he tall, mustache, cocky?"

"That's the guy," I said.

"We flew together. He flew on my wing a few times. Most guys couldn't keep up with me in combat."

"He was good flying wing. I'll say that. Cocky, like you say."

"You know, I've got work to do, so you can leave now."

I ignored his suggestion. "You're right. Talking about old times is good, though. I think I've gotten to know you some. You pilots sure are tough to deal with."

"When's my order coming, then?"

"When I have a check. Like I said. Pilots are tough to deal with."

He pointed his finger over my shoulder. "There's the door. Send that fat Indian next time."

I stood my ground. Looking into his conniving eyes, I waited in silence to add some irritation to his day. He pointed again at the door. I leaned forward and put my hands on his desk with an invoice from A-to-Z.

"Look, pal. I know your POW story is a bunch of crap. You no more flew in Vietnam than I did. You're lucky my buddy Hal isn't here. He lost friends in those operations you claim to have been in. If Freed were here, he'd kick your ass."

"How dare you, you son of—"

"Just shut up! You're a fake. It's obvious. If I don't get my check from you, you don't get your order from me. And God help you if some of your roughneck buddies discover their jet jock boss's hero stories are all BS. How many Vietnam vets do you have in your crew? One is all it takes."

He looked at me with withering eyes. It didn't faze me. I had seen it before. The two of us remained silent. The rhythmic drone of drilling and the voices of men calling out were music to my ears as I waited. Helmut Reihert picked up the invoice, looked it over, then pulled out his checkbook and ledger. We remained silent as he put his finger on the bottom line of our invoice, while his other hand found a pen and filled out the amount on his oversized check. Writing fast and aggressively, he nonetheless signed the completed check and handed it to me. Still without a word between us, I carefully looked over the check. In the place for a signature, he had signed it, *John D. Horseshit.* I looked at him while tearing the check in half but placed both halves in my pocket.

"Write it again."

With a you-got-me smile, he again filled out another check, this time properly. After a quick inspection, I placed the check inside my billfold and headed for the door. Stepping outside, I turned to our fallen hero.

"If you have a girlfriend, I wonder if she knows you are a chicken hawk?"

I didn't wait for an answer. Moving to my truck, the first drops of an afternoon storm began falling.

42

IT WAS A TRIUMPHAL DRIVE back home. I raced eastward and southward toward Oklahoma City, with storm clouds chasing me the whole ninety miles. Between Watonga and Kingfisher on four-lane US Highway 81, the rain finally caught up to me. It quickly gained intensity, rendering driving a difficult situation. Pull over and get rammed by a car or truck from behind. Keep moving and ram an idiot who had pulled over. From experience, I locked on behind an 18-wheeler. I kept close enough behind him to where I could see his taillights. I figured his stopping distance would be long enough that I would have a good chance of stopping before I rammed him. If he rammed someone, it would save me from doing it myself. The semi and I drove south together at 30 mph until the rain let up. Then it was back to some reasonable speed, but still exceeding the 55 mph federal speed limit.

In two hours, I parked the company truck at A-to-Z Oilfield Services. With check in hand, I jubilantly marched into Stanton's office and slapped the check on his desk then plopped myself down in his favorite chair. The first words from Stanton's mouth after looking at the check were reassuring.

"You are kidding me."

"Honest Injuns." My Osage partner shared the joke with laughter and a slap on the back.

He looked at the check carefully, then at me. "We better cash this fast."

"I agree. You want Mary to take it to the bank right now?"

Stanton did not hesitate. "Mary! Get in here quick."

Mary, the best of team players, was in his office within seconds. Stanton paid her well. She earned it.

"I'm endorsing this check, but I need you to take the truck and deposit this before the banks close. We'll deposit the other checks we have at the usual time in the night deposit window. This one needs urgent attention."

She looked at the name on the check. Her eyes brightened. "You got that obnoxious little puke to pay up?"

Stanton looked at me. "Amity here did the deed."

"Mary," I said, "if you hurry back, I'll tell you the whole story. You'll love it." I looked at Stanton and added, "You'll love it, too. Wait till you hear what I figured out about the little kraut."

Stanton and I remained together in his office to discuss the needs for the rest of the week. He was a genius of organization, a legacy from his Army enlisted time. He had our work schedule laid out for each month ahead of time. After not even three months I noted the blurring of our assignments into each other's area of concentration. Instead of our products as a priority, he was now linking me first to the customer. What we sold didn't matter as much as who sold it. I had a knack of winning over our customers, as I was learning.

I expressed concern since I was slowing down my schedule for Suzy and Sean. He reminded me of our two hires that were starting on Monday. Mary returned and interrupted our chatter with news that the bank deposited Helmut Reihert's check. From previous experience, the bank first verified the check was good. I stood up and gave Mary my chair as a gesture of gratitude.

"Okay, Amity," Stanton asked, "how did you pull it off?" Mary looked at me with a grin of anticipation.

"I learned years ago, that if I wanted something, I had to first act like I already had it. Secondly, I find that when someone talks tough, they are likely to respect you more if you talk back to them the same way."

"Oh, boy," he replied. "What did you do?"

"When he asked me why you weren't calling on him, I said, quote, 'because he was a pain in the ass.'"

Mary and Stanton laughed at the unexpected answer.

"You're too nice," Mary said. "I'm trying to imagine this and can't."

"I've interviewed him," he said to Mary. "Rob here is tough as a boot."

"I just matched him word for word on insults. He was quite puzzled by my not being defensive or upset. He does cuss a blue streak, doesn't he?"

"I can't imagine you cursing, either," she said.

"No, I'm a reformed cursing machine. It didn't faze me a bit. Instead, I went right into his aviation record and asked him a bunch of questions. I was trying to interrupt his insults and bring some humanity into the conversation. Stanton, you told me he liked to brag about his war record, so I egged him on."

Stanton laughed. "I'm surprised you got back today. He's probably still bragging and doesn't know you are gone."

"Not after I got through with him. I asked him some pointed questions about his Air Force pilot training and his time in Vietnam. I guarantee you that your little kraut buddy has never served in the military a day in his life."

Stanton nearly jumped out of his chair at that declaration. It was obviously a total shock to him. Mary sat in her comfortable chair, hands to her face, and laughed aloud sounds of retribution. They both said nothing, wanting me to continue.

"If you ask any veteran what unit he served in, he can tell you without hesitation. Helmut was uncertain what year he was in pilot training. He claimed he was flying over North Vietnam in Rolling Thunder, which ended the same year he would have begun his military service. He told me he was over the North for Linebacker, but I had a sense that he was unaware there was also a Linebacker II.

"The next lie was when he told me he was leading a four-ship formation of Thuds on a bombing run as a single-seater. Lead on an F-105 missile strike always has a backseat electronics officer to do the targeting. He didn't know what a Wild Weasel was. Early in the war all the formations were two-seat fighters. Later the wingmen flew single seat aircraft but never as lead. And I'm unaware that F-105s ever did a four-ship attack. They always split up into two-ship formations.

"His biggest whopper came when he told he got shot down. He said the

Viet Cong captured him. First, the Viet Cong weren't even in North Vietnam. Second, he said he immediately went to the Hanoi Hilton as a POW.

"I asked him if he knew a friend of mine, who flew Thuds for a year over Hanoi. Hal is a great guy who shared with me a lot about his combat over North Vietnam. Our kraut buddy claimed he knew Freed, but that was impossible. The timeline wasn't even close. When he described how well Freed flew on his wing, I quote, 'most guys couldn't keep up with me in combat,' I had enough. Only an experienced officer would lead any formation."

"Did you tell him?" Stanton asked.

"I calmly told him that his whole POW story was a piece of crap—that he was a fake." Mary tittered in her comfortable chair.

"And he said...?"

"At first he was indignant, but I told him to shut up and write me a check." I paused, the word bribery on my mind. "I might have mentioned that there were a lot of Vietnam veterans among his drilling crew that would kick his ass if they ever learned he was full of bull."

Reaching in my shirt pocket, I extracted two sheets of paper. "He said nothing after that and wrote me this check, which I immediately tore in two."

Stanton reacted to that with surprise. I handed my evidence to him, waiting for a reaction. He looked at each half of the first check, then double checked them, before reacting.

"He actually signed it *John D. Horseshit!*" The three of us burst into loud animated laughter.

"I made him write another check." I started laughing. "I told him... I hoped his girlfriend didn't know he was a chicken hawk."

Stanton found amusement watching Mary laugh at the reference to what a girlfriend might think. "Anything else?"

"The only thing I might bring up is I told Helmut that I would send him his orders only after he wrote that check. What do you think?"

"He won't get diddley squat from me. We're done with him. Agreed?"

"Agreed," I replied.

"You done good, Amity. You done good."

43

BEFORE I LEFT THE OFFICE for the day, I called Suzy to plan our evening. Although it had been a day of triumph, I still had great discomfort thinking how Mr. Jensen and I would get along together. Meeting him in person had to be done. I didn't know how it would come about.

Suzy was blessedly cheerful when she answered her phone. Hearing my voice elevated her mood another notch. Not since high school had I been this nervous and excited to hear a female voice. She was happy I kept my promise. I was relieved that I had passed the first of many tests of my newly vowed conduct. I quickly told her about my day and the impossible check I got from a shamefully colorful character. Tonight, I was the knight who slayed the dragon, returning in victory to be with the fare maiden.

I parked my Porsche in the circle driveway just short of the Jensen's front door. My first visit was not to see Suzy but to see her parents. If I had to eat crow, I wanted the meal done before bedtime. I rang the melodious doorbell and nervously waited. I exhaled a deep breath just as Mr. Jensen opened the door. My respiration froze, which left me breathless. I stammered for words that were stuck by my respiratory apprehension. I needn't have worried. Instead of Mr. Jensen greeting me, he placed the tottering little Sean at the front door. The boy looked up in recognition and broke out in a big smile and laugh. He turned to playfully run away but fell on the ornate oriental carpet in their entryway. I showed no expression when he looked at me for approval to cry. He turned to his grandfather and got the same response. Consequently, instead of crying, Sean got up and ran away laughing.

"You passed that test," Mr. Jensen said. "Come in here. It's about to rain." The afternoon rainstorm that had followed me home was now regenerating overhead. In my excitement during the day, I was unaware it had never left.

"Thank you, sir." The tension was evident in my voice.

"Son, let's clear the air right here and start with a clean slate. I never had a son in my family, so you're it. We can't afford to be at odds. In truth, I'm relieved to see you back here."

I nodded acknowledgement, then spoke the truth. "I deserved it, sir. Thank you for your call. You, my father, my mother, and our friend Stanton all thought I was an idiot. I decided I don't like being an idiot."

"Suzy's in the kitchen with her mother. She'll be glad you're here." He reached out to pat my back as I walked by him. I stopped when he continued. "I just got off the phone with Stanton BigHeart. He told me what you did today. It makes me proud that I recommended you to him. He is an incredibly happy man."

"I guess we both owe you."

Mr. Jensen waved his hand in dismissal. "She's waiting," he whispered.

I entered the kitchen to the gracious greeting from Mrs. Jensen, wearing an apron over another lovely and cheerful print dress with an array of pastel Paris café scenes.

"I would give you a hug, but I have flour all over me. I don't want to mess you up." I looked down at my own clothes, soiled from my visit to the drilling site.

I was about to offer a greeting, but Suzy moved in front of me with a hug of welcome. As she lingered, the arm of a little boy clutched my leg. We both looked down at Sean, an arm wrapped around each of us. We looked at each other with smiles. While both of her parents watched, she planted a significant and lingering kiss upon my lips.

"Wow! Watch out, Rob," her mother said. "She must mean business."

We unlocked our lips and broke our clutch. I was slightly embarrassed but not Suzy. She was dead serious. In my life, I had never enjoyed such pursuit by a woman. It was now a neck and neck race because my pursuit was equal to hers.

Sean remained next to his mother and offered himself to her for a lift into her arms.

"May I?" I said.

Much to Sean's surprise, I bent down to him and clumsily lifted him into my arms. At first, I had him all wrong, and the look on his face was not encouraging. Suzy gave me quick coaching on proper toddler wrangling, while placing a hand of reassurance on the back of the boy's neck. Sean at first found my face interesting and placed a hand on my nose and lips. After that, I got my first challenge of anchoring a squirming toddler in my arms, who seemed hell bent on breaking my grasp and flying to the floor. Suzy rescued us both, and Sean reached his desired destination—Mama.

"We're having dinner in the big house tonight," Suzy said.

"You are staying, I presume?" asked Mrs. Jensen. It was more an implicit command.

"Of course," I said.

Suzy added her own mandate. "I'm seating you next to Sean. I can either sit by you or on the other side of Sean. Which do you prefer?"

"Can I pick neither?" That caused the Jensen's to stir.

"No." Suzy started a giggle, then turned to her parents. "You'll get used to his humor."

"I'll sacrifice for the child and let him sit by each of us."

"You may need a plastic sheet to cover yourself when he starts to eat," Mr. Jensen said.

"You'll need to get used to Daddy's humor, also."

After we sat down to eat and as the meal progressed, I realized that Mr. Jensen wasn't kidding about the plastic sheet. Sean was hurling food in all directions. They had indeed used a plastic sheet, arrayed on the floor under his highchair to capture as much food as possible. Much of it was impossible to contain.

"I saw him eat last night. He wasn't like this then."

"Different food," Mr. Jensen said. "Real peas are the worst, followed by scrambled eggs, any liquid in a cup or a bowl... oh, and any food you give him as soon as you quit looking. He also likes to bang on the tray and hurl food off the sides. Every man deserves at least one chance to experience this in their lifetime."

As I watched the boy eat, it was apparent that I was the only adult in the room wincing. I had lots to learn. The Serenity Prayer came to mind.

God, grant me the serenity to accept the things I cannot change, courage to change the things I can, and wisdom to know the difference.

It wasn't just for alcohol anymore.

44

SUZY AND I TOOK SEAN with us back to her poolside guest house for some time to relax away from polite conversation that we both enjoyed, until we wearied of it. It is sometimes only after you can happily be together without talking that you know your marriage is secure. We were already there, without yet being married. Sean was tuckered out from the attention. I was worn out from the chatter. Suzy was exhausted from being a single mother. With Sean changed and in bed, we sat down on the couch to hold hands, Suzy's head resting on my left shoulder. The television was off. Neither of us expressed interest in Top 40 music from the radio. The record player remained with the cover lid down. We just sat holding hands. A clock on the end table said 8:30. Was this what wedded bliss would be like? I hoped so.

While the clock ticked away, I began to hear next to me the faint sounds of deep sleep. I listened with joy to those sounds that meant there was life in her still. With each heartbeat and each breath came a countdown to when life ends. I could be pessimistic, or I could choose the Serenity Prayer little Sean brought to mind. Here I sat listening to the sounds emanating from the one woman I dearly loved. I enjoyed this moment. If I were meant to live for the moment, that prayer was the best reminder I could have. At dinner three adults calmly watched Sean hurl food around the dining room floor, as I watched in relative horror at the spectacle. I had to learn to enjoy the chaos as well as the stillness of these trivial things in life. Sitting with Suzy's head on my shoulder was a moment to enjoy. One day we would miss this moment and wish it back. We could replicate it many times, but our special moments would only get better with time. There would be no countdown in our life because each minute of a clock would be ours to share.

At ten o'clock I spoke to Suzy, first with a kiss on her lips. "I need to go, before your mother comes with the morality police to run me out."

Suzy opened her eyes in delayed surprise to see me on her couch. After setting her head straight, she looked at me and kissed me back gently.

"We're quite the wild lovers, aren't we?" she said.

"I'm afraid a movie about our lives would be a flop. We lie around all night doing nothing."

"I think what we did tonight was lovely."

"Do I pass the test today."

"A-plus."

"Do I get to give you a grade?"

"Never."

I looked at her with obvious passion. "I must go. I don't want to, but I must go before I do something and fail the test."

"You can try." Oh, that high school feeling surged through my brain.

"Not tonight."

"No?"

"I love you, Suzy. Not tonight. I promised."

"I love you, Rob. I don't think I can wait much longer."

"Good night," I said. With aching reluctance, I kept my promise and went home to my sparsely appointed apartment to be alone once more.

What is it with women? The question kept repeating in my mind like a song that won't stop playing in your head. *First, she got mad because I had neglected her. Then she put me on probation to prove I was worthy of her love. The probation lasted for two days. Now she makes suggestions that I should stay. Was it a test of my probation? She said she can't wait much longer. What in hell is she doing? I wish she would make up her damn mind.*

My driving was distracted all the way home. I couldn't remember if I ran red lights or looked for cars or kept to the speed limit. My memory was all a jumble. I got home safely if home was what it was. I was ready for Suzy. She said she didn't think she could wait much longer—emphasis on *could* wait, not will wait. Was her will slipping, or was it a trick to test me? The problem with women is that either scenario might have only wrong answers. If I slept with her, I would be an opportunist. If I didn't, I would be told that I didn't understand her obvious signals. Then I'd be the most inept lover in her world. There was only one conclusion. Until I knew what was right and what was wrong, it wouldn't matter. I was plunging into a deep depression, which had no correlation to events. Today I enjoyed remarkable success at work, blessed reconciliation with the Jensens, and obvious signals of passion from Suzy. What should have generated elation was lost in a black hole of despair.

After entering my apartment, I stood to reflect upon what made my mood turn sour. I ached for the warm touch of another human who would love me. I returned to my empty and gloomy shell of a home. I left my car in the parking lot, not remembering if I locked it or not. I didn't care. Entering the funeral quiet of this tomb of a home, I flicked on the lights to see nothing. It was all my own doing. I had nothing on the walls. Nothing on the floors, except a kitchen table, a chair, and a bed. I went to my bed, leaving my clothes on and skipping my routine tooth brushing. Falling onto the unkempt sheets, I closed my eyes, only to feel a dark shroud descend upon my face. My skin began to crawl, the pain of a deep depression. This was not the first time for me, and I once again vowed I would never let this pain happen to me again.

45

I MANAGED TO MAKE IT to work at 7:00 a.m. thinking I could fool everyone. All I wanted was to not think about my desperate mood. I hoped diving into work would make me forget. It did no such thing.

"Rough night?" Stanton looked concerned.

"No. Just the opposite. Suzy and I had a nice evening with the Jensens."

"Sure doesn't look like it."

The words were devastating. I was standing in his office looking outside the window that faced south at a rising sun to the east. I turned away from him, trying to suppress the tears of grief that I couldn't stop and couldn't explain. I had tried to fool myself into sanity, but Stanton had to point out the obvious.

"Have a seat, Rob. You want to talk about something?"

I kept my back to him and stood in silence, struggling to keep my composure and self-dignity. Real men cry, I know, but I was a basket case of tears that made me look wimpy. I wanted to be tough, but my emotions had too often disappointed me with tears at the slightest disturbing moment in my life. I hated how I reacted. It was humiliating. I prayed no one would walk in and see me this way. I tried unsuccessfully to hide a tear when I turned around to face him.

"I can't stop this feeling I have. I've had it since I was a child. I used to think depression was what everyone had—that it was normal."

"Something happen last night?"

"Nothing bad, mostly good stuff. Do you know what that's like?"

"No, I don't, but I know many veterans kill themselves because of it. Are you at that point?"

"Not yet, but once I quit trying to save myself. Sort of a passive suicide, I guess."

My Osage friend looked at me while I stood helpless to crawl my way out of this embarrassment. He was a far contrast from the Stanton BigHeart I encountered at our first interview—not aggressive but empathetic.

"Why should you care?" I asked.

"We Osage deal with this. Our history is filled with examples of our people keeping us strong. Our culture teaches us that. Whenever we are in trouble we go to talk to our elders. They have great wisdom, which can teach us. My best advice came from my father when I returned from that thankless war in Korea. I was in the late part of the war when we lost most of our buddies. Battle lines didn't move. We just kept shooting at each other until the bodies were piled like cord wood in front of each other. Father said, 'go do some of the things you missed while away in the Army. It will help make you better.' So, I did. I hiked for many miles into the prairie lands of our nation and camped out for several days, all alone in the quiet. The winds were gentle during that time. The rustle of the grass and the call of the birds were my only sounds for a week. After months of soldiers and artillery, the prairie was my salvation. I loved the outdoors back then. I still do."

"I like doing a lot of things."

"So, what do you miss most of all?"

"I hate to admit it, but I miss the Air Force. I miss flying. I miss having a real home."

"What could you do tomorrow?"

It would take weeks to return to the military. There's a chance I would fail to be welcomed back, with the reduction in force ongoing. Buying a home would require a lot of effort. Having a flight in an airplane would be easy.

"I have a friend, Brad Kilty, who is an airplane nut. He would take me up in a heartbeat."

"Call 'em up. Right now." Stanton lifted the whole telephone around and placed it in front of me. "You have his number?"

My blank stare prompted him to pull from his drawer the Oklahoma City Bell Telephone White Pages. "Do it now."

"Shouldn't I be working. Don't you need me?"

"Rob, I can't afford to lose you. Do you realize how lucrative you've been to our business? But I can afford to lose you for a day or two. Go fix yourself in an airplane. I need you to keep your head on straight while this crazy oil boom is going on."

I didn't need to look for Brad Kilty's telephone number in the phonebook. I had his business card in my billfold. I pulled it out and was surprised the see the address listed for his home. He was clearly successful already if his location was any indication. Since it was early morning, this was likely the best time to catch him at home. Chances were he was working today at The Great American Railroad where he was manager. I dialed him up, and he answered on the first ring.

"Brad, this is your old buddy Rob Amity."

His enthusiasm was genuine and immediate. *"Tell me you called to go fly with me this morning."*

"That's actually why I called."

"I try to get at least an hour in every morning before I get to the restaurant. I'm heading to Wiley Post in about ten minutes. Why don't you meet me there?"

"I don't mean to butt in, Brad. I was just going to check for something in the future."

"I guess you're working?"

"Yes, well...."

"Screw the boss if he's not looking."

"Screw the boss you say?" Stanton looked at me and grinned wide.

"I don't know what you do, but there's always an errand you can run for the benefit of your company."

"Okay, Brad. When should I be there and where?"

"Can you make it to the tower by 8:30? I'd give you the number of my hangar, but it's too complicated. Just go to the tower, and I'll drive you over to my plane."

"I'm on my way... and Brad. Thanks. I really needed this. I'll explain when I get there."

"You needed a fix, didn't you?"

"Yeah, I needed a fix."

"Hurry up. I'll wait. It'll be great to fly with a real pilot."

We hung up. Stanton sent me some cryptic Army hand signal that I was smart enough to know meant to bug out. I raced to my car and quickly left for my chance to fly for the first time in a year.

46

WHEN I DROVE UP, I found Brad outside in the morning sunshine leaning on a fence and watching a private jet taking off. I walked up behind him and stealthily grabbed his arms in a mock arm lock. He turned around and gave me an enthusiastic greeting. After his welcome ran its course, he looked beyond me to the lone car parked nearby.

"Amity, is that your Porsche?" He was almost yelling at his surprise. Everything he did was over the top with enthusiasm.

"That's my new Porsche. It's a...."

"Don't tell me. Let me guess." He left his airplane interest at the fence and rushed over to get a better look at the vehicle before exploding in a staccato description of my car's details. "That's a Porsche Carrera RSR 3.0 liter. If it's a 1973, you've got an almost one of a kind."

"That's what it is."

"Then we're going to the hangar in your car, not mine. How in the heck did you land this monster? You have to be a millionaire to afford this."

When he stepped into the cockpit of my car, his legs were almost too long to fit in the right seat comfortably. He proceeded to list all the details of this specific Porsche I was driving.

"This has a bigger 2.8-liter, 296 horsepower air-cooled engine, five-speed manual transmission. They only made a few hundred of these. With that special engine and all, you must be filthy rich."

"Well, it is paid for," I said. I loved egging him on, after his filthy rich crack. "I see that you're living in the Lakehurst addition. You own your own airplane. You must be filthy rich, too."

"That I am," he said. When I began idling slowly out to the street, he added, "Could you give this putt-putt a little gas. I want to feel what it's like to ride in a rocket."

Once out of the parking lot, I lined up on the street and floored it in first gear until I reached about 70-mph, before shutting it down. I was already feeling better.

"That's outstanding!" Brad said. His enthusiasm was contagious. He began laughing. "You forgot to turn back there. My hangar's behind us."

I found a place on the road to make a high speed one-eighty, which set Brad to laughing even more. He seemed in adulthood to be an adrenalin junky, which could be a deadly combination with an airplane. We drove up to his hanger, which was directly southeast of the tower. After driving through the coded gate, we reached his hangar door, notable for being the only pristine door among the row of five other units. We parked the Porsche facing the doors between his hangar and his neighbor's. When he opened the hangar door, I was struck by the showroom quality inside. His early model Cessna 172B, looked flawless. In fact, it was 13 years old with the original engine, a 145 horsepower Continental piston engine, capable of going 105-mph. Although it was certified to carry four passengers, only fools would load that many adults into an airplane like this.

The interior of his hangar appeared clean enough to perform surgery on the floor. There was not a spot or a smudge anywhere. His mechanics tools were each marked for a specific hook on his peg board. Anything unsightly I could find hidden in his enclosed metal cabinets.

Brad by contrast was dressed in shabby blue jeans and an old faded t-shirt from high school. With a full head of prematurely gray hair, he stood above six feet, with more of his inches making up his legs than his torso. His height made it easy for him to do his meticulous preflight inspection. He carried no checklist, as we would have in the Air Force. Instead, he recited each item checked, as he went around the aircraft. First, he covered the fuselage and empennage. *Baggage Door... Rivets... Rudder Gust Lock... Tail Tie-Down... Control surfaces... Trim Tab... Antennas.* Next, he moved to the right wing. *Wing Tie-Down... Aileron... Flaps... Main Wheel Tire... Brakes... Fuel Tank Sump... Fuel Quantity... Fuel Filler Cap.* It continued like this at the nose of the aircraft with an engine and nosewheel checklist. He moved to the left wing, where he added extra checks for items only on that wing, such as the *Pitot Tube Cover* and *Stall Warning* which are critical for maintaining a flying airspeed. He spent at least five minutes carefully inspecting items on the outside, then went inside of the airplane. No doubt, he had done the same inspection after each flight as well. Brad was my kind of pilot. He was obsessively cautious but never assumed he had it memorized. After he finished his preflight check, he stood there going over the list again, saying each item aloud. With each confirmation, he replied "check!"

He hooked a tow bar to the nose gear and pulled the Cessna carefully out of the hangar. The condition of the three tires was pristine, like everything else on the aircraft. The tread and sidewalls looked showroom quality. He asked me to shut the hangar doors and lock the padlock, all the while inspecting my work carefully.

With two doors on the 172B, Brad climbed in first to occupy the left seat, where the pilot in charge assumed control. His long legs forced him to carry his knees higher than the bottom of the control yoke. I knew once we were flying the yoke would be further back and out of the way. He began his second chant by rote of his startup checklist. Fast and efficient, we had engine start, instrument double check, and call to Wiley Post Ground Control in a flash. He adjusted the altimeter to the current barometer setting, as stated by Ground. Clearly, Brad wanted all the flying time he could muster before he reported for lunch supervision at his restaurant.

This early in the morning found only a few aircraft taxiing in the vicinity. We soon taxied to the runup area at the takeoff end of Runway 17 Left. Thanks to Oklahoma's prevailing southerly winds, this was most often the takeoff direction at Wiley Post. It was the same I had experienced in South Texas when I was flying jet trainers. Brad turned his Cessna facing into the wind and applied the brakes. We waited there until he noted warming on his temperature gauge, which indicated his Continental engine was warm enough for takeoff. Remaining in place with heavy brake pressure, he ran up the engine to 1800 rpm and checked for proper function of the two magnetos. Designed as a redundancy, he first switched to the left magneto and looked for a drop in rpm. He noted the slight drop, then turned to the right magneto and noted its drop. They were equal and acceptable, so he switched to employing both again. The engine increased to its original 1800 rpm.

After running through a few more routine Before Takeoff checks, he switched his radio to Tower, and taxied to the line short of the runway.

"Wiley Post Tower, Skyhawk eight-two-one-niner-X-ray, Runway one-seven-left, holding for takeoff."

Tower cleared us for immediate takeoff. We carefully checked the approach end in case an unseen aircraft was coming in for a landing. I knew it was smart to double check everything. Brad lined up his Cessna on the center line, applied power and right rudder to counter the yaw caused by a turning propeller, and began his takeoff role. I was reminded that this was not a jet. The acceleration down the runway was anemic. Even the small T-37 jet that I flew pinned me back in the seat on takeoff. This was different. When we reached airlift speed, the aircraft gingerly lifted off the ground and seemed to float. A jet plane doesn't float. It blasts through the sky, making the air bounce. In this airplane the liftoff was more like flying a kite. The air bounced the airplane. I had flown a military version of this Cessna 172, called the T-41 Mescalero. The significant difference was the engine. While Brad's 172 had a 145-horsepower engine, my T-41 moved along with 210 horses. The military version climbed better, flew faster, and didn't feel like a floating kite. Our instructors had warned us that military pilots were more likely to be involved in civilian aircraft accidents than military ones. The reason was that military pilots, used to powerful engine thrust, expected too much of civilian airplanes. Stalls, bent airframes, and damaged landing gear were all part of the mix of ways to ruin an airplane or kill its pilot.

I was glad my friend was flying this kite. After liftoff he went through his mental checklist routine again. I heaved a sigh of relief when he declared, "Now, let's go fly."

"We passed over Lake Overholser, the city's first water reservoir, before we turned right 180 degrees to head north over Lake Hefner, the city's second water source. The winds were moderate this morning. The lakes made waves but no whitecaps.

"We'll head north for a while to keep the sun out of our eyes," he said over the drone of the engine and propeller. "You going to take up flying again?"

"I'm not sure," I replied. "I was happy to quit before, especially because of my sinus difficulties."

I reminded him of my being grounded from flying and how I was happy to pursue other interests as a result. It got me out of the Air Force early, which at the time made me happy. Now? Not so much.

"Let's see how you do with this flight. I don't go as high or as fast as you flyboys do. I bet you do okay."

Brad leveled at 3500 feet on the altimeter, which put us at least 2000 feet above the ground. We flew east of Guthrie, another Land Run city, where he pointed out the Guthrie Airport runway to our left. I was struck by my inability to spot the landing strip. Despite numerous clues and landmarks, he pointed to, I couldn't spot the runway. It had only been a year. I was already forgetting visual memory clues of what an airport looked like from the air. Brad circled back for another pass. Now closer, and with my side less obstructed by a window frame, I spotted it.

"Tally Ho!"

I was amazed how vague the view was from the side of the runway. Then we made a quarter circle around the south end of the runway. As my view grew closer to the position a pilot would have on landing, my ability to recognize what it was became easier. I was reminded that runway sightings come from experience, and that experience can disappear like the runway.

From Guthrie we flew the 20 miles or so to Sundance Airpark, a sleepy World War Two landing field built in 1944. It lay ten miles northwest of Oklahoma City. There we found a couple of other aircraft flying in the pattern, practicing touch and go landings. He expertly entered the pattern in a totally different manner than we entered a military airfield. Instead of flying directly over the field, pitching out in a steep-banked 180 degree turn to a

downwind leg to a circling final turn to landing, Brad was squaring off his
left turns in a box pattern. I had a lot to learn in the civilian world.

Brad completed his traffic pattern with a nice half-flap touch and go
landing. As we took off again, he turned to me. "Your turn. You want to try
a landing?"

I grabbed my yoke and in habitual military fashion said, "I've got it," and
shook the yoke for confirmation. I cleared for traffic in the downwind pattern, made a climbing turn to pattern altitude, levelled off as best as I could,
but I was out of practice and unprepared. Brad made my radio calls, inform-
ing the field and other airplanes where I was and what were my intentions. I
set my power as best as I could.

"What's my speed on downwind?" I asked.

"I don't know," he said. "Try 65."

"Do you know what my final approach speed is?" I asked. These were
numbers a pilot should know.

"I don't know that, either. If the stall warning horn starts screaming, add
power and lower the nose."

I mumbled an uncomplimentary description of his flying skills. I chose 65
mph, then began a military circling turn to final. I looked over to see Brad, a
nervous smile on his face. He let me continue my military style pattern, but
it put him on edge. I slowed the plane to 60 mph on final, lining up my nose
to the runway. I looked for a windsock to no avail. Having no idea what a
correct airspeed was on final, I pulled power off slightly and bled airspeed to
55 mph. This mimicked the relative airspeed changes a T-37 had, although
now I was in a much slower aircraft. No stall warning horn sounded, which
was good. I checked for the VASI lights that would help me stay on the proper glide slope to touchdown. I was way too high. I cut power more, trying to
hold airspeed at 55. My rate of descent increased which prompted Brad to
put his hands on the control yoke.

"I still have it, Brad."

He let go of the controls and watched as I came steeply down to a point a
quarter mile beyond the preferred first thousand feet of runway for landing.
At least we would have walked away—and I didn't slam the airplane on the

pavement. But it was shaky, and I chose to leave the aircraft for good in the hands of its owner.

Brad took the control yoke from me and continued the touch and go takeoff, raising the flaps that I forgot to clean up. After one more practice landing, we departed Sundance for Wiley Post Airport.

"I've got to get to work," he said.

"I was depressed about missing flying," I said as we leveled off at 2,500 feet. "I thought this would help, until you let me fly."

"You did great for a guy who's been off for a year. I wouldn't get depressed over that. I got a little nervous, but I saw you adjust on final before you landed. It was long, but you knew it would be long way before it was too late to correct."

"It's so easy to forget the little procedures that the FAA requires. A lot different than the Air Force. Sorry for my round turns. I saw you fly the box pattern, but stress makes me go to my comfortable past self."

"I think I've seen others fly the same pattern, so it must be okay. You might ask the tower for approval, but an uncontrolled airport like Sundance, who cares."

As we approached Wiley Post and contacted the tower, they cleared us for a straight-in approach, no traffic pattern required. I noted the final airspeed as we descended to land. The speed was all over the dial. Brad was flying by the seat of his pants, not even looking at his airspeed. If I flew his airplane alone, I might be dead. If he flew mine, he would certainly kill himself. What a combination of skills we had.

After a perfect touchdown, we taxied to his hangar. I helped with returning the Cessna inside. He went through his compulsive post flight checklist, repeating many of the same checks he made before our flight. Once completed, he closed the doors and padlocked the hangar, until his flight tomorrow. It was a lot more flying than I would ever want to do every day of my life. I wasn't cured, yet. There had to be something more than flying that I needed to make me happy again.

47

I LEFT WILEY POST FOR a return to A-to-Z. Working might be the best therapy for today. Pulling into our parking lot, more cars than usual filled the spaces. I entered, curious to see who was visiting. Mary met my inquisitive peek with her wonderful smile. Her hair was not as blonde, and her dark roots were missing. I was smart enough to choose my words carefully.

"You certainly look chipper this morning. Did Stanton give you a raise?"

"Not yet, but your new assistants are here. I think you will like them both." She continued her smile. It just begged for a compliment.

"You look so happy. I'm guessing you have a date tonight."

"Yes. How did you know?"

"You just have that look about you. I've seen it before, you know."

"Oh, Mr. Amity. Quit your bragging." Then she giggled at our clever shared joke.

I stepped up to knock on Stanton's closed office door. It quickly opened for me to see a tall, thin, and swarthy man about my age. Behind him sat a raven-haired woman in her forties.

"Come in here, Amity, and meet our new assistants," said Stanton.

"Great! What a surprise?" I replied. "I didn't expect you two until Monday."

"Luther Muttencherry," the man said. He extended his hand in a firm handshake. I could feel the rough calluses on his hand, a sure sign of a man who worked hard.

"To the rescue," I said. "You are a welcome sight. You go by Luther?"

"My friends call me Mutt." He was somewhat taller than Stanton and all bones and muscle.

"Mutt it is." I looked beyond Mutt to the lady who was standing up to greet me. "You must be Lily."

Lily standing looked to be a full five feet tall if she stood on her tip toes. She grabbed my hand in a grip capable of crushing bone. Like Mutt's hand, hers was firm but soft and uncalloused. Work gloves hung from the hip pocket of her blue jeans. The petit Lily looked tough enough to handle a roughneck, with eyes that spoke to self-confidence. She wore less than feminine steel-toed work boots. Her tan long-sleeved blouse was more work shirt than fashion statement. A ballpoint pen and a note pad occupied the left breast pocket. Her long black hair, pulled back into a ponytail, stuck out the back of a nondescript bright green ball cap. Inside her other hip pocket a can of Skoal dipping tobacco formed a permanent white ring on the outer fabric.

"Lily White," she said after releasing her grip on my hand. "I don't have a nickname. Don't need one."

"I get that," I replied. "We're grateful you joined us."

I turned back to my new assistant. "Muttencherry is an interesting name. Where does that name come from?"

"It's Indian," he replied.

"What tribe?" I asked. All three laughed—at my expense.

"Not any tribe in Oklahoma," Mutt said. "Go halfway around the globe to India."

"India?"

Mutt was so thin that the legs of his blue jeans failed to make it to the toes of his work boots. If I hadn't already experienced his grip, I would've assumed he was too weak from starvation. He wore a dark blue hooded sweatshirt that seemed inadvisable for a mid-spring day, destined to get hot before our workday was over.

"My grandparents came to America in 1939. Most people assume we are Hindu, but we're actually Jewish."

"Hey, we could both take Friday afternoon off then," I said. Mutt was uncertain if my words were sarcasm, until I smiled. "I have a girlfriend I'm trying to see. Early on Friday is an ideal time to quit, that is, unless there's some emergency."

Stanton interrupted us to clarify. "We are all going to be on standby in rotation. Amity and I will sort out our schedules. You two assistants can figure out how you would like to arrange your schedules for something like Friday sundown services."

We stood around chatting. Mutt turned to Stanton and suggested that he and I might want to leave and let Lily discuss things. He turned to me.

"I need to discuss some things with you. Can we go to your office?"

"I don't have an office." I looked at Stanton, who made a face of mock irritation. "Stanton is frugal."

"Why don't you guys check your schedule today." Stanton said. "Mutt, you could tag along, or if you like, talk over lunch."

We chose lunch at Johnnie's at May Avenue and Britton Road which was only a quarter mile from The Great American Railroad. Being the area where I grew up, the greatest hamburger joint in America was a popular hangout for its friendly and familiar surroundings. Mutt ate like a starving piranha. He was right. After scarfing down two adult-sized hamburgers with fries, it was evident he was no Hindu. He spoke with the clear and slow cadence of a real Okie accent. I found his range of interests fascinating.

"My grandparents came over here before World War Two officially started," he said. "Not everyone realizes that Japan was already at war in China. They looked at the world situation and left their home in Mattancherry, India. America was the only place they considered."

"I assume it was a difficult trip."

"The only thing they ever talked about was their arrival in New York and seeing the Statue of Liberty. They couldn't take the Pacific route because Japan was on a rampage. They must have gone through North Africa."

"Any problems coming in as a refugee?"

"No. They were both highly-desired physicians trained in London. That's where they met. In the bigger area around Kochi, Mattancherry has the nickname of Jew City. They feared that being Jews might put them in peril crossing the Atlantic. They had no issues but being anywhere near Nazis made them worried."

"Well, Muttencherry is an interesting name."

"That wasn't their name, but after they went through the immigration office, the officer got their city and name mixed up. The man Americanized the spelling of Mattancherry to Muttencherry, and my grandparents got stuck with it. I guess the office liked sheep or something. I wish they had said they were from Kochi. Spelling would be a whole lot easier."

"Either of your parents along on the trip in '39?"

"They had some leisure time apparently. My father was conceived along the journey. He was five or six months along when they reached America."

"Parents still around?"

"Doing well in Tulsa."

"Do your grandparents still practice medicine?"

"Oh, yes. Work is in our genes. So is thinness, apparently."

"You going for a third burger?"

"No, but I think you'll find that I like to work. Because of that, I eat a lot."

"Hobbies?"

"Work." I waited for him to laugh at his joke. He was dead serious. "I said, it's in our genes. It's what I enjoy... that and eating."

"Married? Kids?"

"My parents have arranged for me to meet my bride, but so far, I resist their attempts. I want to be American, not Indian."

I checked the time on my Bulova watch and suggested we could head out soon. Mutt looked at me curiously, like earlier when he was answering my many questions. It was an odd quirk, the way he would look away. This time his curious gaze was prolonged. Finally, Mutt spoke up.

"Rob, I don't know how to tell you this, but your nose is bleeding from your left nostril."

That caught my attention. My nose was frequently runny, but that was common for me whenever I ate anything spicy. I grabbed one of the paper napkins from the booth's dispenser to place against my nose. The blood quickly wicked into the white absorbent paper. To me it seemed copious. I don't know what Mutt's opinion was. I do know that I was more alarmed than he was. I excused myself and went to the restroom at the back of the restaurant to cautiously deal with the blood. From my previous flying experiences blowing my nose could be helpful or it could induce more bleeding. I gently blew into a paper towel and discovered it to be a bad idea. I molded a few sheets of toilet paper into a nasal cork and plugged up the left nostril. For the next ten minutes I held my head back with my toilet paper cork inserted. Mutt finally came to check on me and offered his assistance. He looked over at the sink I had initially used and did his best to rinse the remaining blood down the drain. I pulled out the old bloody cork and inserted a new wad of toilet paper.

"I think I can go now," I said. My nasal voice made both of us chuckle. "Thanks for cleaning up my sink."

"Why don't I drive?" he asked. "Just let me know where we're going. I know these parts like the back of my hand."

We managed to leave Johnnie's without notice. I took the right seat of the company pickup and showed Mutt the customer we were going to see just south of Okarche. He drove out of the parking lot, choosing to navigate north around Lake Hefner before intersecting Northwest Expressway to Okarche.

"Are you okay?" he asked.

"I think I understand why the Air Force grounded me from flying."

"Why? Nose bleeds?"

"No, that's just a consequence. I had a chronic sinus condition. Cigarette smoke made it worse. I never smoked, but half of my squadron did. I got sinus blocks a lot. Sometimes I got a bloody nose as a result."

"And you flew today, I heard."

"Yeah, this morning. First time since my last military flight."

"You still have the touch?"

"Do I have what it takes? Just barely. I felt rather good about it—well, until this happened."

"Well, enjoy the ride. I'll give you a little tour of the potential markets we can find up here if that's all right."

Mutt tapped my shoulder to get my attention. He pointed to a single mobile home on the right of us as we passed by. I read the sign. The single word posted on a temporary pole read *BAR*.

"See that?" he said. "The way to an oilie's heart is through his beer, and the way to our prosperity is through that bar."

"Why don't you call on them Monday on your first official day," I said. "This activity out here is a target rich field of endeavor. I bet you know others out here."

"I'm pointing them out as we go along," he replied. "I've known Stanton for maybe three years out here. I wanted to work for you and him because I saw you were missing a lot of opportunities from people begging for some decent suppliers."

"You're saying I could cut you loose and stand back?"

"I would do my best work on the fly."

"You're supposed to be my assistant."

"As many targets as we have out here," Mutt said, "I can help you best by calling on the one's you haven't found, yet. I already know who they are."

I stuck my head outside the truck's passenger window to check my nosebleed in the right-side rearview mirror. I pulled out my tissue cork. The wind caught it and it flew out of my hand. I waited for a gush of blood, but it was clotted and stable.

"You going to fly again?" he asked.

"Nope. I'm done." I pondered a moment the reasons for my delayed mishap. "I only went up to 4,500 feet in altitude. That's more than 3,000 feet above the ground out where we were. A change of 3,000 feet up then back down in less than an hour is all it took to cause a sinus bleed. If I fly as an airline passenger, I'm going to be in trouble."

Mutt continued to drive us up the Northwest Expressway to Okarche, continually pointing out prospects along the short thirty miles we were on the highway. Possibilities were everywhere. Right away I understood why we needed to hire more good people.

When we arrived at our destination, I let my assistant work his magic on our prospective customer. While I stayed in the truck to make sure I didn't shake a clot loose, I rehearsed the exciting story I would tell Suzy about my new assistant and my day of flying. I feared that Suzy would discover that I was battling depression again.

After only15 minutes, Mutt came back with a signed order from the new customer that Stanton and I feared would be a challenge. Expressing my surprise and delight, his only comment was, "That's why you hired me, isn't it?"

48

THAT EVENING AT SUZY'S GUEST house, we discussed the day's events. Mine were full of big happenings. Hers were full of Sean incidents. The frustration of motherhood hung like a black shroud over our evening. We were both depressed.

Suzy had a forceful suggestion that I should go back to the VA Hospital in Oklahoma City to see about my sinus condition. I was reluctant. I had visited twice since leaving active duty. Each time I grew worse than before my arrival. I hated the cigarette smoke I had to endure in the waiting rooms, and I hated the smokers for making me sicker with each visit. But I listened to Suzy and made my appointment the next morning, which in the best bureaucratic fashion was scheduled over a month away. In the meantime, I worked with a growing team of employees, visited Sean and Suzy every evening, and remained good to my word.

I arrived at my VA appointment the first day after Independence Day. The morning's 7:00 a.m. reporting time, 8:00 a.m. roll call, 9:00 a.m. announcement of appointment times and physician assignments, ended with my 11:45 a.m. scheduled appointment getting delayed over an hour past my lunchtime. All the while veterans of all wars smoked, played checkers, read *Reader's Digest,* and smoked some more. Finally, my name came up, and I eagerly left the cloud of secondhand smoke to the lungs of the afternoon's patients.

My doctor greeted me with the same lack of enthusiasm as I had for the VA. I hoped he was as hungry as I was and would hurry through my exam. The man was under six feet tall, in his late sixties, and as dynamic as a salted slug. He shared my desire to be gone.

I told him my story of flying again one year after my Air Force grounding and of the nosebleed that surprised me, since I only went up to 4500 feet. He listened to my sad tale, scribbled a few notes, and took a few peeks to compare my real nose to my verbal description. After a few questions I had answered a hundred times before when I was still flying, he dismissed me by handing me my chart and saying, "We'll be in touch."

"Before you go," I said, hoping to stop his exit. "Last year my flight surgeon prescribed some Maalox antacid for me. Could I get a prescription for that?"

"Buy it yourself," he said. His impatience was obvious.

"I can do that?"

"Yes."

"I don't need permission?"

"No, you don't need permission. Where did you hear that?"

"Well, the Air Force required that pilots get permission before even taking an aspirin."

"Just go to the drug store and buy it. You don't need permission." The doctor walked out of my exam room, leaving me to wait again. For what, I couldn't tell.

After 15 minutes, a male nurse came to my exam room with a handful of papers. He went through a few sign-out procedures and handed me three prescriptions. One was for Sudafed, a decongestant. The second was for ampicillin. The last prescription was something I couldn't read, the nurse couldn't pronounce, and for what purpose neither of us could decipher.

"You take these to the pharmacy, and they will fill them for free."

That sounded good, so, after he dismissed me, I headed to a pharmacy apparently hidden from any new veteran in the system. I asked more than one person its whereabouts to no avail. I finally spied another harried doctor approaching and cornered him for directions. He was surprisingly upbeat and helpful. It made me wish he was my doctor next time if I ever visited again.

I located the pharmacy only to discover that I had to take a number. There were close to a hundred veterans waiting ahead of me. I talked to a veteran of the VA system who patiently explained that the whole process would take another hour or more of waiting before my prescription would be filled, then I would wait for my name to be called. I left the building and took my prescriptions with me.

This was my third visit to the VA hospital. I vowed it would be my last. To my surprise, at the end of the workday, when I stopped by my apartment to change clothes, I had a call from my father. He called me occasionally when I got a letter of importance. I was still using my parents' address as my home of record.

"*You have a letter from the VA,*" Dad said. "*Do you want me to open it?*"

"Sure, go ahead and read me the gist of it if it's worth reading." I continued to change my wardrobe as he read.

"*Have you been going to the VA hospitals?*"

"Yeah. I just got back from my third visit about five hours ago. I don't think I'll go again. It's a nightmare."

"*Well, this letter informs you that you are now a disabled veteran and have a thirty percent disability rating for sinusitis. It means you're getting a whopping eighty-nine dollars a month for the rest of your life.*"

I had no idea. I didn't know I had made an application. In fact, I know I didn't. Now I understood why I was mandated, after separating from active duty, to make those first two appointments. The VA had done all the work for me.

"Dad, I can't believe it. Should I be glad or embarrassed."

"*I would say that eighty-nine bucks a month beats a kick in the head.*"

"I don't think I deserve it."

"*Nonsense, son. Of course, you do. You served, learned a skill, and your equipment injured you.*"

"At least you got shot at in the Pacific. I did nothing."

"*Don't forget that a lot did less than you did, but all of you gave up something to serve.*"

"I don't know."

"Are you a veterinarian today, like you planned?"

"No."

"You gave up something for your country, then, didn't you?"

"Yes, I did."

"Then accept the disability. Be proud of it. You earned it."

After pondering his words, I told him for the first time about my flight the month before with Brad Kilty and its aftermath with a nosebleed.

"That's why I was at the VA today, so I guess you're right. I'll change my attitude about this windfall."

My father chuckled, then confessed to me that he had never been to the VA Hospital. *"You had smokers to contend with. My generation had alcoholics to go with the smokers. It was a tough time for both our generations of veterans. Despite their problems, we need to show all them our respect. Don't forget that. And that includes you. You served your country well, son. Don't be ashamed. Be proud."*

"Thanks."

"Go see Suzy. Tell her of your day. Let her be proud of you, too."

"Good night, Dad."

He hung up the telephone with a simple, *"uh-huh."*

Dad faced alcohol. We faced drugs. I wasn't about to steal his thunder.

49

STANTON AND I HIRED MORE people, just as Luther "Mutt" Muttencherry had predicted. We had to move to bigger offices further north in the identical twin tower east of Victor Jensen's plush office. Now in July, Luther and I relegated our work no longer to the field but to our desks. I was flying another desk chair, just like I did during my last months at my squadron in Laredo. The difference now was that I had my own corner office. My view looked east and south with a splendid panorama of Oklahoma City's downtown with Oklahoma City University's Gold Star Memorial Building in the foreground. To the east was Northwest Expressway, already giving life to several oil-funded office towers, either under construction or in the planning stages. It was my choice to choose this view because it reminded me of my high school days when I often took a date to Baptist Hospital. We could take the elevator to a specific upper floor with an oversized east facing bay window. At night it was a cheap and safe place to take an impressionable 15 or 16-year-old girl and introduce her to the possibilities of life in the big city. An experience of holding hands while viewing cars on the highway and the lights of downtown made affordable those romantic gestures a young man could win points for.

My last experience at the VA reaped one other benefit for me. For five years on active duty, all my medical needs had been taken care of. Going to a doctor was often an order. The Air Force paid me to fly. It also provided me housing and on-base facilities like the commissary, base exchange, and a package store. The only thing I spent money on were toys. Everything else was free stuff. It was like I never left home. College life had been the same way. So now, 28 years later, I was having an epiphany. I didn't have to ask permission to do anything. I could do it myself. When the VA doctor told me to go get Maalox myself, he was trying to educate me, not talk down to me. Instead of those three on base facilities, I had hundreds of shops to go to in the civilian world. Instead of a commissary, I had a hundred grocery stores, many with better prices. Rather than a base exchange, there were dozens of stores in the malls and in places like Sears, Wards, and Penny's. If you needed a package store, there were scores of liquor stores to visit. For the first time in my life, I realized that I could do what I wanted, anytime I wanted. I was elated at my new understanding and embarrassed at my 28-year-old naivete.

If I could do what I wanted anytime I wanted, there was only one thing now I wanted. I called Suzy on Friday afternoon and told her to get a babysitter and to be ready at five o'clock. Stanton and I were now on even footing. We made decisions together. He was no longer leading the charge by himself. That also meant that the man who had helped him reach the next tier of success no longer asked to go home early. I did as I pleased, and he never questioned. It helped that we had hired well.

After stopping at my bleak apartment and cleaning up for my five o'clock rendezvous, I drove my Porsche over to the Jensen's house and knocked on the front door. Mrs. Jensen greeted me in her consistently elegant style. She dressed like a soap opera star in a beautiful crisp pastel green cotton dress, perfectly fitted with matching shoes.

"Hello, Rob!" she said. Her manner was enthusiastic whenever I chose to arrive at her front door. "Come in. I'm afraid Suzy's still out back. She dropped Sean off just a few minutes ago. Do you need to see her first?"

"Not at all," I said. "I was actually hoping to see you and Mister Jensen first."

"So how is work?" Suzy's father was coming from the kitchen, a lady's apron hanging loosely from his neck.

"We're moved in fine at our new offices. Sorry I haven't stopped by to see you, yet. Moving an office is a nightmare."

"You wanted to see us first?" Mr. Jensen asked. "Come in the kitchen with us. I literally have something cooking in here."

He had some sort of beef in a large frying pan with grease popping everywhere off onto the range. He flinched when a fleck of grease popped on his cheek. Mrs. Jensen seemed unflappable amid her husband's making her kitchen into a greasy mess. He eventually turned off the fire and put the meat somewhere else. I was looking away at the time, for fear of hot grease flying into my eyes. Sean, in his highchair, was already moved out of range of the hot oil fusillade. I remained next to him and waited for the all clear.

"There now," he said. "I'll put that aside, and we can chat. So... you want to speak to us. Did I hear that right?"

I looked at Mrs. Jensen, who seemed genuinely puzzled. Her husband stood there like a man who has something more important to do.

"With your permission, I will ask your daughter tonight if she will marry me as early as possible."

I expected joy and ecstasy. Instead, I got a question from Mr. Jensen.

"How soon is 'as soon as possible?'"

"I mean it literally. Tomorrow would be nice."

I could tell they didn't expect that answer. The two stared at each other. The quiet was uncomfortable. I laid a hand on the top of Sean's head, patting him cautiously. Mrs. Jensen began to smile. I turned to the mister and waited.

"Yes!" They spoke in unison, as if they rehearsed before I came.

"Okay then. I'll go see your daughter. Don't tell her the obvious... and by the way, sir. Do you know of an adoption attorney I could use?"

"Oh, my! That's wonderful," she said. "I know of one our neighbor used."

"We'll find you the best, I'm sure," said Mr. Jensen. "Let's wait and see what Suzy's answer is first."

If I was worried that he was still was angry over how I ignored his daughter several months before, I was soon reassured by the big smile he faced me with.

"I will let you two know how it goes. Now, if I may be excused?"

Mr. Jensen added one more comment as I started to the backyard door. "If Suzy says 'yes,' then you may call me Victor."

"Thank you, sir." I kissed the top of Sean's wiggly head before I left.

50

SUZY WAS LIKE HER MOTHER in many ways. I feared the clothing bill for us would be quite high. I didn't care because each time I came to her door, I was taken aback by her sense of style. She knew how to make my heart melt and loins rally. I suppose every man, truly in love with the right woman, sees her as gorgeous. Suzy looked stunning, whether wearing rags and no makeup or, like now, dressed to kill. She seemed happy and curious when she welcomed me at her guest house door.

"So, what's the occasion?" she asked.

"Big news at the office," I said, wearing my liar face.

I'm not sure it was convincing, but she played along. She never waited for an explanation when I invited her to dinner. She never asked how she should dress. I never failed to match her style. Coming from a military career of wearing flight suits all day and night, I found to my surprise that wearing current fashions was fun with Suzy. Shortly after Stanton and I hit it big, I began major upgrades to my wardrobe. Tonight, I wore a gray summer weight suit with a matching vest and a new fashionably wide tie with a matching pocket handkerchief.

Suzy was stunning in an all-white knee length dress with a point of pastel green lace at her naval rising to cover an empire waste bodice. When she turned to grab her small purse, she revealed her backless dress held on by two narrow lace straps. Like most date nights we had, she wore shoes I had not seen before. Tonight, they were high heels that matched the pastel green of her lace.

"I can't wait to hear what happened at work. Give me a hint."

"Not until we have drinks in hand," I said. She looked at me in mock irritation. I sneered back with my best face.

I walked Suzy to my car and opened the door for her like a gentleman. Her parents unexpectedly stepped onto their front porch, each holding a glass of champagne, and lifted their glasses in a toast to us. Before I could close her door, she asked me, "Did you see my parents first?"

"Yes. I drove up and your mother was on the front porch, so I parked here to talk to her. Before it was over, Sean and your dad came out as well."

The answer satisfied her curiosity, but I took note that she was a good detective—a keen observer of details. We drove east on the street to Pennsylvania Avenue, then turned south toward Penn Square Mall.

"Are we going back to the Magic Pan?"

"Oh, not again. I have unpleasant memories of a boy gone stupid there."

Suzy laughed at my self-deprecating humor. We had long since dismissed our spat as a funny story and unimportant. "Then where?"

"You'll see." I said. "It's new."

We drove into the massive parking lot for Penn Square Mall, an open-air mall undergoing stiff competition from two enclosed malls already in Oklahoma City. We entered the open-air portion and walked east to where the older portion of the massive mall was now enclosed. We went through the doors into cool air and echoes of customers, not evident in the open air.

"Are you familiar with the Red Eagle Room at Valgene's?"

"I hear it's good," she said.

I stopped abruptly and made her turn to face me. I now had her positioned where I could see the façade of the city's most notable jewelry store. Established in 1892, B.C. Clark Jewelers was known for its radio and television jingle so ubiquitous at Christmas, that it was evolving into a secular Christmas carol all its own.

"Come this way," I said. I took her hand and marched her into the store where a nice lady met us with a surprise for Suzy.

"Miss Alexander," she said. "I'm Joan. We've been expecting you. Mister Amity asked us to show you some items he hoped might meet your needs."

Suzy did not flinch. She turned to me, not letting go of my hand. "Is this a proposal?"

"Yes, it is," I replied. She kissed me lightly on the lips. I took her other hand. I kissed her more forcefully on her lips. She let go of my hands, wrapped her arms around my shoulders and smashed her lips into mine in a most welcoming lip lock.

"How romantic you are. We better go in there before I change my mind."

Suzy followed Joan's lead to a counter where a specially selected tray of diamonds and rings waited under the glass for our examination.

"Do we have a wedding date, yet?" Suzy asked.

"You haven't said 'yes,' yet."

"Yes! Now, do we have a date?"

"It depends upon whether the ring fits or needs resizing. How about tomorrow? Is that soon enough?"

Her eyes expressed shock, then progressed into a devil may care look. "What about Sean?"

"If we must, we'll take Sean with us. I'm tired of waiting for your probationary period to be over."

Joan patiently listened to us banter, smiling at each comment we made. I had spoken to her earlier to set up the showing and generously tipped her, asking if she could uncork a bottle of champagne for us as the bride-to-be perused the items I had selected. Suzy was still settling down as Joan uncorked a bottle. The pop of the cork caused Suzy to jump. The unflappable Suzy Alexander was suddenly unnerved. Our hostess poured a half-full flute of bubbly for her. The flute shook in her hand after she took it from Joan.

"You, sir?" Joan asked me.

"Of course," I replied. "You can give me a full glass."

Joan smiled and poured a second flute. As she handed it to me, I noted that it was a fine cut crystal Waterford Champagne flute. "Could you box these up after we make our selection, please? I think they will make a nice memento, don't you think?"

"I already have the box ready for you." She pointed to a table behind her.

"Clever girl you are," I said. She was a pro at this, which I appreciated.

Suzy worked her way through each of the nearly 25 wedding ring sets I knew she would like. I had selected several different diamonds, based upon their quality and size. I was beginning to feel like an *Early Oily*. Joan could almost read my mind. *Spare no expense for my pretty little lady!* Then the shock that all men eventually experience happened.

Suzy stood up, looked at me, and then said to Joan, "I don't like any of these," and stepped to the next counter to look for her own choices.

At first, I was aghast. Then I settled down. I quickly downed my flute and asked for a refill.

"That's an excellent idea," Joan said. She tried to reassure me. "This is usually what happens... but without the champagne."

I worked hard resisting the temptation to scream. This was now my failed attempt to create the most romantic proposal any man has ever achieved for his future bride. It was a total shamble. I found a chair and sat down. Joan handed me my second glass, even fuller than the first.

"I'm going to talk to Miss Alexander," she said. "You stay right here and relax. You two are going to be incredibly happy before we get through, okay?"

Although it sounded condescending, I knew Joan was trying her best to make this moment end up a happy beginning to a happy marriage. I nodded my reluctant agreement and sat alone to ponder my fate. On the good side, we were not going to have a stressful big wedding. Suzy had said that once was enough for her. Since I was best man for that wedding, I totally agreed. On the downside, I had studied a lot about diamonds and jewelry. I knew what she liked. I was disappointed that she showed no appreciation for my good taste. Instead, I sat and sulked.

I had time to think about my own parents and their seemingly irritating behavior. They frequently hurled comments at each other, as I grew up, that made me uncomfortable. Few couples divorced in those days. The prospect of that ever happening to my parents petrified me. I was prone to depression enough as it was. I would desperately try to wipe those thoughts from my mind. The subtle gigs at each other continued during all my formative years.

Over time, I replaced my fears with irritation and later acceptance. I knew they loved each other, but I vowed I would never be that way with my own wife, certainly not in front of children. Now I sat alone, starting to understand that it was a part of the experience of becoming two souls into one. It didn't mean marching in lockstep. I remained composed, although my brain wanted to complain.

I looked up to see Suzy, sitting down in front of a counter and motioning me to look with her. I got up like a sore loser and sauntered over, trying to not look too mopey. Her smile was unusually bright and animated. She held out the back of her left hand. She said nothing. Her expression of excitement said it all. I reached out and took her hand for a close look, knowing that both ladies were watching me carefully for a reaction. My shock was unexpected. It was a better choice than anything I had found and stunningly beautiful and blessedly not in the style of her mother's wedding rings. The large diamond on the engagement ring was bigger than a carat, but smaller than one I would have chosen. It sat in a yellow gold setting bridged on each side by tapered side baguette set diamonds. The wedding band held the same inset diamonds over the entire circumference. It was too classy to look like oil patch overkill. I looked at Joan, then quickly at Suzy.

"I like it," I said. I was trying to remain calm.

"I love it," said Suzy. Joan remained silent.

"Does it fit?" I asked.

"Perfectly."

"You still want to marry me?"

"Yes!"

"Joan, write it up. Suzy, leave that on your finger and have Joan box up the wedding ring."

I was about to learn my first lesson. Suzy looked at me with loving irritation and took off both rings. She handed them both to Joan and instructed her to box them up together.

"You're not going to get engaged to me without a lot more style than that."

With that admonishment, I started to gain a better understanding of what went on with my parents.

"Suzy, I'm sorry. I forgot. You need this presented in a more formal way." I looked over at Joan and added, "Joan would you gift wrap that for me... or what would you suggest?"

"I'll put it in a nice box that will look better than anything wrapped up." Joan looked at Suzy. "I don't think you'll have it long enough to bother wrapping it first." Suzy met my glance with a wide grin.

Joan and I settled on an agreeable price, not helped at all by Suzy's insistent smile. There was no way we could have left without the rings. I would remember that the next time I got married.

51

RING SHOPPING AND PURCHASING HAPPENED so fast, we were early to our reservation at the Red Eagle Room for dinner. The oil boom meant the place was packed as usual. We chose to have a cocktail in the bar until our designated reservation time.

Oklahoma had odd laws on alcohol, which became more bizarre as the years moved forward. Oklahoma had been a dry state since statehood in 1907. The eastern Indian Territory had never allowed alcohol. The western Oklahoma Territory had nearly as many bars as people, many conveniently located on the eastern border for the thirsts of patrons in Indian Territory. With Oklahoma's statehood, the Indian and Democrat votes for alcohol prohibition prevailed. Fifty-two years of prohibition ended in 1959 by a vote of the people. All it took to get the vote of the people was to enforce the liquor laws. Liquor stores sprang up, but liquor by the drink was still unlawful. There was a way around it. Oklahoma allowed citizens to carry a bottle of alcohol into a bar or restaurant and have it served in mixed drinks for a fee.

Beer was banned, although you could buy non-intoxicating 3.2% beer. My high school friends found that drinking boatloads of beer with a 3.2% alcohol content was intoxicating. Our parents were wrong again.

Throughout the state in those years without liquor by the drink, citizens simply ignored the law. We called it *liquor by the wink.* More restaurants flaunted the law with each successive year. At first it was ordering the *special coffee.* The waiter would bring a coffee cup filled with your choice of wines. That was not too sophisticated. Oklahomans soon tired of that in favor of in-your-face violations of the law. It was great. There was no liquor tax during the era of *liquor by the wink.* It was the least expensive alcohol in the nation. It turned the oil boom into heady times for partiers. That's when the state decided a vote was necessary and began to enforce the laws. To combat that enforcement by state and local police, to get a drink, I needed a business card. The way it was explained to us, any undercover policeman was required by law to present their business card if it was requested. Obviously, if the business card said they were with the police department or any other law enforcement agency, the office was told that alcohol was not served there. I handed the Red Eagle Room bar maid my A-to-Z business card, and she cheerfully welcomed us into the world of misdemeanors.

"What can I get you two?" she asked. Her skirt was short and red. Her blouse was white and waist-length with enough cleavage exposed to make laying a drink on the table interesting. Suzy gave me a smile of impish acknowledgement of her assets.

"Champagne?" I asked.

"Let's save that for our table," Suzy replied. "For now, I will take a gin and tonic."

I asked for the same, and we both watched our bar maid parade past more oil men with similar stares to my own. Suzy giggled.

"She certainly knows how to walk."

"You can walk like that for me anytime."

"I just might," she said.

I was beginning to sense that Suzy was never going to be shy when it came to being seductive. My good fortune.

A waiter called us to our table more than a half hour before our reservation. We carried our drinks with us. He politely held the chair for Suzy while I sat down. The chair assist gesture puzzled me. The carpets in restaurants made the gentleman's chair assist an impossible task. The chair legs are stuck on the carpet. The man puts his hands on the back of her chair, and nothing ever moves, until he releases his grip and steps to his seat. Then the man and woman simultaneously hoist their chairs into the air slightly and scoot forward to their desired position. I recalled how my parents had decided years ago to never do that courtesy. It was too ineffective to make any common sense. They were both happier.

With menus in hand, we glanced over the offerings. She commented that the lobster tail looked especially appealing. I looked for it only to find little description, not even a price. It was odd and intimidating to hold a menu without prices. I guessed it was a new way to gouge the oilmen and other would-be bigshots. I wasn't falling for that. I fully intended to ask the prices before I ordered anything. Suzy continued to thumb through her menu, stopping at a page with an insert and running her finger down a list of wines.

"Oh! Let's get the 1959 Dom Perignon," she said. "I definitely want that champagne."

I looked for my own insert but had none. My mind was confused. *Oh well. Get her what she wants.* She looked at the insert, loose so as not to be evidence of alcohol printed on the actual menu.

Our waiter stepped into view. "May I interest you in a bottle of wine, sir?"

"Yes," I said. "We would like the... let's see... oh, yes, a bottle of your, I think '59 Dom Perignon Champagne."

The waiter's eyes grew wide in astonishment, which puzzled me. He recovered enough to ask a question.

"Sir, may I ask. Is this for a special occasion?"

"Yes, it is. We're going to be engaged in just a few minutes."

"Very good, sir!" His manner was enthusiastic. I looked over at Suzy, whose face was now flushed a beet red.

The waiter ran from our table in haste.

"Are you sure you want to order that champagne?" Suzy asked, now in her whisper mode.

"Sure. It's a special occasion. That's what you want, isn't it?"

"It's just...."

Our waiter was back to interrupt. He looked embarrassed. His eyes suddenly looked at Suzy's menu, then at mine.

"Sir, forgive me for having to ask, but our manager wanted to confirm. Have you seen the price of the Dom Perignon you have ordered?"

"No. It wasn't on my menu. How much is it?" Suzy squirmed in her seat.

"The 1959 Dom Perignon is $8,800, sir."

"Well, that's a little high," I replied. My deadpan expression was met by our waiter's face in mixed horror and humiliation.

"My apologies to you, sir and to you, ma'am." He reached for our menus, examined them carefully, and handed the opposite menu to each of us. "I accidently gave the lady the gentlemen's menu... the one with the prices."

"You didn't have prices?" Suzy asked, almost shouting at me.

"No."

"I was joking about the champagne... and the lobster, too. Did you see the price on that?"

I looked at my menu. The lobster was priced at a point I imagined meant it was cooked in 1959 Dom Perignon Champagne sauce. We looked at our horrified waiter. In a spontaneous act, we both broke out in uncontrolled, cacophonous laughter. Our waiter made a hasty retreat from our table. We stopped briefly, bothered by our waiter's chagrin, but continued with un-stoppable bouts of hilarity for several more minutes.

Another man approached our table, interrupting our lack of decorum. The man dressed in a black suit identified himself as the manager of the restaurant.

"Excuse me for interrupting, but may I be of assistance? I want to make sure everything is all right. How may I help?"

I tried to compose myself enough to speak and to explain. "I assure you that we are fine. There was a little mix-up in the menus. Our waiter may be a little upset, but we certainly are not."

"I will be glad to get you another waiter."

"Oh, please don't do that," Suzy said. "This is our engagement dinner, and we would like to continue with our waiter if he will have us. He is a pleasant addition to our meal."

"I agree," I said. "We came for a nice meal, not to mortify your staff."

"I take it then, that you will not be drinking the 1959 Dom Perignon."

I gave Suzy a quizzical glance. She shook her head vigorously. "No," I said.

"Could we interest you in another champagne for your celebration?"

I pulled out the wine insert and read the list of bottles available and their prices. "Bring us a bottle of Veuve Clicquot. That's my favorite champagne, anyway."

Suzy gave her enthusiastic approval.

"Yes, sir. Right away. If it is acceptable to you, we will charge you only half for this champagne, with our apologies."

"That's not necessary, but thank you."

"Happy engagement to you both."

The manager left us to speculate whether our uneasy waiter would return. We started to chuckle again, when our waiter returned, his tail figuratively tucked between his legs. He carried an ice bucket on a stand, with a bottle bearing the yellow label of my favorite brut champagne and two flutes. With laughter suppressed, we welcomed our man back with gratitude.

"I apologize again."

"Please don't." I said. "We asked for you to come back but not to hear that. What is your name, by the way?"

"Johnston, sir."

"Mister Johnston, we are glad you are here."

"Just Johnston. That's my first name." His manner became a little more relaxed as he went to work opening our bottle of champagne. With an extra bit of flare, he popped the cork with just enough overflow to add drama without significant waste.

He set the glasses before us and expertly poured each glass three quarters full. After setting the bottle back into the ice, he quietly slipped away.

We picked up our glasses and held them out to each other.

"Suzy Alexander, will you marry me?" I clicked my glass to hers with my right hand and with the other presented her with an open box containing her chosen wedding set.

"You already asked me that, but the ring is a real surprise."

We started to laugh again, which brought us to the attention of the diners sitting near us. They raised their own wine glasses and vocalized their congratulations.

"Did you say yes? I'm certain the table next to us heard that."

"Yes! I will marry you. The sooner, the better."

52

SUZY AND I SOON FOUND out that getting married was harder than we wanted. Getting a marriage license, something not done every day, required a birth certificate, a blood test, and a waiting period. We didn't know any of the rules. We made more than one extra trip back to the Oklahoma County Courthouse. Although notable locations in Oklahoma, such as Durant, managed to speed things up, we elected to delay our wedding a few extra days. Suzy was more upset than I was.

After acquiring our marriage license over a two-day period, we sat down to discuss who would officiate. We learned judges don't conduct weddings in Oklahoma. Turning to our parents, who all still went to church, unlike us, we arranged for the Jensens' assistant pastor to do the honors.

"Do you have a best man?" Mr. Jensen asked.

"No."

"You know you need to pay the minister something."

"I do?"

"Weren't you best man at John and Suzy's wedding?"

"Yes, but John gave me a checklist, and I just followed the list. I did give an envelope to the minister. I didn't know what it was. I just followed orders."

"Good Lord, I pray for my daughter. Give me strength."

"Is it that bad," I asked.

"I guess I'll be your best man and walk your bride down the aisle."

"Maybe I should ask my dad."

"Excellent choice, son. And see if your father thinks a hundred bucks for the preacher is enough."

"Yes, sir. I will."

It got worse. Suzy informed her parents that she wasn't walking down the aisle. Instead, she preferred the quiet intimacy of the minister's office.

"This is not my first wedding," she said. "I just want it to get done with a minimum of fanfare."

"But Honey, we southern girls don't get married unless it's done properly," replied Mrs. Jensen. Tears of shock ran down her cheeks. "Surely you understand that?"

"I do, but I did a wedding already. End of discussion."

Mrs. Jensen turned to me. She started to speak, but her husband cut her off. "Mother, that's enough! Suzy's a grown woman now, with a child. Step back a bit."

She took his suggestion. Suzy got her way. Now we had to pick a day. Our Oklahoma Marriage License was good for ten days. After that, we had to reapply and repeat the process. It was Wednesday with nine days left. We had to get the job done by the first of August. The Reverend Remington agreed to two dates when he could officiate. Friday, July 26th was his first choice, followed by Wednesday, July 31st. After thinking about the logistics involved with work, care for Sean, and scheduling a honeymoon, we decided the last day of July was our only option. It was one additional week to wait.

Work was getting interesting, so I dove with enthusiasm into my job with our new hires. It served me as suitable sublimation until my wedding day. I assigned Suzy to plan our getaway. I was in my military element, working hard, giving orders, and assigning responsibilities. It was the best antidepressant around.

Stanton and I garnered some attention outside of Oklahoma the month before, after a magazine article singled out A-to-Z Oilfield Services as the best service provider in the Anadarko Basin. The quotes and descriptions of our business model made us out to be organizational marvels of efficiency. Our telephones began to ring more urgently and frequently. Finally, we got the call that we couldn't ignore. A larger nationwide company wanted to buy us. The initial proposal was incredible, with an offer of a cash buyout in the millions of dollars if we continued management of A-to-Z for a period of one year. It sounded good but required a lot of preparation before we could meet with the other company to discuss the offer. With the crazy prices that oil companies offered every day in the oil industry, we knew that with good representation in negotiations, we could get much more than their initial offer. However, we had to act with urgency.

Stanton had the most to gain. He was older and willing to slow down from his urgent pace. I realized that that was why he hired me. He wanted to slow down. Then I bought half interest in a well-run, but poorly marketed, oil field service provider. The net worth of the company skyrocketed overnight. That's part of what made the oil patch such a crazy place. Men could be broke on Monday, millionaires on Wednesday, and go bust again before the weekend. We had to figure out how to do the smart thing and not the stupid.

Suzy was excited and suspicious at the same time.

"What about the wedding? Are we still on?"

"Of course, we are."

"What if you have to hop on a plane and go to a meeting? You said time was critical."

"They will understand."

"I won't."

I was left with no doubts about the importance she placed on our wedding date. How could I help but understand? This was a woman living in a borrowed space, existing in exile from her friends, and caring for a toddler she dearly loved. Having been in this state for nearly a year, she had to be on the brink of giving up. I had to make the dates work.

On the other hand, Stanton was depending upon me to help bring this deal off. With millions of dollars at stake, Stanton was putting unusual pressure on me to perform and to prepare for negotiations. We needed time to talk with the team of acquisition attorneys experienced with handling these negotiations. We calculated that our legal costs would garner twice their fee in added sales price. Remembering that time was money to the buyer, too, we had hopes that the deal could happen before the end of August. How our books looked would make all the difference. Mary at the front desk had been a wonder of keeping records. Her value to the company rose every day with negotiations pending.

I was stuck between two inflexible forces that did not want just a piece of me. They both wanted all of me. I finally made my choice, not between Stanton or Suzy, but between the urgency of getting married versus the possibility of becoming a multimillionaire. Surely Suzy would understand.

53

"I'M GETTING MARRIED NEXT WEDNESDAY, whether you are there or not."

This illogical and impossible threat made it hard to talk rationally with Suzy about the situation. Our whole future was in the cards.

"All I'm saying is that there is a chance I may be called to do some last-minute negotiations around the time of our wedding." I was confused why she would not see the long-term benefits of being flexible to realize the potential for this million-dollar sale.

She had had it with her backyard guest house and single motherhood. I knew the issue was the same one we'd clashed over in the spring. I called Hal, only to learn that he was recently married and happily test flying the still-in-development F-15 Eagle air superiority fighter in his new assignment at Edwards Air Force Base. The man knew how to redeem his career and capture a plum assignment. As a married man, he already sounded different over the phone.

"You still hoping to kick some ass, or have you settled down?"

"No, I'm not calling you to go on another fool's adventure with me. I just need to share an issue I'm having with Suzy. I want your opinion."

"It's only about women issues with us. I highly recommend marriage."

"We have a disagreement."

"Oh, boy."

"I have a chance to land a sale that will secure our future forever, but I may have to skip our wedding… I mean *postpone* our wedding."

"Do you have options?"

"Not really."

"Oh, come on! You always *have options."*

"I have a million-dollar sale at stake, Freed."

"Or you have a marriage at stake it sounds like. Look, Amity. When I was flying in Route Pack Six near Hanoi on a mission, I had a chance to bag a MiG-17. That was going to be my million bucks. It would be an easy gun shot when I caught up to him. Getting an air-to-air kill would make me one shit hot fighter pilot. I wanted it like nothing else. Then my GIB reminded me that we were bingo fuel. I needed gas ASAP. My choices were only two. Get the MiG then crash for lack of fuel, probably get captured, likely get the hell beat out of me. You name it. Or I could go get me some gas and try again another day. There were other opportunities, I assure you. More MiGs than I ever want to see again. What do you think I chose? I'll let you decide."

"It's several million bucks. Suzy only has to wait another week."

"What if the deal takes longer?"

"It probably won't."

"Now that is convincing. By the way. Why did you call me?"

"I wanted advice."

"You wanted me to say okay."

"That, too."

"Then I'll give you some advice. It's harder to find a good wife than it is to earn a million bucks."

"I'm not sure I understand."

"Good gracious, Amity. Just because you don't understand a premise does not mean it is invalid."

"I suppose you're right."

"I need to get back to Lisa, but here's what I'll say. The next time you call me wanting to go kick some ass, instead I'm going to take you out and kick your ass. You need a bay window installed on your stomach."

"Why do I need a bay window?"

"So you can see what's happening around you, while you have your head up your ass."

He hung up the phone on that note. He sounded surprisingly ticked off.

Then I got a call from Stanton. I knew Hell must have frozen over. The perfect disaster was planned for me by Stanton, our buyer, and fate.

"Rob, I know you're getting married Wednesday, but I need us both in Dallas on Tuesday. We may be there a while. It's critical that you be there."

"You've put me in a bit of a pickle here, Stanton."

"What time is your wedding again?"

"Noon."

"That's workable. You can make it."

He was lying. I was certain of it. Nothing ever works out as planned, but I assured him I would be there. I stopped by Suzy's guest house to let her know of my plans and to assure her of Stanton's promise. Was that lying, too?

"Isn't that cutting it a little close?" she asked. "You can't be late for our wedding. Our minister has 30 minutes booked, and then he must leave. Our parents will be there."

"I'll be on time, I promise." I wasn't certain it would work. *But fighter pilots are risk takers.* Not exactly the tip Hal gave me.

My next stop was to see my parents and explain my plans and its tight schedule. I had not told them of our impending sale of A-to-Z. My mother was ecstatic at my good luck and success. My father was more skeptical.

"Aren't you getting married Wednesday?"

"Of course."

"You're cutting it close, don't you think?"

"No. I've got it all worked out."

"What does Suzy say?"

"She is looking forward to Wednesday. She said she would be there."

"How sweet," Mom said.

"Why do I feel that there is more to this conversation?" asked Dad.

"Well, there may have been more emphasis on her part. Perhaps different words."

"I'm sure you will do fine," said Mom. "We're just so proud of you."

I wondered if I deserved the praise.

54

STANTON WAS ON MY SIDE. I sat in my office looking out toward downtown, a gloomy drizzle putting a damper on my enthusiasm for this Monday morning. Stanton sat in a plush chair across from me. We went over the final preparations for our meeting in Dallas with our buyers. Our lawyers had been busy coordinating everything on our behalf. Our plan was to leave tomorrow at noon for a five o'clock meeting. If all went well, we would sign our agreement that evening, and I could return home or stay for a celebration with the new owners. I opted to stay overnight only if the meeting extended late into the night. We were all set. The employees of our expanding team were off on their missions into the oil patch. We sat back for a moment and smugly pondered our futures.

"Everything is going like clockwork," Stanton said. "I think it will work out fine for you. Your warm body will be in Dallas where I need you, and then your rich warm body will be at your wedding where your bride needs you."

Odd coming from a man who had grown up on traditional Indian time in his formative years. The Army had cured him—or so I hoped.

Our assistants Lily and Mutt were humming along as we hoped. They were further adding value to A-to-Z with the people we hired upon their recommendations. They had been out in the real-world oil patch. They knew all the saints and all the sinners. We had collected more than a dozen saints so far to spread the message of our company that would take care of customers fairly and promptly. This collection of good people made our value much higher in the eyes of our buyers. We bent over backwards to make sure none of our saint-like employees left. Of course, we weren't leaving just yet, either. We were part of the package they were buying.

I RETURNED TO MY DEPRESSING apartment that evening, noting I had a message on my telephone answering machine. It was Hal again, asking me to call him back. He had forgotten to tell me something. I called him immediately because I was pressed for time to get to Suzy's guest house.

"What's this all about?" I asked when Hal picked up his phone.

"Hi Rob. I'm glad you called me back." His voice sounded somber. *"I forgot to tell you of some unwelcome news I received when I checked in with my flight surgeon here at Edwards."*

"Go on," I said cautiously.

"I've got some sort of Leukemia."

I was shocked into silence. I agonized over what to say.

"They caught it early."

"This upsets me, Hal. I'm so sorry. Any idea where this started. I thought only children developed Leukemia."

"Air Force is not talking, but the doctors sure are. Remember that defoliant spray we used in Vietnam? It's called agent something or other. I don't remember, but the doctors told me that they are seeing more Leukemia cases then there should be. Nearly all cases were Vietnam veterans during the years they sprayed the stuff."

"Are you grounded from flying?"

"It's pending. Right now, it's just a wait and see."

"What are you going to do?"

"Right now, it's light duty scheduling flights and keeping proficient on the Link Trainers."

"You can't fly? I'm sorry, man. That must be killing you."

"I'm not worried about flying right now. I'm worried about my marriage. I can

live *without flying, but Lisa is better than any airplane, Rob. That's what I'm more afraid of losing."*

"Your priorities are in the right order then."

"Absolutely!" Hal was silent for a moment. I waited. *"I know you have to go now, but I wanted you to know. Savor the here and now,* mi amigo. *Semper Fi!"*

"Maybe that should be Semper *Fly!* Here's hoping you're back on flying status real soon."

We hung up. The unpredictable nature of life hit me hard. At first, I was not overly upset about being grounded the year before. I was surprised, however, to discover how much I missed flying and missed being active duty again. Had I made a mistake? Hal by contrast lived for flying, except that things had changed for him, too. He sounded like he loved to fly but now did not live to fly. In only a few weeks, Lisa, Hal's new bride, had turned his priorities upside down. It was like losing a friend and gaining a totally responsible big brother. My youth was being ripped out of my life one friend at a time.

I DREADED SEEING SUZY THE night before I was to leave on a mission certain to disappoint her. If big weddings were stressful, how did this one top the scale? It turned into a gut-wrenching and mind-numbing exercise. No one was happy, least of all Suzy. She met me at the door with her eyes to the ground and her excitement packed away. She held Sean in her arms. When I reached to take the toddler, she took a step back. Dollar signs and beautiful brides switched back and forth in my head. If Suzy was momentarily angry, I was temporarily insane. It was a terrible way to start a honeymoon.

We were going out to eat, with Sean tagging along. Was this our last meal? Her expression said it was. I chose a nice and inexpensive Chinese Restaurant on May Avenue because it was near to her place. It was a restaurant where the staff would not look down on a child capable of hurling food against their walls or on the floor. A man at the front desk welcomed us in fractured English and escorted us to a seat at the far back corner of the dining room. We came here frequently and liked the food. This was our table anytime Sean went with us. The darkly lit interior was predominately red curtains, red walls, with lots of cheap Chinese art and iconic images along the walls and on the tables as center pieces.

I unwaveringly ordered the same thing at this restaurant. If I wanted variety, I would go to another establishment, where the waiters had my standard order memorized, just like here. Once I found something good, I never wavered. Tonight was special, but Suzy gave every indication that it was not special for her. When our Chinese waiter, named Bob, took our order, it was a standard order for me, the same old Sweet and Sour Pork and Fried Rice. For Suzy, it was different. Tonight, she ordered Moo Goo Gai Pan, whatever that is? Suzy was tired. Her voice said all.

"I don't like to see you sad," I said. "I promise I will be on time."

I wanted to be truthful, but I was also capable of past immature and last-minute moves that I later regretted. I was impulsive. I feared I was capable of anything, even lying to myself. I began hearing my own voice in my head giving me hell.

Grow up for once. You're not some dumb jet jock carrying out pranks on people. You're supposed to be a responsible adult. You'll be a dad. What example am I going to show? Is my first major responsibility as a married man going to be skipping my own wedding... and after making a promise. Would John Alexander be ashamed of what I was doing to his widow?

I switched to a more tempting area, with the angel saying *don't miss the wedding* and the devil saying *think of the money you will make.* Each weighed heavily on my shoulders.

My life will be better, no matter which way I go. I win with a happy marriage. I win with a ton of money. Either one will make me happy. Money can find me another wife. So why should I care?

I care because I made a pledge of love and loyalty. I may be happy either way. But the selfish choice is a betrayal of Suzy. The selfless choice makes us both happy. Why would I ever think such evil thoughts?

I might be able to pull them both off if I'm lucky. That's what I need to do. I'll make them both work. We'll both be happy!

"Suzy, you need to relax. I'm leaving tomorrow for Dallas. I will be back for our wedding well rested and ready for our honeymoon."

"You don't even know our plans."

"Where are we going?"

Suzy's eyes shifted down to her plate. "You're so preoccupied with your work, you've forgotten where we planned to go?"

"I thought you would be happy to plan it yourself."

"That's not how it's supposed to work on a honeymoon."

My stomach was churning. Suzy was pointing out the same flaws in me that I knew needed reform. Everything she said was true. I needed to grow up to block my impulsive nature. Some men never do grow up. They are laughed at. But behavior patterns are hard to break.

We ate our dinner, Sean happy to share our food bits that we gave him to chew on, throw out, or choke down. Rice, pork, and whatever Moo Goo Gai Pan consisted of formed a ring around the floor beneath him. By the time we consumed everything, I was one beat up fiancé. Sean's mess seemed quaint, compared to mine.

I took Suzy and Sean back home, reassuring her as well as I could as I drove. Tales of the stress present before a wedding were not new to me. Perhaps this was all it was with us, too. After I parked at the Jensens, I made it a point to lift Sean out of the tiny back seat of my car and carry him for Suzy to her guest house's front door. The rain of previous days made the night air muggy and depressively hot. Suzy opened her door and turned to take Sean from my arms. I kissed the boy lightly on his Chinese food-encrusted lips, then wrapped my other arm around my love, kissing her just as lightly on her forehead. Tonight was not the night to exhibit passion.

"I won't let you down," I said. "Then it will be all over." We transferred the boy into her waiting arms.

"Okay." Suzy was not convincing.

"I love you."

"I hope you do," she said and closed her door to my anxious gaze.

55

STANTON AND I LEFT FOR Dallas at 7:00 a.m. the next morning, taking separate cars. He suggested we drive together in an A-to-Z Chevy pickup, but I knew better than to accept. If we went together, I would be out of options if the deal were delayed. Stanton no doubt knew that when I vetoed his idea. We told our buyers of my wedding plans in hopes of getting an earlier meeting. It was Stanton's sole concession to me for our meeting. After he told them, we immediately regretted it. The buyers could now hold out for a better deal, knowing we were in a hurry to sell.

We were slated to meet our buyers at offices at Braniff International Airways on the site of the recently opened Dallas-Fort Worth Regional Airport. We had rooms booked at the newly opened Hyatt Regency, located adjacent to the airport's Terminal C.

The Texas sky was hot, humid, and hazy in the late morning sun, making it difficult to see much distance ahead of our vehicles. With temperatures forecast in the low 100s, it was not a day to wear a coat and tie. Yet, this is how we were dressed for the most important day of our lives—or was it getting married. For the moment I focused on the road going through Gainesville, where a stretch of highway had been under construction since George Washington was a boy. Approaching Denton, I-35 picked up speed as the highway split in two, with I-35 East to Dallas and I-35 West to Fort Worth. We chose the Dallas route, although it would not matter. One was no faster than another. Stanton was way behind me. Driving a Porsche behind a pickup I deemed unworkable. That was another concession he made. I took the lead.

Texas speed limits were suggestions, more than laws. No one obeyed the posted speed. For Texas highway patrolmen, it was impossible to issue tickets for the entire population. Naturally, the most egregious offenders were pulled over, leaving those driving only 99-mph or less not likely to pay for their crimes of speeding. I arrived at our Hyatt Regency Hotel an hour before Stanton pulled into the parking lot. Once again, my irresponsibility was on display. Could I not control my impulses to push the limit of everything?

For a price we got early check-in for our two adjoining rooms. After dropping our small bags in our rooms, we considered doing some work in our rooms ahead of our attorney's arrival to finalize the negotiations. It was awkward to work upstairs in our rooms. We quickly elected to do any necessary discussion over an early lunch. If Suzy were to call me on my room phone, she would be out of luck.

We had a lunch in the hotel café of hamburgers, fries, and Cokes. Beers, martinis, and champagne would wait until later. At one o'clock we received a message at the front desk that our buyers were still on for five o'clock, which set my mind at ease. *I'm going to pull it off.*

By three o'clock we were bored out of our minds with waiting and decided that going to the bar would be all right. We were only going to watch the television. At four o'clock we ordered our first beer. A half hour later, we got in Stanton's Chevy pickup to go to the Braniff headquarters, where we would meet with our attorney and then join our buyers in one of the conference rooms.

Stanton was on edge. He nervously worked the accelerator and brake pedals as we headed out of the parking lot. He turned on his truck's radio, a luxury I didn't want in my Porsche. It was a sportscar for goodness' sake. Porsches didn't need a radio. The radio I had installed, I never turned on. He had his truck's radio tuned to a Dallas AM country radio station, the music unfamiliar to me. I was a city slicker. I didn't listen to that stuff. I hardly listened to any music at all.

We found the correct building entrance at the Braniff International Air-ways headquarters. Stanton parked the truck, and I made sure the country music radio station got turned off, hopefully for good. We quietly stepped inside to a splendid and inviting lobby. Wearing suits, the comfortable cool air conditioning was a relief. I was sweating from my own nervousness. Within five minutes our legal negotiator arrived. He recognized us immedi-ately, came over, and grabbed each of our hands in a tight grip.

"Hi, my name is Sladek. I know we've talked on the phone."

"Yes, sir," Stanton said. He seemed calmer now, possibly more in his el-ement of comfort.

"Mister Sladek, I'm Rob Amity. I believe you've talked with me, also."

"Indeed, I have," Sladek said. "I know you have been to our Oklahoma City office and talked to the boys there. I live here in Dallas, so I will be your man getting this deal finalized pronto."

"I assume the negotiations are over?" I asked.

"For the most part. There is always some small detail you or they like clarified. I know what their concerns are. We are ready with the answers they want. I see no issues at all. You two boys have a really top-notch com-pany to sell."

"Any changes to the negotiated price?" I asked.

"That's one of the issues they want to discuss. They may have to pay you more, and they know it." Mr. Sladek was looking at me, not Stanton. "They want more of your involvement if you are agreeable."

Stanton spoke to me. "I have already told our attorneys that after our year of obligation to help with the transition, I want out completely."

"If I could have gotten hold of you this morning," Mr. Sladek said, "I could have shared that information with you, but I guess you were already in your car to come here."

Stanton turned to look at me. "I might have told them that you are a dy-namo at organization and personal relations with customers."

"What are they offering?" I asked.

"I don't know," Mr. Sladek replied. "They just put out a feeler to us if there would be any interest. Your answer might change the sales price upwards if you signed a second contract to extend your obligation as an employee and part owner."

My look of surprise must have been evident. "Part owner? Is that what you said?"

"Yes," Sladek said. "To keep you on the team, they're offering you quite an incentive."

"Should I consider it?"

"It sounds like it would be a terrific opportunity for you. It's up to you. That's why it was important that you be here today."

Sladek looked at his watch, announcing that it was nearly our meeting time. We followed him to the elevators where we rose to the third floor and into a lobby that hosted several attorney practices. He stepped over to the young and attractive receptionist and introduced himself with reference to our five o'clock meeting. She came to attention, obviously aware of who we were. Without explanation, she rose from her chair and opened a door behind her front desk. She tore a sheet off a fax machine, looked at it with surprise, and brought it out for us to see.

"Mister Sladek, it appears they've postponed your meeting until nine o'clock tonight."

She handed him a faxed message, which he read with irritation. Our attorney took charge.

"I'll contact their attorney right now. In the meantime, go back to your hotel. Have a stiff drink for all I care. This will not last long, I promise you."

"I want to stay here, until you make that call," Stanton said. His voice became angry. "We're not leaving until you find out what the hell they're trying to pull."

I nodded my own agreement and kept my impulsive mouth shut. What type of company would they be to work for with these shenanigans going on?

Stanton and I found two leather chairs to sit in and wait while our attorney made his call. We hoped he would keep his cool and remain the superb negotiator we were paying for. Our chairs enveloped us in coolness, which allowed us to cool off ourselves. They were comfortable enough for us to calm down, but not so much that we would fall asleep.

We waited out of range of our attorney, who chose a telephone far from the lobby's front desk.

"I'm so sorry for this mix up," the young receptionist said. "If you had been up here earlier, I could have saved you some time. I tried calling earlier, but everyone was out of reach."

"We're at the Hyatt nearby if someone wants to reach us," Stanton said. It was a moot point since it was already after five o'clock, and our receptionist was packing her purse to depart for the day.

"I'll leave a note here with that information," she said. Jotting down our names and room numbers took a few minutes of her donated free time. We thanked her for her kindness and watched her sprint for the elevator. We waited in uncertainty for another ten minutes.

55

WHEN MR. SLADEK RETURNED TO the lobby, he brought us worse news. His face was beet red. His fists gripped in anger.

"Well, it gets worse," he said. "Apparently, the attorneys on the other side are rewriting the whole contract. The typist putting this together is new and was using white-out. The documents must be pristine, no errors. Attorneys can't type either, so they are franticly trying to redo the contracts. The time is uncertain. They will call us when they are ready. It's nothing but a Charlie Foxtrot in their office right now."

"You think they will get 'er done tonight?" Stanton asked.

"To be honest, we'll be signing everything in the morning, not tonight."

Stanton looked at me. My face flushed red hot.

"Don't do it," he said.

"I won't," I replied. My heart was pounding with anxiety.

"You boys go to your room, and I'll call you if things change, okay?"

We agreed. Stanton stormed out of the lobby ahead of me. Cursing with rage, he walked over to our pickup and kicked the passenger door with his steel-toed boot, hurting his foot more than the door. He angrily limped around to the front of the car, lobbed a few more curses at the hot muggy skyline, and stopped to stare my way.

"I'm driving the truck back, Stanton."

"I'm just going to shut up for a while," he said.

"That might be good. We'll talk when we get back to our room. Let's just try to stay calm."

It was a short drive to the hotel. Neither of us wanted to talk. I was taking a risk in agreeing to stay and wait, but I knew I could pull it off. An experience I shared with Hal on our road trip came to mind. I almost ran out of fuel on a flight, but I managed to land on fumes. I knew what to do without being told what to do. I was successful then. I would be successful now. But in the back of my mind, I was growing tired of the conflicting demands everyone from Stanton to Suzy to the Jensens and more were telling me to do. I didn't need their help to know what that right thing was.

I turned on the truck's AM radio for distraction. The country station was still tuned in. I would have changed to another station if I had known any Dallas frequencies. A popular balladeer sang a song that was new to me, so I turned up the volume and listened. His voice was melancholy. The lyrics spoke to me.

> *You should be mad*
> *You were so gentle*
> *But you must know*
> *Life goes on*
> *We had potential*

I glanced over at Stanton, who was in his own world and not paying attention. I inched the volume up a slight turn.

> *We will move on*
> *There will be others*
> *But I know I will miss you*
> *If you change your mind*
> *You can always call me*
> *Then I will know*
> *That you still love me*
> *But it will never*

Be like those past times
Only goodbyes
Suzy's fears were true. I was choosing money over a promise to her.
Feel my tears upon your shoulder
Rolling gently down the curves
that smooth your form
Feel the touch of my warm lips
as they faintly
brush your soft skin
Think of how you loved me once in time
It was sublime

I fantasized for many years the feel of Suzy against me, her warmth and naked skin against my own. A chance to embrace her all over. The tender brush of our lips. A lingering shared ecstasy. I had daydreamed all of it many times before.

Life will go on
There will be others
but I know I'll miss you
If you change your mind
You can always call me

The lyrics pulled at my conscience. Could I ever abandon her and the son I was to adopt? They love me. Would testing them once more ever be forgiven?

Then I will know
That you still love me
But it will never
be like those past times
Only goodbyes

If she left me, I would never get over it. After so many pledges to each other, her abandonment would never stop hurting. Could I ever do that to her?

Feel my tears upon your shoulder
Rolling gently down the curves
that smooth your form
Feel the touch of my warm lips
as they faintly
brush your soft skin
Think of how you loved me once in time
It was sublime

We parked the truck. Still no words passed between us. I turned off the radio. We climbed out without even a glance at the other. Walking around to the passenger side, Stanton looked defeated. I turned away to walk over to my car.

"Don't do it," he said.

I continued to my prized Porsche. "Don't do it, Rob."

I got to the driver door and unlocked it. Stanton was walking my way. He shouted something, but I was not listening. Taking my place in the driver's seat, I buckled myself in and started the car. As I sat there, I began to cry. I cried for the loss of Suzy's husband, whom I failed to save from the flames of a burning jet. I cried for the plight that the crash put Suzy in, to raise a newborn baby alone. I cried for my own folly in leaving her for someone else back in college. I didn't want to make-believe anything anymore. I wanted Suzy to once again wrap her arms around me, not to say goodbye, but to stay forever.

I pulled the car forward and waved to Stanton. I wiped away my tears, after driving out of his sight. It was a clear choice. I would be a fool no longer. I was going home to be married, where I should have been all along.

CPSIA information can be obtained
at www.ICGtesting.com
Printed in the USA
BVHW070920020623
665280BV00012B/325/J

9 781633 738133